SLICED, DICED AND DEAD

SLICED, DICED AND DEAD

A
Charcuterie
Shop
Mystery

J.C. Eaton

LEVEL
BEST BOOKS

To the wonderful readers and staff at Desert Foothills Library in Cave Creek, Arizona
Our sincere thanks and appreciation for introducing us to your community, knowing it would be the backdrop for murder!

Praise for The Charcuterie Shop Mysteries

"Take one cantankerous ghost, add a laid-back beagle, and top it off with a cast of eclectic characters and you have J.C. Eaton's delicious new mystery—*Laid Out to Rest*. This first in a new series cozy was so much fun to read! The suspects were as varied as the offerings on a charcuterie board, and the culprit eluded me until the final reveal. The ending was such a delightful surprise that I didn't want to "give up the ghost" or the mystery! I can't wait for the second installment in this charming new series."—Linda Reilly, author of The Deep Fried Mysteries, The Cat Lady Mysteries, and The Grilled Cheese Mysteries

"*Sliced, Diced and Dead* is a deli-licious romp of a cozy with all the right ingredients. Author J.C. Eaton serves up a delightful story guaranteed to leave you hungry for more."—Anna St. John, author of The Josie Posey Mystery Series

"Lively characters rule in this hilarious, action-packed caper featuring smart and sassy charcuterie chef Katie Aubrey who won't let anything get in the way of solving a murder. Wherever Katie goes, so does her roommate Edith, a feisty ghost who shares her two cents every chance she gets. All this makes for an imaginative, expertly crafted, and deliciously entertaining read, with clever dialogue that flows effortlessly. Buckle up and enjoy this fun-filled ride!"—Lida Sideris, author of A Southern California Mystery Series

Chapter One

No sooner did I finish cubing a chunk of Havarti when a crystal-clear image of Edith Ellory appeared in front of me. Not a ghostly phantasma image or a hologram, but a sharp image of a woman in a flowing yellow caftan that gave no indication Edith was dead. Thankfully I was the only one in my sandwich and charcuterie shop at the time.

"Would you look at that? I can snap myself in, and I can snap myself out," Edith said as if she had just mastered a three-point turn. With that, she snapped her fingers, and although it was soundless, it was like watching someone who had been working castanets since birth.

"What the heck, Edith! I all but sliced my finger off!"

"And I can materialize with a snap of the fingers. It's not the same as a wave or flourish. Too filmy. Watch. I've been practicing."

She brushed her hand in front of me, and in an instant, she was feathery and ghostly. Another flourish, this time with a full arm extended, and not much difference.

"Now watch." No longer soundless, a sharp click like a "pin-pan" was followed by the crisp image I'd seen a few seconds ago.

"See what I mean? It's a new skill I believe I've mastered. More or less."

I looked at the unfinished mini-charcuterie board and tried not to raise my voice. "Can't you master it someplace else? I've got to get these mini-boards done before we open. Lilly-Ann and Matt will be here any minute, and they have enough to do before customers arrive. My meeting with the fashion show organizer at Hidden Boulders is in forty-five minutes, and I can't be late. I was lucky to land this catering job even if Tambra Wright is a—"

1

"Stuck up snob, who wouldn't know a charcuterie board from a chess board? And before you say anything, the answer is yes. I've watched her in action when you didn't know I was there. She's almost as bad as Imogen. At least Imogen doesn't speak with a Transatlantic accent. Someone needs to tell Tambra the 1930s are long gone."

And someone needs to tell me what a Transatlantic accent is, but I don't have time right now.

I reached for the dry sausage and kept working. "We can talk about this later. I don't have much time. Especially if you're going to bring up Imogen."

"Don't tell me you're going to cube the sausage? It needs to be round. Round."

"If you keep this up, I may lose more than a finger. I may wind up slicing my hand off."

"No need to be dramatic."

This, from the drama queen of the century.

Some people have to contend with obnoxious roommates in order to pay the rent. In my case, Edith Ellory didn't chip in a dime. Seventy-seven years young (her words), when her lifeless body was found in the house I now rented, Edith insisted she'd been murdered and refused to move on in the netherworld until I found her killer.

Long story short—been there, done that, and she still wouldn't move on. Something about being forced to learn humility first until the decision makers from the great beyond present her with a "Move On" pass to get farther up the chain or whatever it's called.

Then, there's Imogen. Some people carry grudges all their lives, while others, like Edith, take it to the grave and beyond. Edith was a renowned food critic who had a rather unpleasant experience with local restauranteur Imogen Brodeur when they both attended culinary school. Yeesh. At least I moved on with my life.

I'm Katie Aubrey, thirty-two years old and the new owner of a burgeoning charcuterie business and sandwich shop. I traded my business position at Chan-Tech Industries for a career that promised creativity and flexibility instead of heartburn, stress, and the unrelenting pressure to make a new sale.

I also got dumped by a loser of a boyfriend who got his walking papers a few months later from his then-to-be fiancée. Payback's a you-know-what.

Now, with only a few more minutes for me to finish the mini-platters, I had to figure out a way to get rid of Edith.

"Listen, if you leave me alone, I'll let you play a big part in designing the charcuterie boards for the fashion show. As long as they're within reason as far as taste and cost are concerned. Last thing I need is for you to insist on exorbitant and pricy items."

"No, Tambra will be doing that. And if you're wondering how I know, I listen in to the gossip that surrounds you. Don't worry, if anyone dictates the food we serve, it should be me. I'm the one intimately acquainted with the culinary world."

"Right now, Edith, you're the one intimately acquainted with the netherworld. I'm the one who has to put up with you. We can talk about this tonight. Snap yourself out before my employees come in."

"They can't see me. Or hear me. Only you can. And I'm bored. I'll be back before you leave for the Hidden Boulders. I'm still working on getting that Jean Harlow gown. I suppose now is as good a time as ever. This caftan doesn't do anything for my figure. Ta-ta for now."

"Wait! No!" But it was too late. Edith vanished, and next thing I knew, Lilly-Ann opened the front door and called out, "Good Morning! Can you believe it? It's in the eighties already, and it's only six fifteen in the morning. So much for cool late July mornings." Her shoulder-length auburn hair, usually loosely draped around her neck, was pulled into a high ponytail that made her look as if she was in her forties, not fifties.

She walked into the kitchen, put her bag under the counter, and washed her hands before donning one of our new Char-Board aprons. "Matt should be here any second. I watched him nab a parking spot across the street."

The Char-Board was located on Cave Creek's main drag, a throwback to earlier times in Arizona when main drags consisted of watering holes, grub stations, and small sundry shops. Of course, we still had those things, but they're considered classy and trendy now. Pricey, too.

It was the town's ambience that first drew me in. Semi-secluded between the Continental and Black Mountains but only a stone's throw from its prestigious neighbors: Scottsdale, Fountain Hills, and Paradise Valley. That meant I'd have plenty of opportunity for the catering portion of my business to grow.

"Hey, everyone! I nailed the last parking spot on this block. What are the chances of that? Must be the entire town is getting an early start today. Wonder what it is with Tuesdays. It was like that last week." Matt walked toward the sink, then paused to take a look at the mini-boards. "Wow. Those boards look tasty. New kind of ham?"

"Smoked Black Forest, but I rolled them into zigzags so it looks a tad different."

"I can finish them," Lilly-Ann said. "I know you've got that meeting at Hidden Boulders."

"Yeah, I've got to be out of here like five minutes ago. If Sterling Moss from Randolph's Escapade calls, tell him I'll be back by lunchtime. That poor man worries so much, he makes me nervous. I told him we'd have a splendid charcuterie tray delivered on time for his event this Saturday."

"Make it two trays. Didn't you read my text? I sent it to you last night. He called here a few minutes after you left."

"Rats. No. I didn't check my messages. Forgot all about it. I took Speedbump for a short walk, then met my friend Maddie for dinner in Carefree. She had a house showing over there. What did he say? I mean, other than two trays."

Lilly-Ann burst out laughing and tried to close her lips, but it wasn't working.

"What? What? What did he say?" I asked.

"He wants you to meet his nephew from Colorado. Thinks you'd hit it off. The nephew is relocating to Phoenix."

"Oh, heck no. That's all I need. A fix-up with Sterling Moss's nephew. The guy is probably as neurotic as his uncle, although I have to admit, I really like Sterling. He's down-to-earth even though he owns the classiest and most high-profile restaurant in Paradise Valley. Araragh. I hope he doesn't take away his catering business from us if I don't go out with the nephew."

4

Then I looked at Lilly-Ann and Matt before I found myself laughing. "This is so superficial. I can't believe I've stooped so low."

Matt crinkled his nose and shrugged. "What are you talking about? You lost me."

"Sterling looks exactly like Peter Ustinov when he played the role of Hercule Poirot in Agatha Christie's 1978 version of *Death on the Nile* and a slew of other Christie mysteries. I wondered if the nephew shared the same, well, you know."

"Physique and mustache?" By now Lilly-Ann was practically rolling on the floor.

"We're awful," I said. "Petty and superficial."

"So you're going to go out with the dude?" Matt grabbed an apron and tied it behind his back before he washed his hands and placed a dozen eggs in the large pot for boiling.

"Huh? No. I'm going to forget I even got that part of the message. Yikes. It's late. I'd better get a move-on before Tambra Wright pitches a fit."

Suddenly Lilly-Ann's face turned ashen, and she pursed her lips. Something I've never seen her do. "Tambra Wright? Don't tell me she has something to do with the Hidden Boulders fashion show. I thought you were meeting with Deirdre Billings."

"She's on the committee, but the woman in charge of the fashion show is Tambra. She's the one I've been meeting with. Not Deirdre. Is something the matter?"

Lilly-Ann walked to the fridge and began to put the veggies on the counter for slicing. "It was a long time ago. Almost thirty years. But I'd watch my back if I were you. Once a snake, always a snake. And even the non-venomous ones bite."

Matt looked up from the pot where he had just placed the eggs. His eyes were directly on Lilly-Ann's. "Thirty years? That's a long time to stew over something. I've never seen you angry at anyone for longer than a minute or two, and we've worked together for over a year. What'd she do? Steal your husband?"

"Worse. My reputation."

I opened my mouth but found myself struggling to say something. All I was able to spit out were five words. Six, if I counted the "um" that preceded them.

"I've got to get going."

Chapter Two

I couldn't imagine what the issue had been between Lilly-Ann and Tambra, but I didn't have time to ask. I was already running ten minutes later than I had planned for my drive to Hidden Boulders.

Making a quick dash out of the place, laptop in hand, I charged to my car. Thankfully I was able to park a few yards from our shop, having arrived at sunup. With a short-sleeved white top and form-fitting capris, I was both professional and practical. Even though I heard Edith mutter "boring" and "predictable" when I grabbed the clothes from my closet. I wasn't about to succumb to her dress preferences, no matter how much she nagged. Dizzying designs with eye-piercing colors might have been the norm for her, but I was neither flamboyant nor famous.

In a matter of minutes, I took a left-hand turn onto North Spur Cross Road and from there to East Fleming Springs Road, where I spied the entrance sign to Hidden Boulders. Sign? It was more like a handcrafted metal sculpture that could have easily graced the interiors of most art museums. Provided they had cathedral ceilings.

The road north meandered over small berms that morphed into sizable hills before the first cache of boulders off to the sides of the road became visible. They were small, maybe three or four feet in diameter, but they were plentiful. Behind them were a few mature jacaranda trees that stood like sentinels. The boulders grew in size the farther up the hill I drove. Now six or eight feet but still towered over by jacarandas.

Another metal sculpture appeared, only larger than the previous one. The same lettering, though, Hidden Boulders. I kept driving. Off to my left was a fancy wooden sign, framed in metal. It read, "Welcome to Hidden Boulders, a community of distinction."

Distinction. Interesting word for moola. The road curved slightly, and when it did, my jaw dropped. Even the word "breathtaking" didn't come close to what I saw. Whoever the architect was who created a towering masterpiece of natural woods and floor-to-ceiling windows, was probably off the coast of Santorini by now in a private yacht or enjoying a lovely sojourn in the Seychelles Islands. No doubt the ginormous bill was still being footed by the Hidden Boulders community.

As I approached the eye-catching structure, I was taken back by the rock gardens that graced the driveway. Another sign appeared. This time off to the right. Like the other one, it, too, was framed in metal, but instead of displaying the community name, its metal arrows, and accompanying text told visitors where to find the recreation centers, the aquatic areas, and the residences.

The mammoth building that stood in front of me was the Mountain View Recreation and Performing Arts Center. It was also the venue for the Hidden Boulders Fashion Show and my meeting place with Tambra.

I pulled my KIA Sorento next to a red Maserati and looked around the parking lot. It reminded me of Randolph's Escapade in Paradise Valley, where Mercedes, Audis, BMWs, and Ferraris were the key players. As I removed the key from the ignition, a filmy blue haze filled the interior, augmented by a familiar raspy voice.

"You should date the nephew from Colorado. He probably has beaucoup bucks."

"Edith! Don't tell me you overheard all that. I thought you were gone."

"Only for an instant. I tried to replace this hideous caftan with that Jean Harlow gown. Unfortunately, I wasn't successful."

The filmy haze took form, and Edith was now in a billowy sailor suit and yammering as usual. "I know. It's worse than the caftan, and it appears as if I may be stuck with it during our meeting with Tambra."

"*Our* meeting? You mean *my* meeting, and I asked you not to interfere. And speaking of interfering, don't you dare do something that somehow results in me being thrown face-to-face with the nephew on Saturday when I see Sterling Moss. Last thing I need is a blind date."

"Honey, you need a date period. Blind or otherwise."

Terrific. Now Edith Ellory is stepping into my social life.

"Look who's talking. You went to the grave single."

"That didn't mean I went there celibate. I heard you complain about the lumpy mattress when you moved in. You couldn't wait to replace it. How do you think it got lumpy in the first place?"

"Ew! Too much information, Edith."

Just then, a sapphire blue Lincoln Navigator slid into the spot adjacent to mine, saving me from a conversation I'd rather not have. A shapely woman with long chestnut hair and an off-white shirtwaist dress exited the car, and moved gracefully across the parking lot, two-inch heels and all.

I muttered, "don't be a nuisance" under my breath, and hoped Edith got the message. Then I hurried to the entrance of the recreation center. A spectacular chandelier reflected the light from the floor-to-ceiling windows, and I noticed the benches in front of the glass panes had the same metal design as the entrance signs on the road. Large Ficus plants flanked an oval reception table, reminding me of a similar one at Chan-Tech. A middle-aged woman with tight brown curls and hoop earrings looked up from the computer screen and asked if she could help me.

"I'm Katie Aubrey from The Char-Board in Cave Creek, here to meet with Tambra Wright. I'm providing the charcuterie boards for the fashion show."

"She's in the Cimarron room to your left with Deirdre Billings and Cherie Simms. I think Meredith Mason is with her as well. Would you like a Tums before you head over there?"

"Huh?"

"You heard me." The woman motioned me over, and I leaned toward her. She adjusted one of her earrings and smiled. "Better to prevent indigestion than deal with it once your meeting gets started."

I grimaced. "That bad, huh?"

"Let's just say Tambra doles out stress as if it was Halloween candy. But you didn't hear it from me."

9

"Uh, thanks for the heads-up. I'll pass on the Tums for the time being."

She pointed to the Cimarron room, and I took a deep breath before pulling open one of its carved wooden doors and stepping inside.

"Katie!" Tambra exclaimed, motioning me over to one of the round card tables where she, Deirdre, Cherie, and Meredith were seated. "You know Deirdre and Meredith from your shop. This is Cherie Simms. She's also on the fashion show committee."

I nodded and waved before pulling out a leather captain's chair and plunking myself down. A large pitcher of iced tea with lemon and an empty glass were inches from me.

"Help yourself," Tambra said. "I don't care if it is breakfast time. No hot coffee for this gal. The monsoon humidity is dastardly. All I want to do is make myself comfortable with a cold drink and the air-conditioning set on high."

"And enough alcohol in that drink to take her into November." Edith was especially snarky, and I reacted without thinking.

"I'm not here to talk about alcohol."

"No worries," Deirdre chirped. She brushed a strand of her dark chin-length hair to the side, and I could see a large lapis earring in the shape of a dolphin. "We have our own beverage service at the club. All you need to do is supply those wonderful charcuterie boards of yours."

I bit my lower lip and made a mental note not to react to Edith's comments when we were in public. "I understand you'd like three of our 2 x 4 rectangular boards. At least that's what my notes say."

Tambra cleared her throat and placed her chin in the palm of her hand, elbow flush with the table. "These boards of yours must be exquisite. Deirdre and Meredith raved about the ones you provided for their bunco games, but this isn't some casual chip-and-dip eating party. It's a sophisticated and elegant event that defines the culture of Hidden Boulders."

"More like the pocketbooks of the attendees."

I turned and flashed a look at Edith, who had now materialized behind Cherie. Same billowy sailor suit, only this time with a matching cap and red ribbon. It reminded me of one of those 1950s cartoons, and I tried not to react.

With my eyes fixed on Tambra, I took a quick sip of my iced tea and spoke. "Charcuterie boards can be designed to reflect anyone's taste, style, appetite, and budget. I've worked with black caviar boards that showcase triple crème spreads, dried beef salamis like soujouka, or even fennel-flavored pork salamis like juniper. Some boards showcase cured eye of roast beef, known as Bresaola, while others introduce a zing or wow factor, by adding slices of Nova Scotia lox. Add sea salt crackers and flatbreads, along with cornichons or caperberries, and you've got a show-stopping, eye-catching masterpiece. Not to mention, a delectable one."

Tambra was unphased. "If I wanted lox, I'd go to a delicatessen in Scottsdale."

An unexpected gust of air caught her hair, and for an instant, thanks to Edith, that cute bob of Tambra's looked more like the top of a troll doll. "If she really wanted lox, maybe she should swim upstream with the salmon."

It took more restraint than I realized to ignore both women.

"Tell me," I said, looking at Deirdre, Cherie, and Meredith, "what *did* you have in mind for your charcuterie trays?"

Meredith adjusted the Byzantine-style gold chain that hung from her neck and looked at Tambra. "We were hoping for a European theme that would—"

"I'll take it from here," Tambra cut in. "What Meredith is trying to say is that our fashions will reflect the latest styles from France, Italy, and Spain. Those boards of yours should do the same."

"No problem. None whatsoever. Those are three of the most popular designs. If you have specific cheeses or meats in mind, you can email me, or you can give me a price range that you'd like to work with. Keep in mind, The Char-Board is not the party platter section at Costco's." *Two can play that game, lady.*

I pulled out a binder that I had placed in my bag and handed it to her. "These are photos of trays we've done for other occasions. It will give you an idea of what to expect. Take a look, pass it around. I'm open to any and all suggestions."

Tambra eyed the binder and flipped to the first page that showed the charcuterie trays Lilly-Ann, and I designed for Olivia DeLonde's engagement. Too bad that was one marriage that was never going to happen. Similar trays followed. Parties, presentations, you-name-it.

As I watched her face, I could see it soften as she studied the photos. She rubbed the bottom of her chin and took a breath. "Those rosettes you made out of that meat are fabulous. Put that down as a must."

"No problem."

"And soft cheeses. Nothing says money like soft cheeses."

"Or diamonds. Watch out she doesn't want those on a platter." *Oh no. Edith is back in the game.*

"How about this?" I asked. "I'll rough out four or five trays, provide an estimate, and then you can render a decision. But I'll need it this week. Oh, and one more thing. We reserve the right to make substitutions if an item isn't readily available. That's sometimes the case with specialty cheeses, but there are so many options, we'll be fine."

"What do you say, girls?" Tambra asked the ladies. "I think we can get this done in time."

Edith was relentless. "She's picking charcuterie trays, not painting the Sistine Chapel."

"Enough already!" The words flew out of my mouth, and I gasped. Edith's little retorts had finally pushed me to the point of exasperation. "I mean, is it enough...uh, four or five trays to decide?"

Tambra nodded once. "I think that will do."

"Great. I'll send you an email with the attachments. I've got your email as well as the one for your recreation center. Tell me, did you want these prepared on-site or done ahead of time? They're actually much better done on-site since room temperature is best, but we can always create them off-site, refrigerate them and deliver them."

"This place has a phenomenal kitchen," Cherie said. "I don't see why it can't be done right here."

Tambra gave Cherie a cursory look and turned her attention back to me. "That's fine with me. I'll let the facilities director know. Above all else, please inform your staff that under no circumstance are they allowed to snoop around the social hall and fashion runway. The models and their dressers don't need the stress of uninvited lookie-loos."

Again, I tried to keep my composure. "I can assure you, my staff are trained professionals who have a job to do. *And,* for *your* information, we don't want anyone in the kitchen other than this facility's food service manager during our charcuterie preparation. And that includes committee members. Perfumes, hairsprays, lotions, and the like all interfere with the integrity of our ingredients."

Edith positioned herself inches from my face. "She's wearing Byredo's Gypsy Water. It's a woodsy little number that usually sells for upwards of two hundred dollars an ounce. Trouble is, once the wearer perspires, the bergamot in that aromatic eau de parfum will have them reeking like a lumberjack who just completed a log-sawing contest. You can thank me later."

I smiled, lifted my chin, and inhaled. "Is that Gypsy Water I detect? All the more reason to steer clear of the kitchen."

Tambra stood and leaned across the table. "Those charcuterie boards had better be worth the price." With that, she exited the room, and I let out the breath I was holding.

"That went well," Deirdre said. "Usually, she's much more—"

"Obnoxious?"

"Actually, I was about to say *venomous,* but obnoxious works."

I looked at Deirdre and then at Meredith and Cherie. "Why do you all put up with her?"

Cherie ran her finger up and down the watery film on the outside of her iced tea glass. "It's difficult to explain. Let's just say Tambra is good at putting puzzle pieces together."

"Huh?" By now, I was completely lost.

"What Cherie means," Meredith said, "is that Tambra knows how to find out bits and pieces of information about each of us and then puts it together to hold over us."

I gasped. "You mean like blackmail?"

Meredith shook her head. "I wouldn't go quite that far. More like social intimidation. No money involved. Just our reputations."

When I heard the word *reputation*, I froze. Whatever had happened all those years ago with Lilly-Ann, these savvy women weren't about to let Tambra do the same thing to them. Even if it meant letting that she-witch have her way.

Chapter Three

"Too bad the olives on the charcuterie boards are pit-less. It would be fun watching Tambra choke on one of them."

"Edith! That's a horrid thing to say. Although I agree."

I had exited Hidden Boulders and was now on East Fleming Springs Road on my way back to The Char-Board. Edith's phantasmic form was in the front seat, still in that ridiculous sailor outfit. She must have read my mind, given what she said next.

"If they're going to be so obtuse about the Jean Harlow gown, then I'll see if I can get one of Carole Lombard's. I do like the form-fit and those fabulous trains. Nothing says elegance like a shimmery train flowing from the back of a form-fitting gown. Preferably in silver, although champagne would do as well."

"I wouldn't know. The last gown I wore was for my senior prom. And it was—" I glanced to my right, but Edith had vanished. Just as well. I needed some quiet time to decompress before getting back to the shop. There was no way I was about to let Tambra get under my skin, even though she came awfully close. Unlike the bunco group women, there was nothing Tambra could hold over my head, and I intended to keep it that way.

Catering the fashion show at Hidden Boulders would do wonders for my charcuterie business, especially since so many of the attendees had connections that I could only dream about. Connections in banking and movie production, not to mention retail. I figured if I could handle a feisty, demanding ghost, I could certainly manage Tambra Wright. Little did I know at the time that I was wrong. Dead wrong.

"How'd it go at Hidden Boulders?" Lilly-Ann asked when I stepped inside our sandwich shop. It was only ten thirty, but I felt as if I'd put in an entire day.

"About as pleasant as a root canal. I knew Tambra held the reins for that committee, but I didn't know they were attached to choke collars. Boy, if ever the expression 'my way or the highway' needed a venue, that was it."

"You'll have to tell me more when things slow down. Look around, we've still got the breakfast crowd, and now the lunch crew is trickling in. Wow. It isn't even eleven."

Matt stepped out of the kitchen carrying two plates with giant cinnamon rolls. He gave me a neck roll and smiled as he walked the breakfasts to a table near the front window. Straight ahead of him, an elderly couple walked in.

"Please feel free to take a seat wherever you like," I said to them. "I'll be with you in a few minutes."

Lilly-Ann was certainly right about the day's pace. It seemed as if none of us could catch a breath, not even to grab a quick bite. It was a little past three when she finally put the closed sign in the window and sank down at one of the tables. "Wonder what brought on that frenetic pace?" she asked Matt as he raced to the door.

"I don't know, but if I don't kick butt, uh, I mean, get a move on, I'm going to be late for my Intro to Psych class. I'll click the bottom lock, and you guys can deal with the deadbolt when you leave. See you tomorrow."

Matt juggled a full schedule at The Char-Board as well as taking classes at a local community college. He planned to transfer to Arizona State University once he earned his Associate's Degree two years from now. Needless to say, the kid was determined. No doubt, I was lucky to have him on staff, even though I knew it wouldn't last once he had that diploma in his hand.

I pulled out the chair across from Lilly-Ann's and sat. "Our clientele seems to be expanding. More retirees, I think."

"That's because two new fifty-five-plus developments opened up."

"Hmm, it may be time to think about adding a part-time worker. Especially if the charcuterie catering thrives. Something to think about this fall, I suppose. Meanwhile, I've got enough on my plate with the upcoming events."

"Yeah, speaking of which, you were going to tell me about your experience with Tambra, although I can pretty much fill in the blanks. Then again, I'm itching to know what you thought."

"Hang on. This may take a while. I'll grab us some Cokes."

Once back at the table, I propped my elbows on it and described in detail Tambra's snarky comments. "And that attitude of hers," I went on, "talk about haughty. Tell me, what did you mean when you said she threatened your reputation? Not that I'm trying to pry, but when Tambra left the room, the remaining three ladies made similar comments. Like the three blind mice, only instead of the farmer's wife cutting off their tails, Tambra was stepping on them and holding them down with one heavy stiletto heel."

Lilly-Ann let out a slow breath. "Sounds about right. I really hope what I'm about to tell you doesn't compromise the arrangement you made to cater that fashion show. I'd feel awful if it did." She took a sip of her Coke and held tight to the can. "Tambra, by the way, is the combination of her given name, Tammy Barbra, and we used to be partners in a women's accessory business thirty years ago. We were both single, in our late twenties, with experience in retail. It made sense for us to pool our resources, acquire a small business loan, and open our own shop in North Phoenix."

Wow. This is sounding kind of close to home.

I nodded and let Lilly-Ann continue. "We worked hard. We worked efficiently. Tambra used her public relations skills full tilt and made lots of connections that enabled our burgeoning business to grow. Until it didn't."

"What do you mean?" Thoughts of my charcuterie shop plateauing sent a small shiver down the nape of my neck.

"We had lots of customers, sold a great deal of our inventory, paid our bills, yet never seemed to go from point A to point B as far as profits were concerned. Tambra kept saying it took time for any establishment to get going, but it had been a couple of years and still nothing. One afternoon I realized why."

"Uh-oh. Doesn't sound good."

"I discovered two sets of books. Well, spreadsheets. She'd been skimming money for herself all this time. I confronted her, expecting her to ante up, but instead, she threatened to use her personal connections against me."

"Huh? How so?"

"I was friends with a local councilman who was married. Friends. Period. Tambra must have figured the day would come when I'd find out what she was up to, so she planned ahead. She had someone follow me and take photos of me with the councilman. Snapshots. Film. Long before cell phones. In any event, she made sure those photos were poised and ready to sit in the hands of her contacts—newspaper columnists, radio talk show hosts, you get the idea."

"Why didn't you go to the police?"

"I did. That's when I found out there was nothing they could do unless an actual crime was committed. It was all 'he said, she said,' and I knew Tambra would deny everything. In fact, she'd play the role of the injured party."

"So then what?"

"What anyone would expect. We dissolved our business relationship, shored up the details with the help of the bank, and went our separate ways. At least the business was in a rental building, so we didn't have to deal with real estate sales."

"I'm so sorry. I had no idea. I thought you were a teaching assistant and hadn't considered the fact you'd had a different career earlier on."

"Sometimes things are just meant to be. I met a wonderful man who was in the service. We married and had a daughter. Chloe. She's the one I told you about who lives in Houston with her own family. She was only six when her father was killed in Iraq. Don't ask me how, but I managed to survive. I became a teaching assistant, which afforded me the luxury of having the same school hours as Chloe, and I remained in that position until I retired."

"I had no idea. Thanks, Lilly-Ann, for sharing that with me. I'm so sorry about your loss."

She rubbed one of her eyes, and I wondered if she held back tears. "It was a long time ago. And if that business had survived, I probably never would have had my daughter and now my grandkids. Anyway, I wanted you to know about Tambra. Not that she can touch your charcuterie business, but I'd make sure that fashion committee, or whoever's running the program, pays you upfront even though we usually send them an invoice."

I shrugged. "I think I'm stuck in that regard, but at least I'm forewarned. And don't worry, Tambra's not about to call off the deal just because you work for me. Besides, I'm not even sure she knows. It's not like she frequents our shop like Deirdre and Meredith."

Lilly-Ann laughed. "If Deirdre and Meredith know, then Tambra does."

I winced. "Yeesh. I forgot all about the gossip train."

"I hate those self-serving bureaucrats in the outer realm! Imagine the gall telling me I'm not Carole Lombard gown worthy. If I can't wear the Jean Harlow, I want the Lombard gown with the long silky train."

I jumped back and nearly knocked over my chair. Edith had materialized, no warning whatsoever. Not even a filmy haze. She was still in that comical sailor suit, but the hat was missing.

"Are you all right, Katie?" Lilly-Ann asked. "So what if Tambra knows? It's only one business transaction, not a full-time commitment. Besides, she's got a vested interest in that fashion show. Last thing she'd want to do is undermine it. Remember, she's the one with the reputation to protect now."

"Reputation!" Edith shouted. "They said I had a *reputation* and not a very pleasant one. I happen to think I can be quite pleasant. At this rate, I'll never move on. They want humility. That's why I'm stuck here. We'll need to figure out a way for me to do that."

"Humility doesn't come easy," I said before I realized who I was really talking to.

"Don't I know it. Too bad Tambra hasn't figured it out. By the way, how did your noontime conversation go with Sterling Moss? Did he convince you to meet the nephew?"

"To be honest, I didn't give him a chance. We spoke about the charcuterie trays for this Saturday's event. I'm having Desert Delectable Food bring the major ingredients to the restaurant so we won't have to deal with transporting them. We'll only have to bring the edible flowers, the boards, and a few canned items. I told him that you and I would be there around four thirty to prepare the boards. That will give us plenty of time. Then, just as the poor guy mentioned his nephew, I faked a coughing fit and told him we'd chat at a later time."

"You're impossible, Katie, when it comes to your social life."

"I'll tally your vote along with my friend Maddie's."

"Tally it right up there with mine!" Edith shrieked. Still inches away from us. "At the rate you're going, the only male you'll see in the bedroom is that beagle of yours."

Chapter Four

The next three days flew by like a hurricane barreling up the coast, and it was Saturday afternoon before I knew it. Matt agreed to tidy up the shop and lock up so that Lilly-Ann and I could go to our respective homes and take a quick break before returning to gather the materials for the charcuterie boards. I always preferred making them at the site, and Randolph's Escapade had a terrific prep area.

I took Speedbump for a quick jaunt down my block, ate a small bowl of black cherry ice cream, and grabbed a change of clothes before driving back to The Char-Board. Since Lilly-Ann and I wore the fancy black Char-Board aprons for special events, I resorted to wearing white tops and pants underneath so as not to detract from the detailed logo on the apron.

Both of us had designed the boards together, and we were pleased with the patterns. At least on paper. Sterling had requested somewhat traditional summer grazing boards with meats, cheeses, seasonal fruits, nuts, and some spreads. To offset the tartness from the plums and nectarines, I had chosen to make a bowl of candied walnuts. I figured it would mesh nicely with the fig jam and blackberries. Along with two varieties of mild salamis, prosciutto, and the ever-popular brie, Gouda, and mozzarella cheeses, I would add an assortment of mixed nuts, stemmed cherries, and raspberries and compliment it with bread sticks, crostini, and flatbreads.

The boards would differ only slightly, as one of them featured peaches and sliced seedless watermelon instead of the nectarines and plums. I had a thing about not using repetitive charcuterie boards, even if it meant varying the items only slightly. The additional cost was worth the wow factor.

Once inside The Char-Board, we scrutinized our lists, put the additional ingredients in a cooler, grabbed the two larger wooden charcuterie boards, and took off for Randolph's Escapade.

"What are you going to do if Sterling confronts you face-to-face about the nephew?" Lilly-Ann asked as I headed south on Cave Creek Road to the 101.

"She'll tell him to pick the time and place."

Oh no. Not Edith again.

I turned to see where Edith had positioned herself, then back to Lilly-Ann. It was only a second or two, but still, I hated taking my eyes off the road. "I'm not picking a time or place."

"So you're agreeing to meet the guy?" Lilly-Ann's voice was optimistic and anxious.

"Huh? What? No. I was thinking about something else. My mind seems to wander all over the place these days."

"I suppose what I told you about Tambra might have something to do with it. Sorry if it was upsetting, but I figured you should know."

"It's fine. Really." What wasn't fine was having Edith lurking around and appearing at will. Not only was it annoying as hell, but it made me jumpy. I ignored it the best I could and tried to focus on how we'd create Halloween charcuterie boards. Especially since October was less than two months away.

"Believe it or not, I'm chomping at the bit," Lilly-Ann said. "It's my favorite fun-time holiday. And guess what? I saw an adorable design in one of those ladies' magazines where cheeses are cut out to resemble cute little ghosts. Sculpted edges and all."

"See? Even your assistant likes sculpted edges. Don't I always tell you to flute the edges?" A greenish haze drifted over the steering wheel.

"Not everything has to be fluted."

"I know that," Lilly-Ann sounded deflated. "I just thought the ghost shapes would look better that way, and sliced cheese is so easy for that."

"Yes, you're right. Absolutely." *I have got to start counting to ten before I open my mouth. Reacting to Edith's comments is like letting out a belch.*

22

Stretching out her neck closer to the window, Lilly-Ann looked up and down the road. "We must be getting closer. The only cars I see are Mercedes and BMWs."

"We're close, all right, and you nailed it. Two of those fortunes-on-wheels just turned into the driveway. Lucky us, though. We get to park in back with the Chevys, Fords, and Toyotas."

It was a while until dusk, but the sun had angled down, so the heat wasn't as oppressive when we exited the car. I started to reach for one of the wooden boards when I remembered the kitchen staff had a dolly. "Sterling said his staff would bring our boards and miscellaneous food items inside for us. Come on. I'm taking him up on the offer."

"No objections from me," Lilly-Ann smiled.

We walked across the macadam to the rear kitchen door and went inside. Three or four sous chefs were engrossed with salad preparation but looked up when they heard us.

"You must be the charcuterie chefs," a heavyset man, fortyish, with a white jacket, said. He stepped away from what appeared to be a shrimp dish in progress and snapped his fingers at two younger chefs who were a few feet away. "Mr. Moss directed us to assist these lovely ladies. One of you needs to grab a dolly and follow them out to their vehicle."

"Thanks. I'm Katie Aubrey, and this is Lilly-Ann Wentworth."

"Thomas Cauldon at your service." He reached out a hand, and I shook it. "I missed you the last few times you were here, but I heard the boards got great reviews."

A wall phone rang, and a young sous chef answered. He brushed a lock of his chin-length hair away from his ear, and I spied a small gold stud. Holding one hand over the receiver, he said, "It's Mr. Moss. He wanted us to let him know when Miss Aubrey arrived. He wants her to meet his nephew."

I froze, and even without a mirror, I was pretty certain all coloring had left my face. Then I shook my head. Adamantly. The sous chef winked, and I heard him say, "Certainly, sir. As soon as she arrives, we'll let her know."

When the receiver was back on the wall, I let out a long, slow breath. "Whoa. Thanks for that."

"No problem. I've been dodging set-ups for, like, forever."

"That obvious, huh?"

He laughed. "Want one of us to give you a signal if the boss decides to pop in? Your prep area is through that archway on the other side of the kitchen. Plenty of time to duck under something."

"I think we can save Miss Aubrey from ducking under things if Mr. Moss decides to make an appearance," Thomas said. I could see the laugh lines at the sides of his mouth.

The nephew must be a real piece of work. Seems the entire kitchen staff is covering for me.

"I'll follow whoever's going to take the dolly to my car," I told him. "Lilly-Ann can get started since most of our ingredients were already delivered. We got a text from Desert Delectable Foods."

Thomas motioned for Lilly-Ann, and the two of them walked toward our prep area as I headed toward the car with the sous chef who took Sterling's call.

"Act hospitable to the guy. Maybe he'll ask you out. He can't be that much younger than you. And he's certainly a looker." I didn't need the greenish haze to tell me Edith was hovering near us.

"I don't need to worry about my social life right now," I mumbled under my breath, but the guy heard me.

"Don't blame you. Same deal here. I recently graduated from Diablo Valley College in California with a degree in culinary arts. I totally freaked out when I got the job here. I applied to a zillion places, but I really wanted to get the heck out of California. Who on earth can afford to live there? And besides, I wasn't about to move into my parents' basement."

"Sounds like you've got a plan to move up in the industry."

He nodded. "That's why I put my social life on hold. What about you?"

I studied his face and realized Edith was right. The guy *was* cute. Earring and all. In the five or six minutes it took him to load our boards and ingredients, I figured *what the heck* and gave him the salient details of my former life at Chan-Tech, followed by the horrendous break-up with Evan.

"That wasn't a breakup. That was a full-blown escape. Hey, I'm Ian

Monroe."

"Katie Aubrey, but you know that already."

It was awkward, but we shook hands in-between loading up. Then it was off to the prep area where Lilly-Ann was already fast at work. We had both boards going at once since they were virtually the same, and by now, Lilly-Ann had a firm handle on the process.

"Cute sous chef, huh?"

I sighed. "Cute and at least eight years younger than me. It would never work. Besides, we're both too career centered."

Lilly-Ann put down a small paring knife and looked directly at me. "You got all that in five minutes?"

"He's a fast talker."

I don't know how Thomas and the kitchen crew managed it, but Lilly-Ann and I were able to make our retreat from Randolph's Escapade without meeting "the nephew." Thomas told me someone would drop the charcuterie boards at The Char-Board sometime on Monday, and that was fine with me. He also mentioned being in my neck of the woods the following Saturday for a high-profile fashion show where Randolph's Escapade was to provide the canapes.

"I'm not looking forward to it," he said. "I've worked a number of catering jobs for Randolph's, but something tells me this one is going to be fraught with tension."

"The one at Hidden Boulders?" I asked.

"That's the very one. Don't tell me you're supplying the charcuterie boards?"

"I'm afraid so."

Not a hunter-green haze this time, more like mint-green. "Ask him if the hot little whipper-snapper is going to be there. At the rate you're going, you'll be joining the former nuns at the cat sanctuary."

I caught myself just as I was about to deliver a clever retort to Edith and instead took a step closer to Thomas. "Um, you mentioned tension. It wouldn't happen to have anything to do with the organizer, does it?"

"Anything and *everything*. I served in the army before getting my degree in hospitality, and frankly, that woman made our drill sergeant look like Mother Goose. Hey, I've been around the block a few times, so I don't get easily intimidated. But there was something I couldn't quite put my finger on."

"What do you mean?" As if Tambra's attitude and steely demeanor weren't enough.

"I had the distinct feeling she looked for something to hold over my head. Odd, wouldn't you say?"

"No, not really. My initial encounter with her was unpleasant, to say the least. I dread subsequent ones. At least she'll be too busy at the event to get in our hair."

"I wouldn't count on that. Some people derive pleasure from that sort of thing. I'd stay on my toes if I were you. I already informed my serving staff to do the same."

Mint-green haze again. "He said *serving staff*. Ask if that includes the hunky sous chef."

"I don't care who it includes—Uh, what I mean is, thanks. I'll let them know."

Once Thomas was at a safe distance and Lilly-Ann out of sight, I put my hands on my hips and huffed. "Boundaries, Edith! Boundaries! We've been through this before. You can't keep popping in out of nowhere to put in your two cents."

The minty haze materialized, and Edith was now standing directly in front of me. This time in a mint-blue suit with matching kitten heels. The 1960s would have been proud.

"Don't sweat it, honey. And lock up your valuables around that woman. Wouldn't surprise me in the least if that cobra accused you of stealing them from her."

Like it not, Edith made a good point. But as things turned out, worse things were in store.

Chapter Five

"Do you think she'll change her mind again?" Lilly-Ann asked on Tuesday morning. The sun had risen about an hour ago, and she, along with Matt and me, was in The Char-Board's kitchen preparing more chicken and tuna salads. We had less than an hour before we opened for breakfast, and the three of us hustled.

"Are you guys talking about that tambourine woman or whatever her name is?" Matt asked. "It might have looked as if I minded my own business yesterday, but I heard both of you all day. Geez. All you did was complain about her."

"And with good reason." Lilly-Ann motioned for him to send a few green peppers her way. "The woman happens to be a conniving witch, and we're gearing up for Saturday."

Matt shrugged. "Too bad you couldn't sprinkle something on her food that would send her to the restroom for the evening."

I winced. "Bite your tongue. We'd lose our food license. Nah, we'll weather the storm, or in this case, the gale-force wind. Hidden Boulders holds fancy events like this year-round, and I want The Char-Board to be number one on their catering service."

"Okay. Guess I'll sit back and listen to you two dish the dirt. Got to admit, it's more interesting than the usual conversations about body lotions, hair products, and make-up. And hey, before you say anything else, I can't help it if I'm a multi-tasker."

Lilly-Ann and I both laughed. I had to admit, in the short time I worked with those two, we'd become a family of sorts. We were able to kid around with each other without overstepping our boundaries and most certainly had each other's backs.

"It's too late for Tambra to change her mind," I said. "Everything has been ordered, including the black caviar. When she found out how trendy that tray was, she insisted it be one of the two trays we prepare."

Matt put the finished chicken salad bowl in the fridge and turned his attention to some eggs that needed peeling. "I can stay late and close up on Saturday if you want me to. I don't have any real plans for the evening. Just hang out with friends and grab a pizza."

I looked at Lilly-Ann, then back to Matt. "You've got a deal. Just keep track of your time. Clean-up takes a lot longer when only one person is working."

"No worries. Like I said, I don't have any real plans."

Just then, the phone rang, and I grabbed it. "It's her!" I mouthed. Then I quickly put a finger over my lips. Matt and Lilly-Ann moved closer to where I stood and didn't move an inch.

"Katie." No hello. No how are you? "It's Tambra. I wondered if you could tweak those charcuterie boards and add red caviar in addition to the black. We had dinner with some friends of my husband, and they mentioned a fabulous red caviar from Russia. I can text you the name."

"That really won't be necessary. Acquiring red caviar is not the easiest thing. It usually takes two to three weeks. That's why I insisted you select the boards when you did."

"Oh, come now. You have connections. Everyone does. Make some calls. Get on the internet. Oh, and when you get the red caviar, be sure to have some sort of cream cheese spread in addition to what you have already. By the way, I simply can't wait to try one of those pancetta rosettes. They looked divine."

"Tambra, there's no way I can—"

"Of course, you can. You can and you will. Ta-ta for now."

The call ended, and I stood, mouth wide open, holding the end of the receiver.

"We heard that," Matt said. "Loud and clear. But mostly loud and obnoxious. Glad I'm not making those charcuterie boards for her."

I put the receiver back on the phone and rolled my eyes. "Trust me. I'd never make a board for her. But this is for the Hidden Boulders. At least that's what I keep telling myself."

"I liked Matt's idea." Edith sat herself on the counter and crossed her legs at the ankles. "Too bad you can't disguise Ex-Lax. Hmm, what about Imodium?"

My first instinct was to tell her to get off and reach for some Clorox wipes, but I remembered she was only spirit and mist. I also remembered to keep my mouth shut. Securely shut.

In the three days that followed, Tambra called with all sorts of "tweaks," and each time I listened patiently and waited for her to end the call before I could respond. Yep, two could certainly play that game. When Saturday morning finally rolled around, I had successfully avoided any real conversations with her.

"I wouldn't worry about all those additions and subtractions that miserable vixen demanded. They probably breezed out of her brain seconds after she rattled them off."

"Thanks, Edith. That was very comforting." I was at my kitchen table finishing up my coffee and getting ready to head over to The Char-Board. Edith sat, or materialized as the case would be, opposite me. This time in a crimson boho top with matching harem pants. I tried not to look too closely. Some of those styles had large gaps between the tops and the bottoms.

"It was, wasn't it?" she asked. "Say, does that count for humility?"

"Um, I don't think so, but still, it was nice of you."

"Oh, posh. I need to rack up some humility."

"And I need to get to work. I suppose this goes without question, but you'll probably hover over me tonight, won't you?"

A puff of red mist filled the room and vanished a second or two later. "It's not as if I have a full dance card waiting. Besides, I can offer advice. Remember, I'm the one with the culinary degree."

"How can I possibly forget? You remind me every day."

With that, the red mist appeared again, but Edith was gone.

Like the prior Saturday, Matt closed up shop so that Lilly-Ann and I could grab a quick respite before heading over to the Hidden Boulders. At least the location was in Cave Creek, allowing us to catch a breath before we had to prepare the charcuterie trays. Desert Delectable Foods had delivered our supplies, but this time there'd be no helpers to assist with the boards and miscellaneous items. Thankfully, I had one of those rolling milk-crate carriers that I used for presentations at Chan-Tech. It would have to do the trick.

Traffic was heavier on the roads that led to the Hidden Boulders. I imagined it was people returning to the community after work or shopping. The fashion show wasn't for another three hours so I doubted that was the reason. Lilly-Ann had her hair up in one of those semi-loose buns with a few long strands dangling. A good look for her. Especially with this heat.

I knew I had to do something with my own reddish locks if I was going to survive in this heat, but for now, they'd remain as is—wavy and chin-length. Too short to pull back and too long to be comfortable in the heat. I never thought about it when I worked at Chan-Tech since the air-conditioning was always set in the low seventies, and I rarely left the building. Unless, of course, I was on a business trip. Now, with catering venues all over the east valley, I needed to reconsider my style.

A few cars dotted the parking lot along with a cadre of vans, complete with detailing that announced their place of business—Diva Womenswear, Desertique, and a few others whose lettering I couldn't read.

"Wow, those are certainly the highest of the high-end stores in Scottsdale," Lilly-Ann said as I circumvented the front parking lot and, instead, drove to the back where the kitchen was located.

"Too high for my budget, but exactly what I expected we'd find." No sooner did I finish my sentence when a burgundy van pulled up behind me and waited until I parked before the driver took the spot next to mine. I glanced over and recognized the logo immediately—Randolph's Escapade.

Seconds later, another car showed up. This time, a beige Hyundai sedan. Four college-age coeds jumped out before the van's driver had even turned off the ignition. From my side window, I recognized the serving uniforms from Randolph's. Guess Sterling didn't waste any time making sure his staff arrived in plenty of time.

No sooner did Lilly-Ann and I get out of the KIA when I heard a familiar voice. I had just opened the hatchback to retrieve the boards when Ian called out, "Hold on, I'll give you a hand with that."

Next thing I knew, a gust of wind came out of nowhere, followed by a raspy voice that still annoyed the daylights out of me. "He likes you. Don't muck it up. So what if he's younger. It's *in* these days."

"Says who?"

Luckily Ian didn't hear me and stepped closer to my car. "I know those boards are heavy. I'll bring them inside for you two."

Lilly-Ann winked at me, and I tried to ignore her.

"He's adorable," she whispered. "I know what you said last week, but still...Won't be the first time a woman dated a younger man."

"Oh no, not you, too!"

"You mean other people told you the same thing? When?"

"Uh, not Ian. Just in general. Dating in general. You know. My mother, my friend Maddie. They weren't specific. Come on, let's grab our other stuff and get inside. It's getting hotter the longer we stand out here."

Heat. That was one of the weird things about living in the Sonoran Desert. The heat of the day came late, usually around five or six, and it managed to stay well after the sun went down.

Once inside the kitchen, a food service worker from the Rec Center directed me to the area where Lilly-Ann and I would be working. Desert Delectable Foods had delivered our products, and they were all stored in the large stainless-steel refrigerator a few feet from an enormous butcher block table.

"This is perfect," Lilly-Ann exclaimed. "And would you get a look at the set-up? I've never seen anything like it."

"Me either. Deirdre described it, and I really wanted to check it out but didn't get the chance. I told her as long as it had a large workspace with the sink close by, we'd be fine."

Lilly-Ann looked around as if we landed in Disney World. "Oh, we'll be fine, all right."

The Mountain View Recreation and Performing Arts Center took kitchen design to a level I'd never seen. The kitchen was actually three separate circular areas that joined hips at the middle with a reference area, complete with cookbooks and a computer station. Talk about visionary.

The nice thing was that the separate kitchens allowed us the privacy to concentrate on our charcuterie boards without distraction from the other kitchens. A far cry from the galley format that was so popular.

Lilly-Ann got started immediately by retrieving the meats and cheeses from the fridge and setting them out on the long table so they'd have ample time to reach room temperature. Meanwhile, I delved into the products we had brought with us to make the candied walnuts. Step by step, we followed the pattern designs we had sketched out and filled in the charcuterie boards as if they were jigsaw puzzles. Only there was no guessing on our part.

"Think Tambra's going to pitch a fit when she realizes we're not using red caviar?" Lilly-Ann asked.

"Let her pitch all she wants. If red caviar means that much to her, she can pull out her black Visa card and book a one-way flight to Helsinki."

We both burst out laughing when I heard Thomas's voice a few yards away. "You two are having way too much fun. How's it going?" He stepped into our kitchen area and surveyed the charcuteries in progress. "Looking good."

"What about your end?" I glanced over his shoulder toward his kitchen area.

"Working on the cold canapes now. They'll be served first. My staff is itching to get out to that fashion runway. Have either of you seen that setup?" I shook my head, and Thomas continued. "One thing in our favor is that it'll make serving a dream. Instead of rows of seats facing the runway, they've got large circular tables. Really easy for our staff to get around. You should check it out."

I laughed. "Tambra was quite adamant we don't set foot in the fashion show area. However, I do plan on a quick look-see once the Hidden Boulder staff moves our charcuterie boards out there. What decadent hors d'oeuvres are you serving?"

"Sausage stuffed mushrooms, mini quiches, spicy and Swedish meatballs, pierogi, chicken livers in wine sauce, caramelized onion and feta tarts, shiitake and cremini mushrooms with Gorgonzola in mini pastries. Oh, and mandarin orange slices dipped in chocolate and sprinkled with sea salt."

"What? No little pigs in a blanket? I love those."

"Me, too, but they were too pedestrian for Tambra."

"She used that word?"

"Not exactly, but I didn't want to repeat the one she *did* use."

I chuckled. "Well, better get back to work. Catch you later."

I reached for a block of Gouda when I heard shouting coming from the hallway just past our kitchens. It was followed by a litany of expletives that made Lilly-Ann gasp. *And she had been around school kids forever.* One of the voices was definitely Tambra's, but I couldn't tell who her sparring partner was. Only that the voice belonged to a woman. A woman who threatened to "make sure Tambra would choke on her own words."

Chapter Six

"I'm dying to find out what that was all about," I said to Lilly-Ann, "and who Tambra was arguing with. Maybe Deirdre will fill me in when I see her. I know for sure the other voice wasn't hers."

"And how. I don't know how long she's been living in Arizona, but her accent smacks of New England. By the way, we weren't supposed to bring the serving utensils to this venue, were we? Because if we were, we forgot."

"No, fortunately, Hidden Boulders will use their own serving forks. Same deal when we cater at Randolph's Escapade. I guess there aren't any hard fast rules, but the more casual the charcuterie tray, the more laid back the serving stuff. And for picnics and tailgating, plastic forks and toothpicks work just fine."

I went back to my block of Gouda and started to cube it when I nearly sliced a finger off.

"A corner of blocked Gouda chunks on the tray is boring. Set a few of them aside and slice the tips off. Nothing says class like hexagon shapes mixed in. You're welcome."

"Not now," I replied to the crimson haze that had engulfed my workspace. Lilly-Ann looked up. "Not now, what?"

"Oh, I was thinking out loud. I thought maybe we'd sneak a peek at the serving area for our charcuteries. That way, I can make sure the forks are there. But it can wait."

We continued filling in the board as if we were creating mosaics in the Middle Ages. Every section and every free space had to be utilized perfectly for a color and texture blend that would be enticing and inviting. It was a painstaking process made worse by Edith, who kept muttering, "No gaps. No gaps."

At one point in the process, Ian ducked into our section with sliced mandarin orange sections for us. His grin went ear-to-ear. "Thomas said your eyes lit up when he mentioned these. Enjoy. Got to get back." In a flash, he was gone. Replaced by Edith. Raspy voice and all. "He's practically screaming to take you out on a date. I can hasten things up for you."

Thoughts of microbursts, clanging pots, and ice cubes spewing out from refrigerators flashed in front of me. I started to respond but caught myself in the nick of time when I stopped with the word "don't," to which Lilly-Ann replied, "Don't what?"

"Don't waste another second. Let's dive into these."

The sugary citrus juice, coupled with the salted dark chocolate, teased every taste bud in my mouth. "Yep. A taste of heaven for sure." I tapped my cell phone to check the time and glanced at our nearly finished boards. Then I took a few steps back to see what the overall design looked like from a short distance. "We're good to go. Just need to add the edible flowers. This is your domain, Lilly-Ann. Have fun. I'll start on the clean-up."

When Lilly-Ann first started designing charcuterie boards with me, she asked about adding edible flowers. Up until then, I had always relied on herbs like sprigs of garlic, parsley, dill, and chives. She convinced me to go for a color boost, and it really added pizzazz. The only issue was to make sure the flowers we purchased were chemical-free.

As it turned out, our local florist, Petals, and Plants, worked with a few organic growers, so we were in luck. And luckier still that Lilly-Ann had an amazing gift when it came to color infusion.

I wrapped the unused cheeses, meats, and veggies in plastic wrap and put them in the small containers we brought with us. Seconds later, a tall Latino server from the Rec Center walked into our kitchen and asked when the charcuterie boards would be ready. His dark man-bun was tightly gathered at the top of his head, and his beard was carefully trimmed. The guy couldn't have been much older than twenty-one or twenty-two. He wheeled in a stainless steel two-tiered cart that had ample room for both boards. I pointed to them and announced, "They're all yours."

Lilly-Ann and I were so engrossed in our own clean-up process we hadn't noticed the servers from Randolph's Escapade loading up their round cold canape trays. "Wow, the time blew by fast," I said to her. Then I turned to the guy with the man bun. "Mind if we follow you? We'd like to see the setup." *And make sure there are forks before people decide it's okay to eat with their hands.*

"No problem. Right out the door and to your left. Can either of you give me a hand getting the board onto the cart? If not, I can—"

"Sure thing," I answered. "I'm used to lifting them."

Lilly-Ann stood back and watched as we placed the boards on the cart. True, they weren't breakable, but one wrong move and it would have resulted in a mish-mosh of meats, cheeses, fruits, veggies, and nuts.

"All set, follow me down the corridor. The guests for the fashion show are arriving now so we need to keep our voices down. Wouldn't want to upset the she-witch who's in charge of the event. But you didn't hear that from me."

I darted my eyes at Lilly-Ann, then widened them when I looked at the guy. "Sounds like you may have had an unpleasant experience with her."

"Unpleasant? That's an understatement. Toxic is a better word. If I didn't need this job, I would have left in a nanosecond, but I've got one year left before I graduate from ASU and need the extra income. Most of my classes are online, so it works out well."

"I'm curious. What did Tambra do? We *are* talking about Tambra, aren't we?"

"Is that her first name? With heels, she's about my height. Short brown hair? Every single strand in place? Uses a perfume that smells kind of woodsy?"

"That's her, all right. I'm surprised you hadn't made her acquaintance sooner, I mean, since you work here and she's in charge of this major event."

"Two separate areas. I work in food service. She's involved with the events programming. And lucky me. She's the director of this fashion show."

"If you don't mind my asking, how did you cross paths?"

"Exactly that. Crossed paths, I mean. A week or so ago, she marched into the kitchen to meet with someone about that fashion show, and I happened to be there working. She walked right up to me and said, "Don't they pay you enough so you can afford a haircut?"

I widened my eyes and motioned for him to continue.

"Honestly, I was so stunned I didn't say a word. But that didn't stop her. She looked me up and down as if she was inspecting cattle and added, 'Men with beards shouldn't be around food. Think of all those germs you could be spreading.' At that point, I regained my voice and told her I wash and comb my beard daily and keep it well-trimmed. I also told her that my appearance should be of no consequence to her."

"Good. You stood your ground."

"Nope. More like a sinkhole."

"Huh?"

"She said I better not be working the night of her precious fashion show, or it would be the last night I worked."

"She threatened you?"

The guy nodded.

"Did you tell the director? Report her to HR?"

"HR? There's no human resource department here. Hidden Boulders is formidable but not *that* large an operation. And besides, the director happens to be her husband. She made sure she shared that little tidbit of information with me. At least I now know her full name—Tambra Wright."

By now, we were a few feet from the main venue. I reached over and grabbed his wrist. "Maybe you can find another job. People like that suck the joy out of everyone's life."

Just then, I felt a strange whirling sensation around my ankles. Sure enough, it was followed by that reddish haze. *Guess Edith is still in the same outfit.* I stopped, dead cold, waiting for whatever proclamation Edith was about to make, and naturally, she didn't waste a second.

"You said you needed to hire another person. This guy looks as if he's a quick study. Tell him to call you."

"I, I, um, er...I'm Katie Aubrey. I own The Char-Board in Cave Creek. We may be in need of another employee. Call me. I don't have a card handy, but The Char-Board has a website. If you're interested, call me."

"Are you serious?"

"Yes. I am."

"I will. Monday okay?"

"Fine."

"Oh my gosh. I didn't even introduce myself. I'm Javier Rivera, but everyone calls me Javie."

"Nice to meet you, Javie. This is Lilly-Ann, and please call me."

The red haze all but clouded by vision. It was immediately followed by that annoying guttural voice. *"Please call me. If you can say that to Javier, you can say it to that sleek little number from Randolph's. Three easy words. Please call me."*

I held my breath and tried not to show any sort of a reaction. If nothing else, Edith was doing a great job teaching me patience. Too bad I had no luck with the humility skills she needed to master. Heck, I wanted her to move on more than she did.

Javie wheeled the charcuterie boards into a large banquet room with an eye-stopping fashion runway. It was framed with the round tables Thomas told me about, and I stood, momentarily mesmerized, as they began to fill up. Like most banquet tables, they had the usual white tablecloths and skirts, candles, and floral bouquets. I took my time and walked to the front of the room where my boards were to be placed. Darting my eyes to each corner, I wanted to be sure to take it all in.

"It's over here," Javie said. "This should only take a second." Again, I helped him lift and place the boards on a long rectangular table with a white tablecloth and skirt. At both ends of the table were gold-plated three-prong forks, small white porcelain dishes, and cocktail napkins.

Lilly-Ann bumped my elbow. "You can relax. The forks are here. I don't think anything can go wrong now."

Worst words in the history of mankind. "I don't think anything can go wrong now."

Chapter Seven

"Think again. That's Tambra by the front table. Quick, let's step behind these curtains. She won't be able to spot us in the semi-darkness but we can take a few seconds to bask in the glory of our creations."

"I didn't know you were so poetic, Katie."

"I'm not. I was just being overly dramatic."

"Um, you ladies going to be all right?" Javie asked. "I've got to get back to my own crew. The guests are already making their way to the food."

As he spoke, I noticed two servers, both female, add more forks to the ends of the table. "Think they'll have enough for this crowd?" Lilly-Ann asked.

I shrugged. "Look over there. Servers are backed up against the walls. They're not serving; they're waiting to clear the mini-plates. They'll put the cutlery in the dishwasher, run them through, and get them back to the charcuterie table."

Instinctively, I pressed myself against the curtain as far back as it would allow. By now, the attendees had drifted toward our boards, and I could hear comments that made me glad I'd given up my position at Chan-Tech.

Lilly-Ann inched toward me and whispered, "How long should we stay here?"

"Long enough to make sure Tambra has her look-see and gets out of here. I don't want a run-in with her either. Not that I couldn't hold my own, but still, who needs the aggravation?"

"We're getting quite a crowd. Guess the fashion show will start soon. The only area with more action is the bar across from us. Those bartenders are going to be hopping all night. And fancy drinks, too. I can see them from here."

"The last fancy drink I had was in college. A Singapore Sling. It was the cool thing to do when you turned twenty-one. Now I'm satisfied with a semi-dry Riesling."

The area between the charcuterie boards, the bar, and the tables was now buzzing in full force. Minutes before, an announcement was made over their PA system that the program would begin momentarily. What wasn't announced was the fact that no one was about to let that program begin on an empty stomach.

"That's her," Lilly-Ann said. "She's on the farthest side of the charcuterie table from us. What's she doing? She's got her arms crossed, and she's butting in front of people or peering over their heads to scrutinize. Can you believe it?"

Just then, the soft music that had been playing in the background diminished to the point where I could barely make it out. A spotlight appeared on the runway, and a robust gentleman sporting a tuxedo stepped into the light.

"Esteemed guests," he said, "Welcome to the Hidden Boulders Fashion Show. I'm Eric Wright, establishment director. On behalf of our staff, I'm pleased to present this popular event to you once again. But the real stars are the ones you'll see on the runway. Special thanks go out to Diva Womenswear, Desertique, Dilliards, Macy's, Neiman's, and Nordstrom's."

A round of applause followed, and he waited until it dissipated. Then he looked around and continued. "Of course, none of this would have been possible if it wasn't for the stellar job that our fashion committee did. And that wouldn't have been possible without the leadership from my lovely wife, Mrs. Tambra Wright."

"Gag me."

Wonderful. Edith's hovering.

"I think I might actually barf," Lilly-Ann whispered.

"See? Your assistant shares the same sentiment. That buffoon and his battle-ax wife must be a real pair."

"Not now!"

Lilly-Ann took a step back. "I was only kidding."

"Sorry. I didn't mean you. I meant—"

And at that precise second, the strip lights lit up, and the first model stepped out of the entranceway to the runway platform. An announcer introduced her and the fabulous gown she wore. Wavy golden hair hung down past the model's shoulders, and she commanded a figure that resembled one of those statues of ancient goddesses. I gasped when I realized her heels were taller than most midsize dogs. Unfortunately, her gown bore a resemblance to the Jean Harlow one Edith coveted.

It was a satin bias-cut evening gown with a V-neck and slightly flared skirt.

"If I can materialize," Edith said, "maybe you can snatch that gown from her when she goes back into the dressing room. I'll see if I can slither into it."

"I'm not about to pilfer a gown," I mumbled under my breath. "Besides, it's not about to travel to the afterworld with you."

Thankfully Lilly-Ann didn't hear me. But she did hear something else and shook my arm so I'd take a look. Off to the side of the charcuterie table, Tambra and Eric were squabbling. Well, maybe not so much as squabbling as having a contentious conversation. It consisted of Eric accusing her of going through his cell phone messages and Tambra blasting back about Eric's obsessive need for control, even when it came to her daily expenses. The spot they picked for their exchange of words was far enough away from the runway action that the attendees couldn't hear them. However, the folks who were grabbing tidbits from our charcuteries turned their heads every now and then.

"The Jean Harlow gown can wait. I want to watch those two lock horns." Edith stood next to me, hands on her hips. Still in the crimson boho outfit but with large hoop earrings that almost looked comical.

"Knock yourself out," I mouthed, hoping no one saw me.

Two female servers carrying trays of unused utensils placed them on either side of the charcuterie trays before returning to the kitchen. Same uniform as the one Javie wore.

"Probably fresh out of the dishwasher," I said out loud.

"What is?" It was Ian's voice, and I looked behind me to see him standing there. "I wanted to catch a glimpse of your charcuterie boards, and I have to say, you don't disappoint."

"That was a compliment," Edith said. As usual, she materialized out of nowhere. It didn't faze me. I had gotten used to her unannounced entrances, hazes, smoke, whirling colors, and all. "I don't think he meant the boards, Katie. Are you going to ask him out or do you want me to—"

"I don't want you to—" Ian looked directly at me, and I caught a breath. "To, um, feel as if you have to compliment my work." *Talk about fast thinking.*

He walked toward me and took another look at the charcuteries. "Every compliment you get on those is well-deserved."

The low lighting accentuated his facial features by offering more dimensionality to them. Ugh. Edith was right. The guy was a hunk. But he had to be at least six or seven years younger than me. Or even eight. *Gulp.* Then, I started to play the math game. One I hadn't thought about since college.

If I'm 32 and he's 25, I'll be 40 when he turns 32. Then again, it might not matter when I turn 68. He'll be 61.

"Are you okay?" Ian tilted his head, and I could see what appeared to be a dimple when he spoke. *A dimple. Talk about secret weapons.* "It looked like you were daydreaming."

"What? No. I was just thinking. About how the boards looked. And thanks for the compliments. As a chef, you know what that means to us. Oh, and by the way, thanks for the orange slices. They were marvelous."

"If we do have any leftovers, which I seriously doubt, you'll have to try our milk chocolate ones. Glance over at our servers. They're going non-stop, so that must mean so are the canapes. Listen, I need to get back in the kitchen. Catch you later, okay?"

"Uh, sure."

Ian was out of there in a flash, leaving Lilly-Ann and me to our hideaway by the curtains. I studied the tables, and that's when I heard a thud, only to see Eric Wright storm off from the far end of our charcuterie table. He held one hand in the other, and I was fairly certain the thud came from him banging one of his fists on the table. I cringed. Visions of the meats cascading into the cheeses and such.

Tambra stood in place, a tad closer to the corner of the room, but still, within arm's reach of the food. She brushed a lock of hair from the side of her face and picked up one of the small appetizer plates.

Lilly-Ann watched her as well before elbowing me. "She's engrossed with the food selection. Think we can make a quick getaway?"

I looked around. "I don't see why not."

The two of us skirted the edges of the room like escapees from the county jail, waiting to make our break. We had gotten as far as the first of the banquet room's entrance/exit doors when I heard a thud similar to the one Eric made when he exited the room, only much louder.

"No worries," I said to Lilly-Ann. "Nothing of ours is going to make that noise. Most likely, someone dropped a piece of furniture. Like a chair or something."

Then I heard a screech. Followed by three or four more. High pitched and endless.

"Think someone saw a mouse?" Lilly-Ann asked. "I had an aunt who screamed like that any time she saw one. Or thought she did."

I was about to respond but next sound was more of a scream than a screech and it was followed by the words, "I think that woman's dead."

Lilly-Ann and I left our wallflower positions and raced over to the serving area for our charcuterie boards. We weren't alone. A crowd gathered, and I could hear the fashion show announcer say, "Ladies and Gentlemen, please remain at your tables." Her voice was clear and succinct, but I could detect a slight nervousness.

The sound of chairs being shoved into tables multiplied exponentially as the "gathering crowd" fast became the "gathering mob." I grabbed Lilly-Ann's wrist. "What woman? What woman are they talking about?" As if she would know.

In seconds, we wasted no time joining Hidden Boulder's first mob scene.

"They're pointing to the spot where Tambra stood. The last I looked."

Lilly-Ann and I darted and swayed, sashayed, and elbowed until we made our way to the front of the room.

"I'll save you the trouble," Edith announced. No ghostly apparition, only thick reddish haze. "It's the she-witch, all right. But that's not your problem. *Your* problem is that she's holding one of those pancetta rosettes of yours on her fork. And from my vantage point, it appears as if she took a bite before she kissed the floor."

"It's Tambra," I said to Lilly-Ann. My voice was robotic at best.

"How do you know?"

I can't very well tell her Edith pointed it out. "She was there one minute and not the next. Educated guess."

Next I knew Edith's haze gravitated to that area. "Look over to the left. Just past the charcuterie board table. Isn't that her husband? He just shoved something into his pocket."

I stood on tiptoes for a birds-eye view before nudging Lilly-Ann. "Look! Her husband stuck something in his pocket. Oh my gosh. Too bad we don't know what it was."

Chapter Eight

I f I had any thoughts of getting home before midnight, they evaporated the minute sirens cut through the night air. They culminated with a slew of Maricopa County Deputies and members of the Cave Creek Marshal Service thundering into the room like a herd of elephants. It was immediately followed by a deep, gruff voice that filtered through the rec center's audio system.

"Ladies and gentlemen, please return to your tables if you are guests. This is not a request. This is a directive from the Maricopa County Sheriff's Office. Regrettably, this evening's program is, at least, temporarily postponed until we can gather sufficient information to determine why one of the attendees keeled over and died suddenly at the cheese and cracker table."

Cheese and cracker table? That's the worst insult ever!

Lilly-Ann recoiled the minute he said that, and we both gave each other the "I-can't- believe-he-said that" look while he continued to speak.

"This area is now an active crime scene. Again, I repeat, 'Return to your tables and await further instruction.'"

"Where are we supposed to wait?" she asked. It was more of a statement than a question, and I shrugged.

"My guess is the kitchen. I suppose that would make sense."

The lights flickered for a second, and I knew it wasn't an electrical issue. "Don't stand there like a ninny. Ask! Use your voice. And don't raise your hand. You're not in grade school."

"I, uh…"

"I can always turn off the lights."

Sure you can, Edith.

"And create a riot?"

"What did you say about a riot? I couldn't hear you with everyone talking." Lilly-Ann looked around the banquet hall as if a hoard of looters crashed Cinderella's ball.

"Just clearing my throat." By now, the deputies and marshals were ushering everyone to the tables. "Meet you halfway, Edith," I mumbled under my breath. I rushed to the bar, grabbed a large wine glass and small paring knife that was next to a bowl of limes. Then I clanged on the glass as if I was about to make a wedding speech.

"Excuse me. Excuse me." After a few attempts, I was finally heard. "Where do the waitstaff go? The house employees? The caterers?"

No response. By now, a full cadre of forensic techs had made their way to the serving area. The fluorescent lettering on the back of their jackets was a dead giveaway. No pun intended. They took photos of Tambra's lifeless body as well as my entire charcuterie display. Then, in a slow and solemn moment, they stood back as another two county employees placed the body into a dark bag and hoisted it on a gurney.

Once Tambra had been removed from the room, two deputies unrolled a cord of yellow crime scene tape and wove it around the area.

"I'm not about to stand here all night," I said to Lilly-Ann. "Let's head for the kitchen, and if they want us someplace else, they'll let us know."

Apparently, I wasn't the only one with that notion. A few servers slipped out of the banquet room, and my take was that they were kitchen-bound as well.

Lilly-Ann nudged me. "You know, if one of those servers was the killer, he or she could easily slip out of here. Who would know?"

"Surveillance? Time sheets? Someone's iPhone photos? Trust me, it won't stay a secret for long." *Who was I kidding?*

I watched as the deputies and marshals circulated around the tables, pausing to talk with the guests. Most of them were holding iPads, so I imagined they were in the process of getting names and addresses.

"They're not about to stay here all night to question everyone, are they?"

Lilly-Ann moved her neck from side to side, then rubbed the back of it.

"I doubt it. Once they get the contact information, they'll probably send everyone home. Besides, they can always substantiate it with the official guest list."

Then, not unexpectedly, a handful of models and assistants walked onto the runway. One of them, a tall, dark-skinned woman sporting a peacock blue and teal dress, called out, "What happened? Is this over? No one tells us anything in the changing area."

A formidable-looking deputy who looked as if his sideline was playing defense for the Cardinals marched to the runway and immediately walked toward a small podium that housed the microphone for the fashion show. He yanked it from its resting spot and positioned himself midway down the runway.

His abrasive voice gave Lilly-Ann the answer she needed – We were going to be here all night. Period. "Upon cursory inspection from the coroner, there are indications of foul play. Everyone in this building must remain here until our preliminary questioning is completed."

A barrage of questions followed. Along with some rather unsettling comments.

"Are you saying the woman was poisoned?"

"Poisoned? My God! We could all be poisoned."

"What did she eat?"

"Call an ambulance! Call 911! Get us all checked out before we wind up like she did!"

The deputy was unfazed. "Unless anyone is experiencing distress, there is no need for medical assistance at this time. Please remain in your seats until this active crime scene is resolved."

"What does that mean?" I asked no one in particular.

"It means those food trays are going to be carted off for analysis like nobody's business. Glad I wasn't the one who prepared them. Unfortunately, I'm the one who's got to deal with all of this." I turned and was face-to-face with a lanky gentleman. Long-sleeved black shirt with jacquard-patterned formal business tie. I'd seen enough of those at Chan-Tech to know he was in management.

"I thought Eric Wright was the establishment's director." My voice was soft but somehow steady.

"He is. But if you look over your shoulder, you'll see he's with two deputies and a marshal. Not a good sign."

It'll be a worse sign if the guy's not a good actor.

The man continued. "I'm Lance Baker. Assistant director. If you'll excuse me, I need to make my way over there."

Lilly-Ann put her arm on my wrist and gave it a squeeze. "They won't find any evidence on our charcuterie boards. Anyone could have done the deed."

I gulped. "Yeah, but they could have chosen to use our charcuteries as their weapon of choice. Oh geez. This is the worst night ever. Come on, let's head into the kitchen. Less chaos."

Clusters of waitstaff and kitchen personnel from Randolph's Escapade and the Hidden Boulders were everywhere. Ian spied us immediately and rushed over. His eyes were wide, and I swear, the guy had longer lashes than I did.

"What's going on? We only caught fragments of an announcement, and two of our servers rushed in to tell us Tambra was dead. Is that true?"

I nodded. "Oh, it's true, all right. I imagine any second now, someone from the marshal's office or the county will charge in and bark orders. That seems to be what's going on in the banquet room."

"Accidental or deliberate?"

Lilly-Ann looked at Ian and bit her lip. "Guess you missed the gist of the announcement. Her death didn't appear to be natural, so the entire Cave Creek militia was called to the scene. Looks like it's going to be one long night."

Just then, two deputies entered the kitchen area. One of them cleared his throat in such a way as to mean business. "Ladies and gentlemen, do not touch anything. Nothing. Please remain where you are for questioning. All food items are to remain right here on the premises."

"If they're concerned about food items, they must have a reason to believe Tambra was poisoned," Thomas said.

I was so busy looking at Ian that I was unaware Thomas had approached us and was standing directly behind me. I turned and saw the stricken look on his face.

"You know what this means, don't you?" he asked. "Our establishments and our employees will be under suspicion for her death. Of course, I can't think of a single motive, but apparently, there was evidence of foul play."

"Like frothing at the mouth or blue lips?" I'd read my share of crime novels.

"Or redness around the mouth that might be confused with lipstick. Not to mention drooling or pupils that are too large or too small. The coroner must have observed something to make the determination that Tambra didn't die naturally. And if you're wondering why I'm so familiar with such a macabre subject, I was an EMT when I was in the service."

"That determination was made pretty darn fast."

Thomas shook his head. "It may seem that way, but the coroner will take a pulse, body temperature, and do a cursory check of the body for ligature marks, burns, or blunt force trauma. Plus, in this case, there were witnesses all around who saw Tambra ingest something and fall to the floor."

I rolled my eyes. "Yeah, well, she stood at the charcuterie table. Three guesses what she ingested."

Thomas put an arm on my shoulder. "What she ingested at the charcuterie table and what actually killed her may be two different things. Don't jump to conclusions."

Jump? I'm pole-vaulting.

Ian took my arm and gave it a squeeze. "Thomas is right, you know. Come on, there are some chairs over there by the computer station. What do you say we grab them?"

I looked at Lilly-Ann. "Might as well."

"I need to have a word with the rest of my staff," Thomas said. "In a few minutes, none of us will be able to say anything to anyone. Hang tight. Okay?"

As Thomas strode toward his servers, I made my way to the computer station and took the first chair, turning it so it no longer faced one of the Acer computers. Lilly-Ann positioned herself to my right and Ian to my left.

All three of us stared straight ahead.

Suddenly a pinkish haze drifted past me, and my stomach churned. Without warning, the computer turned on, and a video of Ricky Martin singing *Que Tal* appeared. I swung my chair around to power off the machine, only to find Ian trying to do the same.

"Funny how that happened," he said. "Unless it was pre-programmed or something."

"Or something."

Just then, the deputy with the abrasive voice and matching demeanor walked into the kitchen and called out, "Is there a Katie Aubrey in here?"

I raised my hand as if I was back in elementary school.

"Good," he shouted. "You need to come with me."

Lilly-Ann stood. "I'll go with you."

The deputy held up his hands as if he was blocking traffic. "Not at this time." Then he motioned for me to follow him. "You'll need to answer a few questions."

Ian sat up straight. "Shouldn't someone be with her?"

The deputy stretched his arms back. "She's not under arrest. Our office needs to clarify a few things."

"Clarify a few things." The euphemism for "build a case."

"I'll be fine," I said to Lilly-Ann and Ian. "Absolutely fine."

And absolutely the worst lie I ever told.

Chapter Nine

My hands were clammy, and there was no moisture in my mouth as I was led to the Hidden Boulders office. The normally pleasant room I saw when I first visited this place was now semi-dark and foreboding. The fact that a second deputy sat facing the door did very little to lighten my mood.

He pointed to a chair on his left and directed me to take a seat. *This is so not good.* I swallowed a mouthful of dry air and did as I was told. Especially since the deputy who brought me here now stood directly behind me, and who knew if his gun was drawn.

"Katie Aubrey?" the second deputy asked. The man was probably in his fifties, maybe a tad younger, but with a five o'clock shadow on his face, it was hard to tell. "Your company catered this event?"

"We, um, I mean, my charcuterie business provided the boards. Yes. Cured meats, cheeses, fruits, nuts—"

"I get the idea. I'll make this as brief as I can. I'm Deputy Vincent. Travis Vincent. The reason I'm speaking with you is because the victim was found to be holding one of your tray items when she succumbed. An item that appeared to be tasted."

Suddenly, I regained my composure. "Are you implying we tampered with the food she ate, because if you are, that's preposterous. Why would we do such a thing? And how would we have known which item she'd select? If we were to poison her, it would have meant poisoning everyone. No one is as imbecilic as to do something like that. They would have figured out a way to ensure she got the poisoned piece of meat, or cheese, or whatever was poisoned." At that moment, I knew I had dug myself deeper and deeper into the pit. No way out now. I was a goner.

"Miss Aubrey, I did not use the word *poison*. I said she succumbed. Once an initial toxicology screening is completed, our office, along with the marshals, will have a better idea as to what transpired."

"Oh."

"Right now, we are in the preliminary stages of our investigation. Preliminary."

He emphasized the word preliminary, but I knew all it meant was that he was gathering evidence and wasting no time.

"How did you know the charcuterie boards were prepared by me?"

He cleared his throat, rubbed his chin, and looked me directly in the eye. "Questioning and substantiating what we learn. That's why a team of deputies arrived on scene."

I caught a whiff of rose petals and hibiscus before I was subjected to a pinkish-red mist that felt damp on my skin. "Cut to the chase and ask him who ratted you out."

"Not now." I brushed my arm off to the side, hoping Deputy Vincent didn't notice. Lamentably, he did.

"Not now, what? Are you all right?"

"I'm fine. Really. But I'd like to know who informed you that The Char-Board catered that portion of the fashion show."

Deputy Vincent pulled out an iPad, tapped it, and looked up. "The establishment's assistant manager had that information on file. Randolph's Escapade and The Char-Board."

"So if you had that information already, I don't understand why I'm being singled out for questioning."

"Good girl. Show a little moxy."

"Shh."

Deputy Vincent looked around. "Why are you shushing me?"

"I thought I heard a noise. Never mind." *Terrific. I'm fending off an obnoxious ghost and getting interrogated at the same time.*

I watched as the deputy scrolled through his iPad notes, pausing every few seconds to crinkle his brow before he spoke. "According to my notes, you had a rather unpleasant dealing with the victim a week or so ago. Care to expound on that?"

"Where did you hear that?" *Although I can wager a good guess.* I clenched my fists with both hands at my sides, then gradually released them. *He's trying to intimidate me. Edith's right.*

"Tell him you have unpleasant dealings with people all the time." Ugh. Edith again.

And then, it slipped, "only with you."

"I beg your pardon?"

"Sorry. It's just that I feel this is more than information gathering, and I'm the only one getting grilled. For the record, I had one in-person dealing with Tambra. It was when I met with her and the fashion show committee to discuss the charcuterie trays. Someone on that committee must have said something. Frankly, if I were in your shoes, I'd start with them. Are you aware how intimidating Tambra was? How controlling?"

"Miss Aubrey, please don't deflect the question."

"Deflecting? I'm offering you more suspects. I mean, other suspects. Not that I should be a suspect. Am I? Don't tell me I'm a suspect."

The pinkish-red vapor whirled around us, compelling me to close my eyes and count to ten.

"Keep it up, and he'll drag a full-blown confession out of you. Quit while you're ahead. Or, in this case, before they slap those plastic handcuffs on you."

"As I mentioned earlier," the deputy said, "we are in the preliminary stages of an investigation. Until an autopsy is performed and a preliminary toxicology report is handed over, we need to follow protocol. What I need from you is a complete timeline from the minute you arrived with those trays until the victim was found on the floor."

"I didn't arrive with the trays. We created them here. I arrived with some ingredients but the main ones were delivered by Desert Delectable Foods in the valley."

"Fine. Describe the entire process. From start to finish. And be sure to tell me if anyone approached you while you prepared those trays."

For the next fifteen minutes, I went through every detail, every nuance, every single step. If he was bored, he didn't show it. He merely took notes and made a few guttural sounds from time to time.

"I don't think anyone approached me while I worked with my assistant."

And I'm not about to mention Ian and those mandarin orange slices. Bad enough I'm getting beat up around here.

"Who moved the trays from the kitchen to the staging area?"

"An employee from Hidden Boulders."

I'm not blowing in Javie, either.

"Male or female?"

"Male."

"Describe him."

"I really wasn't looking that closely. Tall, I guess. Dark hair."

"All right, Miss Aubrey, if we have any further questions for you, we know where to find you."

"Does this mean my assistant and I can leave?"

"Only if the deputies in the kitchen area have completed their questioning." Then, he looked at the other deputy in the room. "Please escort Miss Aubrey back to the kitchen. If they're done speaking with her assistant, then she's free to go."

I stood, nodded at Deputy Vincent, and followed Deputy-with-the-abrasive-voice back to the kitchen. We had gotten halfway down the corridor when Eric Wright appeared from the opposite direction. He looked pale and shaken, but there was something else about his demeanor that I couldn't quite place.

As the deputy and I approached him, he lunged toward me and shouted, "The Char-Board, I see the logo on your apron. You're responsible for my wife's death. Her *murder.*"

The deputy held one hand up and, with the other, moved me out of Eric's range. "I understand how distraught you are, sir, but this is neither the time nor the place. I suggest you call your relatives and return home. Our office will contact you tomorrow morning."

"Tomorrow morning? I'm not waiting until tomorrow morning. I want answers, and I want them now. Answers and justice." When he said the word *justice*, he glared at me and held his stare longer than I would have liked.

The deputy turned to me and, in a low voice, asked, "Can you walk back to the kitchen by yourself, or would you like me to page someone to escort you?"

"It's only a few yards. I'll be fine. Thanks."

I moved from that spot with more speed than I imagined I had in me. Meanwhile, I heard the deputy say, "Don't make this worse on yourself. The cause of your wife's death has not been determined. We can discuss this in your building's main office. So you know, our deputies will be on scene for most of the night gathering every bit of evidence and information we can."

A quick turn of my head and I watched as the two of them walked toward the office I had just left. Then, I pushed myself forward and didn't stop until I reached the kitchen.

As soon as I stepped inside, Lilly-Ann and Ian were practically on top of me, firing questions nonstop.

"What happened?"

"They're not placing you under arrest, are they?"

"Did they say it was poison?"

"They're not going to shut down our sandwich shop, are they?"

And finally, from Ian, "Can I get you a glass of water? You look really washed out."

Washed out. What every woman wants to hear.

"Yeah, actually. Water would be great."

By now, many of the waitstaff and kitchen crew were gone. Only eight or nine people remained, including Thomas. I presumed the deputies had gotten the information they needed and were trying to move through the first leg of their investigation as timely and efficiently as possible. Still, I couldn't help but shake the feeling that they weren't going to look much further than me as far as a suspect was concerned.

As Ian walked to the fridge, Thomas approached. "Long night, huh? Not what any of us planned on. I saw you had a personal escort out of here. Everything okay?"

"Not really." I told him and Lilly-Ann about my being questioned and about my unsettling experience with Eric Wright in the hallway. With a palm against his chin, Thomas rubbed both of his cheeks. "Someone on my crew said they thought he pocketed something while he was perusing the charcuteries, but they couldn't be sure. I told them to let one of the deputies know."

"Yeah, I kind of caught that, too. But what? A piece of meat? An olive? What was there to pocket?"

All of a sudden, Thomas's jaw dropped. "Whoa. Maybe he wasn't so much as *pocketing* something as he was *placing* something."

Then, not totally unexpected, given what I had gotten used to where Edith was concerned, small grayish-white dust devils appeared from floor to ceiling and intensified in speed and size.

Oh, brother. This, on top of everything else.

"We need to follow that bugger home and see what he's up to."

"I'm not following anyone." Then I caught myself. "I mean, I'm not following this."

Thomas placed an arm on my shoulder and took a breath. "Maybe he planted something he knew his wife would take."

Edith was relentless. "All the reason to find out."

"I need to take Lilly-Ann home."

Thomas shook his head. "I understand. It's been a grueling night. Did you get the all-clear to leave?"

"Yes." Then I looked at Lilly-Ann.

"I'm free to go," she said. "No sense packing up anything. It's all evidence."

Evidence that might not get paid for. Aargh!

Ian rushed over, out of breath, but smiling. "Sorry it took me so long. I wanted to nab bottled water for you but surprise, surprise. Anything in those refrigerators is now evidence. I was, however, able to find a wrapped plastic cup and use tap water."

"Tap water's fine. Thanks." I took a large gulp and then a second. "By the way, what happened to the crew from Hidden Boulders? Were they questioned in here as well?"

Ian and Thomas both shook their heads before Thomas replied. "Nope. They were ushered out of here like nobody's business. I have no idea where they went."

"Further down the dungeon," Edith announced. "And if you're not careful, that's where you'll end up, too."

Chapter Ten

"I think I'd better get on the horn and order three more large charcuterie trays," I said to Lilly-Ann when I dropped her off. It was after midnight, and we were both exhausted. "I have no idea how long they'll keep everything for evidence."

"I'm so sorry. Those are expensive, too."

"I'll write it off as a business expense. And who knows? Once this nightmare is over with, I'll get them back. By then, if the business grows, I'll need them."

"That's what I like about working for you—your optimism."

"Wish I could be more optimistic about tonight. All fingers are pointing my way."

Lilly-Ann sighed. "Things may change once they complete the tox screen."

"We can always hope. See you on Monday."

"Hey, by the way, Ian's really sweet. Give him a chance, will you?"

"That'll be my next arrest—cradle robbing."

"You're both adults. See you Monday."

The second Lilly-Ann shut the car door, Edith materialized in the passenger seat. She was no longer sporting the bizarre boho outfit and instead wore a horrible brown turtleneck and dungarees. Not jeans. Dungarees. Like the kind John Wayne wore.

She must have noticed the expression on my face because she was in defense mode before I could utter a word. "Fine. So I managed to tick off a few of the middle management clerks up there. Don't you dare say a word. The sweater is itchy, and these cowboy jeans are scratchy."

"You can feel the clothes they give you? That doesn't make any sense at all."

"Tell that to middle management. They're the worst. Always passing the buck. Listen, it's not even two a.m. and if we don't see what Eric is up to tonight, it might be too late."

"Two in the morning *is* too late."

"Fine. I hope you have a good lawyer on retainer."

I pulled away from the curb in front of Lilly-Ann's house and started for my own place.

"I know where he and the late Tambra live. Or lived, in this case."

"How did you manage that?"

"While you were on the receiving end of Deputy Vincent's personal colonoscopy, I had myself a good look-see in the files. Some ding-dong in their office left the computer on. I told you I was good with electronics."

I knew where this was going. Edith would get under my skin like a splinter if I didn't acquiesce.

"You win. But I'm not getting out of the car."

"A lot of good that will do you."

"Okay. But I'm not breaking in."

"It's not breaking in if a door is open. It's *entering*."

No wonder she's conversant with keeping a lawyer on retainer.

I let out a slow breath and rolled my eyes. "What exactly do you think we're going to find?"

"Anything that would incriminate him."

"Like a poison? No one in their right mind is going to keep that in their house. And what kind of poison? For your information, there's like a zillion of them. That's why Agatha Christie was able to write so many murder mysteries."

"Not that. The motive."

"Huh? You lost me, Edith."

"We need to scout around for a hefty insurance policy. Or notes he left to himself that he thought no one else would see."

"What about what he might have pocketed? Do you think it could have been a vial of something?"

"Never hurts to go through someone's pants pockets. I'm open to anything and everything."

"Sure, you're not the one who's going to have their mugshot plastered all over the news."

"Not if you're careful. So, are you going to head back to Hidden Boulders or not?"

The clock on my dashboard read 1:47. I turned and stared at that godawful sweater and tried not to laugh. "I suppose so. But by 2:47, we're out of there. Deal?"

"Okay. Unless, of course—"

"2:47. No unless."

Edith rattled off the address, and I put it on my cell phone. From there, I pulled up a map and took the shortest route back to Hidden Boulders. The estate of Eric and Tambra Wright was exactly what the word implied—oversized and luxurious. Framed by rocket junipers that were set off by custom lighting, it stood back from the road, and I imagined a spectacular mountain view from the rear.

"Only the coach lights are on," Edith said. "Must be the master bedroom is in the back. If those lights are on, we can't see them out here in the front."

"The place is probably armed. Let's turn around now."

"Since when does an electronic monitoring system stand in my way? A little flicker here and there, and voilà!"

Little flicker. The place will look like a strobe light hit it.

I parked the car in a dimly lit spot between Eric's house and his neighbor's. Then, with Edith hovering over me like something out of a bad 1960s horror movie, I walked up his drive and quickly skirted to the side of the house, hoping I'd find a kitchen door or even a side door from the garage. If not, I braced myself for the fact I'd have to check the other side.

My take was that, like most Arizona homes, the rear of the house would have sliding patio doors or, worse yet, those heavy French doors. Not to mention, a master bedroom that all but encompassed the entire second floor. And one look out the window, and I'd be a goner.

A bluish-brown haze clouded my vision for a split second before I heard Edith's raspy voice. "No one's in the kitchen, and the locks are automatic. A little electrical disturbance, and we're home free."

I stood, fixed to the ground, my eyes on the door.

"What are you waiting for? An engraved invitation? The door's open. Go in. And be quiet about it."

Be quiet about it? This, from the queen of pot clanging and ice cube spewing.

The only visible lights were the metallic green ones from the microwave and the stove. Still, there was enough illumination for me to find my way into the kitchen without knocking anything over. My heart raced, and I had to focus and take deep breaths every few feet.

"What am I supposed to do now?" My voice was more of a squeak than fully-formed words. But before Edith could reply, I heard another voice—Eric's. And I had no idea where it came from, only that it was as crystal clear as if he were standing next to me.

Rats! Where is he? Please don't tell me he's going to walk in here any second. I'm deader than dead. And who knows if he's got a loaded gun. It's Arizona, for crying out loud.

"He's upstairs. On a balcony landing between the floors. Stay still."

"Stay still." What does she think I'm going to do?

For someone who just lost a wife under suspicious circumstances, Eric sounded robust and steady. "I told you not to come here. Of all the stupid things. Do you have any idea how this looks?"

"To who? And I pulled my car into your garage. Handy to have the code." It was a woman's voice. Youngish but not overly adolescent. Deirdre? No, her voice was way too Bostonian. Meredith? Nope, too girlish. My mind began to replay the voices from the bunco group, and I came up empty. Then again, I never heard Eulodie or Deborah's voices. Only Deirdre, Cherie, and Meredith. And under very different circumstances.

"You need to leave. Now! For all I know, those deputies could show up any second with a search warrant. The spouse is always the first suspect."

"You certainly played the part of the distraught and angry spouse."

"Look, maybe Tambra and I didn't have the best marriage, but still—"

"But still—nothing. That marriage was on the rocks like a Johnny Walker Black, and you know it."

All of a sudden, a cold draft hit me in the face, and Edith's voice blew straight in my ear. "That chickee's got enough eye makeup on to keep the cosmetic industry going. Probably late forties trying to be late thirties. What are you waiting for? Take out your cell phone and record the conversation. Any minute now, he's going to confess to doing away with his harridan of a wife."

"I was staying still." I reached into my pocket and pulled out my iPhone in time to record the remainder of the conversation. Fat lot of good it did me, though. Although if Eric ever needed a defense attorney, he or she would have been thrilled to get their hands on it.

"If you're insinuating that I killed her, go no further. Not my style."

"You could have fooled me."

"Look, you can't stay here. You need to leave. We'll continue this conversation another time."

"That, and the other little matter that you've been putting off. I'm not running a lending library, you know."

"Whatever. Come on. I'll escort you to the garage."

"You don't trust me."

"You have to ask?"

And then the voices faded, replaced by the sound of footsteps on the stairs. I looked behind me and realized I was staring at the utility door to the garage. The one they'd need to access. Wasting no time, I darted out of the kitchen and into an office.

"Good thinking. Now you can start snooping around."

"What? He already made it clear he didn't kill her." *And what if he decides to kill me, thinking I'm a burglar?*

"Nonsense. Since when have any murderers confessed to doing the deed?"

"Even if that's the case, it's pitch black in here. If I so much as turn on a desk lamp, he'll be in here."

"Not if he has a plumbing problem upstairs."

"You mean you can mess with water, too? I thought sending ice cubes out of the fridge was about as far as it went."

"Honey, I'm just learning my new skills. Time to put them to the test."

And in a flash, a cascade of brownish smoke made its way up the stairs. Seconds later, I heard what sounded like Niagara Falls.

"What the—" Eric's voice was almost as loud as the gushing water I heard.

"How many bathrooms are you messing with, Edith?" I whispered under my breath.

"All of them. Get moving. And you can thank me for booting up his computer. My way doesn't require a password. Quick! He's thundering up the stairs."

Chapter Eleven

The pounding in my chest was almost as disconcerting as the tremors I felt in my hands. Still, that didn't stop me from tapping the enter key and doing a quick search for his screen icons. Sure enough, WORD stood out, but I had no idea which of the zillion files would yield any useful information.

Tax information, personal correspondence, Hidden Boulders information. It was all clearly documented in the titles. So what the heck was I looking for? A recipe for murder?

"Look for any anomalies. It's not what's in front of you. It's what isn't." Edith's voice was somewhat muted, and when I looked around, I wasn't blinded by haze, smoke, or any noxious announcements of her presence.

"Why don't you look?" I was so exasperated and nervous that I actually shouted.

"Because I'm stuck up here, Missy, using all my energies to keep the water flowing."

"How did you—"

"It's a skill set."

I scrolled through the files and tried to hone in on anything out of the ordinary. Seconds later, I could hear Eric's voice. "Damn it! Why the hell won't this faucet turn off? Stupid wrenches are in the garage."

Then, the thundering of footsteps down the stairs and out the utility door to the garage. I held still and waited until I heard him retreat upstairs. This time even louder with more "hells, craps, and damns" imaginable. It was followed by, "This is all I need. First Tambra face down and dead, and now a flood!" Not exactly the grieving husband.

As he rustled around above me, I turned my attention back to the computer screen. Only two files didn't fit in the scheme of things. One was labeled "Options" and the other "Honey-do list."

I opened Options first, only to find it dealt with remedies for golf course issues like drainage, tree management, and turf control for healthy grass and desirable putting speeds. Nothing at all that smacked of a motive for murder. With a quick click, I was on to the Honey-do list.

It struck me odd that someone would have to create a file for household repairs, and my hunch was right. The file had nothing to do with chores. But it did contain something else—a list of people who were being blackmailed or at the very least, intimidated. And this list had nothing to do with Eric Wright. In that split instant, it occurred to me that Eric and Tambra both shared the computer. And her list was more chilling than anything I could possibly imagine.

Not wanting to turn on the printer, I did the logical thing. I held my iPhone to the screen and snapped a photo. Then, I emailed it to my address. Call it overly cautious, but I wasn't about to take chances. Especially the way this night was rolling out.

I moved the mouse to the x on the top right hand of the computer monitor when my curiosity got the best of me. I itched to read the details. Or at least get started. In the grand scheme of things, what did another few seconds matter? I squinted at the screen to get a better look and covered my mouth with my hand, so I wouldn't gasp.

Kiara, manicurist—Nails 'n Such—giving the salon manager more than work hours.

Judi, masseuse—Pressure Points Plus—watched her pilfer over-the-counter meds at Safeway.

Ricardo, personal trainer and co-owner of—Up and Running, two-timing his partner

Alon, colorist and owner of New You—bought generic dyes and rinses, not brand as advertised

Eulodie—dented car and covered up accident

Cherie—owed gambling money

Deirdre—dirty weekend and not with sick relative as stated

Deborah—had face lift, not on cruise

But the real shocker came when I scrolled to the bottom of the page and read the following sentence, "If you're reading this Eric, which one of those trollops, and don't think Ricardo isn't included, are you doing?"

Whoa. Talk about toxic. By now, my hand was no longer over my mouth, but my jaw nearly hit the floor. I was so engrossed I didn't hear Eric make a return trip to the kitchen until I heard something slam. A cabinet door? It was followed by, "I don't need this crap. Worse than the mess from last year's monsoons. Serve-Pro's number is on my desk somewhere."

The word *desk* was like a hot poker in my chest. I clicked that x like there was no tomorrow and looked around the room for a good hiding spot.

"Back of the futon. And move it, Missy. The guy's a regular storm trooper."

"Then do something, Edith," I whispered.

A horrific gas smell permeated the air, and I gagged. "What happened to smoke or haze?"

"I'm trying something new."

"Now? Now you're trying something new?" I dove behind the futon, managing to bang both elbows just as Eric charged toward the desk and shuffled papers around. "Now what? A damn gas leak?"

I leaned forward and caught a glimpse of him reaching into his pocket before I heard him.

"This is Eric Wright, and I'm calling to report a gas leak at my residence. Two eighty-three Horizon Drive in Hidden Boulders. It's a bad one. Place reeks of sulfur gas. I had a water leak and maybe—What? No, don't put me on hold. Get over here. Before my entire house explodes."

The pain in my elbows shot through me, but I was too scared to rub them. The guy was on edge as is. Finding me behind his futon would most definitely give him cause to do something unthinkable. If he hadn't already done that with Tambra.

"He won't stay in here much longer. The stench will get him," Edith announced.

I rolled my eyes and kept still.

"What did I tell you? He's out the door already. Probably halfway down the driveway."

Suddenly, all noxious odors vanished. Kaput. Just like that.

"I told you I'm learning new skill sets. What did you find out?"

"Laundry list of possible blackmail victims. Hers, not his. It's a veritable treasure trove of suspects."

"That's probably what the husband counted on. Look, if the marriage was on the rocks, he'd stand to do better financially if he didn't have to pay alimony. Or sell the house and split the difference. You heard that conversation with his uninvited guest. You need to find out that "other little matter."

"I can't very well do that if I don't know who it was." Then I remembered something. "She got into the garage with a code. And this house has camera surveillance. Holy Moly! That system's on his computer. I've watched my friend Maddie use hers. I should be able to figure this out."

I ignored the slight tremor in my hands as I pulled up his security system on the computer. "How long do you think it will take for Southwest Gas to get here?"

"They're here already. Been to any discos lately?"

"Huh?"

"I can strobe the lights and slow them down, but you need to work fast."

Using one hand as a visor over my forehead and the other wrangling with the mouse, I pulled up a grainy photo of a woman behind the wheel of the car as she pulled it into the large tandem garage and got out of the car.

"Nice style choice." Edith now hovered behind me. "Banded-waist maxi dress with a rib-trimmed cardigan shrug. Hmm, could be ombre dot fabric, but it's hard to tell."

For a food critic, Edith was fast becoming a fashionista as well. I shrugged. "What's ombre dot pattern? And with this strobing, everything looks dotted."

"Dip-dyed color variation. Think a Paris runway's version of tie-dye. Not as glam as the Lombard gown I've been eyeing, but a distinct possibility. Then again, the way things are going with those pencilpushers up there, I'll wind up wearing something Jimmy Hendrix wore at Woodstock."

I did a mental eye roll, squinted, and gave the screen another look. "The Mountain View Rec Center has security cameras by the outdoor entrance. Oh my gosh—all I'd need to do is view the footage and find the mystery woman in that dot-whatever dress. Someone's bound to know her." Then reality sunk in. "I have no authority to do that."

"Since when has authority ever stopped you? Tomorrow's Sunday. Perfect time to waltz in there with some concocted story."

A loud bang jolted me momentarily, and I realized it had to come from a door being slammed against the wall. Most likely the front entrance door.

"Patio doors to your left, honey. I'd make a break for it if I were you."

"Thanks, Edith." I was out of the den, through a great room, and over to the sliding glass doors like nobody's business. "Aren't you going to bring back the sulfur smell?"

"Just run, before you get company."

I ran all right. And I honestly don't know how many small barrel cacti and agave plants I smashed on the way to the street where I parked the car. I only know I pressed my car clicker with so much force my finger hurt. Ten seconds later, I revved the engine and took off as if I was being pursued by the zombie apocalypse.

"That should keep the scoundrel occupied for a good hour or two." Edith leaned back and stretched her filmy legs on the dashboard. I was about to mention germs. An automatic response when anyone does something yucky. Even a ghostly spirit. But before I got the chance, she continued yammering. "We needed to find an insurance policy, but we didn't."

"No. We found a mystery woman instead. And that list of Tambra's."

"Go with the mystery woman first. It'll save you some time."

"What makes you think that?"

"You really have to ask? Maybe she's not getting under the covers with Eric, but trust me, she's getting something from him. Or she did. That's why she swooped into his house faster than a Cooper's hawk after a mouse."

"You think she could have done the deed?"

"That's what you're about to find out as soon as you have a little chitchat with whoever's in charge of security footage at Hidden Boulders."

"Look, I'm not good at fabricating stories."

"You're not writing the great American novel."

No. Only living the Abbott and Costello version of it.

Chapter Twelve

Speedbump was all over me when I walked into the house. It was 4:46, according to the clock on the microwave, and for some inexplicable reason, I was alert and functional. Edith had vanished somewhere between the time I got off Cave Creek Road and turned onto my street. Just as well. There was only so much of her I could take in a single setting.

I gave the dog a handful of kibble before gulping down some iced tea and making my way to the bedroom. "If I'm lucky, I'll crash until nine. That'll give me a good four hours of shuteye."

Not unexpected, Speedbump jumped on the bed and curled into a ball at the foot. As soon as I tossed my clothes onto the floor, I pulled back the covers and crawled in. *That's what washing machines are for.* Then, total oblivion. Total welcome oblivion.

Maddie's chipper voice on my landline woke me at a little before ten. "I should have phoned sooner. You've probably been up for hours doing all sorts of energetic things. Call me when you get back."

I reached across the bed, fumbled for the receiver, and tapped her phone number into it. "I never left."

"Katie? You sound awful. Are you hungover or something?"

"Not hungover. The 'or-something.'"

"What?"

"I may be the prime suspect in a murder."

"Come again?"

"You heard me. It was horrible. They think I poisoned a woman at that fashion show in Hidden Boulders. She keeled over and died after biting into

70

one of my pancetta rosettes."

"Oh my gosh. I'm speechless. Do you want me to come over to your place today? Is there anything I can do?"

"I may need a criminal defense lawyer. Know any good ones?"

"Not personally, no. But we both know how to use social media to find a reputable one if need be. You said *they think*. Who's *they?*"

"The Maricopa County Sheriff's Office and the local marshals. Deputy Vincent to be specific."

I went on to give Maddie the unfiltered details of everything that happened last night, beginning with my arrival at Hidden Boulders. The only thing I left out was my unorthodox visit to Eric Wright's house. After all, she thought I was a rational and clear-headed friend, not a kook and nutcase when it came to bossy apparitions.

"Katie, you may be jumping to conclusions. You weren't arrested. You weren't told to not to leave town like they always do on TV shows and in crime novels. Believe me, if they thought you were implicated in any of this, they would have taken you into custody."

"That's because the toxicology report hasn't been completed. Same with the preliminary autopsy. Geez, what I wouldn't give to find out she had an aneurysm or coronary."

"One can always hope."

I chuckled. "Pretty grim, huh? Listen, as much as I'd really like to see you, I've got a million things to do today. They confiscated our charcuterie boards, food, and all. I need to order more. And I need to—"

"Get your pretty little derriere over to Hidden Boulders and zero in on that surveillance system."

"Edith!"

"Eat what?"

"Sorry, I need to eat something. I haven't had a bite since early last evening, and my stomach is in knots."

"Okay. I'll let you go. Call me tonight. If I don't hear from you by nine, I'm driving over."

"I'll call you. Promise. Maybe by then, I'll know something."

71

"Hey, if it's bad news, call or text me. Don't worry. You'll get through this."

"I suppose the only good thing is that my parents don't know about it. And I don't see how they would. It's not as if they knew I catered that particular event."

"If it's any consolation, it wasn't on the morning news."

"That's because it's Sunday. By tomorrow, Tambra Wright's unexplained and questionable death will be plastered all over the media. Heck, it's probably going viral on social media."

"I doubt it. Chances are those deputies put everyone they questioned on a gag order. Violating it would be almost as bad as tampering with a crime scene. Wouldn't it?"

"Maybe. Ugh. This is a nightmare."

"Look, get something to eat and take deep breaths. I'm here if you need me."

"Thanks, Maddie. I needed to hear that."

Once I made sure Speedbump was fed and I had a double dose of McCafé, I jumped into the shower and let the cool water remove any vestiges of the prickly sweat that clung to my skin. Nervous sweat. Not the kind from hard work, although I certainly did my share last night. Then I returned to the kitchen, made myself a toasted bagel with real butter, and took the dog for a short walk to clear my head.

It was mid-morning, and the neighborhood was as eerily still as those episodes from *The Twilight Zone* where aliens have taken over. Then I remembered it was Sunday, and most likely, folks were at church or enjoying a leisurely brunch.

Speedbump lifted his head and sniffed when I opened the door to let him inside. I didn't need to sniff. I knew he sensed Edith poking around somewhere. Sure enough, a dizzying display of magenta and red plumes danced around the kitchen. Seconds later, Edith materialized near the sink. Flapper outfit with purple and red boas.

"Don't try anything funny," I said. "We had enough plumbing displays last night."

"Not *we*. Eric. And if I didn't intervene, you'd be waiting on a bail bondman to come through."

"Don't remind me. I suppose you're hankering to get over to Hidden Boulders so we can scope out the video surveillance."

"It's not as if that mystery woman is about to barge in here and introduce herself. And need I remind you, this was your idea."

"I, um…"

"Oh, don't get me wrong, honey, it's a good one. If you can pull it off."

I hated to admit it, but I'd become used to Edith's unconventional interference. Interference that usually got us closer to whatever scheme we had to devise.

"You mean to tell me you're not going to put on your usual Edith act and disrupt something?"

"Honey, do you have any idea how exerting that is? No wonder I don't have the energy to pitch a fit over the wardrobe choices I'm stuck with. Just use that noggin of yours, and you'll come up with something."

Yeah. Indigestion.

There was no sense in putting it off. One way or the other, I needed to get a glimpse of the footage from last night's fashion show to see if I could recognize someone wearing a banded-waist maxi dress with a shrug. Ombre dot or not.

"Okay, Edith. But if everything goes south—"

"Move to Plan B."

"I don't have a Plan B. I don't even have a Plan A."

"Then think of them on the drive over."

Chapter Thirteen

I expected Hidden Boulders to have a flurry of activity on a Sunday, considering all of the activities it offered its residents. What I didn't expect was that the flurry of activities would include a lineup of sheriff's vehicles by the main entrance. At least I had worked out a viable premise for me to appear on site, even though it had nothing to do with sneaking a peek at the security video.

Not wanting to get cornered by official vehicles, I drove around back to where the staff parked and edged my car between a semi-new blue Mazda and a faded red older model Toyota Corolla with enough bumper stickers to hold the thing together if all else failed. I scanned political signs that dated back to two elections ago to a few signs that touted organic farming and herbal medicine. A larger one read, "Put Big Pharma where it belongs—Out to Pasture." It showed a herd of cows stomping on prescription bottles, and I chuckled. Yep, whoever that worker was, he or she missed the hippie age by a few decades.

When I got inside, the same middle-aged woman with tight brown curls was at the oval reception table. Only no hoop earrings this time. Instead, long dangle earrings all but touched her shoulders.

"Hey there, I recognize you," she said. "You had to contend with—Oh goodness. I was about to say something catty, but Tambra's left this world, so it would be like speaking ill of the dead. Then again, it wouldn't be as if it wasn't deserved. By the way, I heard it was a regular fiasco here last night. The place never closed down. The morning shifts and the clean-up crew arrived, but I don't think the sheriff's deputies ever left. Or maybe they sent in another crew. All I know is that things have been popping ever since I got to work at eight."

"Would you happen to know if anyone reviewed the footage from last night? The security footage?"

"Lance Baker, the assistant director, was with the director of security when I got to work. The only reason I know is because he phoned me to let me know he was not to be disturbed. I figured they had to be reviewing the camera surveillance."

"Were any of the deputies with them?"

"Two deputies arrived about ten minutes after Lance called me. They informed me that they were here for that very purpose. I phoned Lance and then escorted the deputies to the security director's office. He's a nice guy by the name of Liam Nelson. He used to work in IT for Chan-Tech. You must have heard of them. They're like one of the biggest firms in the valley."

Liam Nelson. Holy cow. Talk about a stroke of luck. Liam really was one of the good guys, and he bolted from that pressure cooker a few months before I did. Maybe I wouldn't need Edith's help after all.

I nodded. "Who hasn't? Um, I actually came here to see if I could retrieve my charcuterie boards. Do you know if anyone is in the kitchen area? I can ask them."

"Our morning staff is there. You know your way, right?"

"Um-huh. Is the security office near there? Curious, that's all."

"It's a few yards past the kitchen on the left-hand side."

"Thanks. I appreciate it."

As I turned to head out, the receptionist blurted out, "You think the husband did it?"

I spun around. "The husband's always the primary suspect. But I didn't think it was officially deemed a murder."

"The scuttlebutt around here is that Tambra's death was suspicious. We all know what that means. Rumor also had it Eric would need a blowtorch to warm her up."

Whoa. TMI. TMI.

"Um, well, I wouldn't put too much credence into the rumor mill."

"Not exactly the rumor mill when someone's heard it firsthand."

I widened my eyes and inched closer to the receptionist. Close enough to read her name on the gold-plated name tag she wore—Stacee Thorne.

"What someone?" And just like that, one of the marshals I saw last night walked up to the receptionist's table and cleared his throat.

"Guess I'd better get a move-on. Thanks, Stacee."

She gave me a quick nod before turning her attention to the marshal. So much for information-gathering. I'd have to gather it circuitously. At least I had an "in" this time, and it didn't involve a pesky ghost.

The door to the security office was closed, but as Edith so bluntly put it, "Since when has authority ever stopped you?" I turned the knob, took a step inside, and watched as four men moved their heads away from a series of computer screens and faced me. Thankfully, the one with a smile on his face stood and walked toward me.

"Katie! What are you doing here?" Then, before I could answer, he turned to the two deputies and Lance. "Give me a minute, please. Katie is an old friend from Chan-Tech. We both served time there."

"Yeah," I smiled. "But I got off for good behavior."

"I'll only be a minute or two."

He took my elbow and walked me out the door, closing it behind him. "Seriously, what are you doing here?"

"Trying to keep myself out of the Fourth Avenue Jail."

"Huh?"

"I think I'm a suspect. My pancetta rosette was the last thing Tambra ingested. And we all know how that went."

"What do you mean *your pancetta rosette?*"

"I started a sandwich shop and charcuterie catering service here in Cave Creek when I moved out of Chandler. The fashion show was one of our events."

"Okay. Take a deep breath. We should be done in less than a half hour. We've reviewed the footage from last night. A cursory look." He grasped my wrist. "Let's talk."

"Honestly, Liam, I had no idea you were the director of security here. I only found out this morning when I spoke with the receptionist. Got to admit, you sure are a sight for sore eyes. How's Bari?"

"You know Bari. Loves her nursing job and was elated when I got out of the rat race. We're living in Carefree now. That's only a stone's throw from here. Listen, I've got to get back inside. Stop back in thirty. Okay?"

"Absolutely."

At least I had one stroke of good luck. I wasn't banking on another when I stepped inside the first of the three kitchens. A young, twenty-something woman with a layered blond bob stopped sponging down the stove and looked up. With her shirt rolled up, I could see she worked out. Not huge muscles, but muscles nonetheless. Really toned. Something about her seemed familiar, and I realized I'd seen her last night, assisting at the bar.

Even though I knew the answer, I needed an opening. "Excuse me, I hate to interrupt you, but I'm Katie Aubrey from The Char-Board. I came by to see, if by any miracle, my charcuterie boards were returned from the sheriff's office."

The young woman shook her head. "Everything's been wiped clean. Literally. All food items, all storage containers housing foods, you-name-it, those forensic tech guys took them last night. And by last night, I mean up until four in the morning. Can you believe it? I got a text at a little past four asking me to come in ASAP to help clean."

"So you're not alone?"

"Nope. Javie Rivera just took a load of trash outside. He'll be back any second. I imagine the other workers punked out. Can't say I blame them. All of us worked our tails off last night and then wound up playing a waiting game for those deputies to interview us."

"I know. I was stuck here, too." *And getting skewered in the main office.*

"I mean, how many times can you tell someone you didn't see anything suspicious? I helped serve drinks, and all I saw were hands reaching out to nab whatever I served. It was all a blur. I didn't even know anything happened until the crowd went haywire."

"Were you acquainted with the deceased?"

"You mean, 'Did I steer as far away from that witch as possible?' And the answer is yes to both. When I had to assist with special events, I made it a point to find out where she was seated and rushed to cover another area."

"That bad, huh?"

"If her husband wasn't my boss, I would have registered an official complaint. Not that he's any prize with an ego as large as Jupiter, but still, I couldn't picture him married to that shrew."

A thud, and we both turned to the door. Javie elbowed it open and dragged a large trash bin inside. His eyes widened the second he saw me. "Katie! I thought you'd be pretty wiped out after last night. I, unfortunately, got called in to work along with Twila." *So that's her name.*

He shook his head ever so slightly and, at the same time, flicked his palm. I got the message—Don't mention anything about Javie wanting to leave.

I winked, and he gave me a quick nod.

"You two know each other?" Twila crinkled her nose, and I wondered if I detected a tad of jealousy.

"We met last night," I said. "Javie helped bring the charcuterie boards to the banquet room."

"Oh." No nose crinkling, only a long stare. It was obvious she was interested in him.

"Um, I need to get going. If they do bring my charcuterie boards back, can you leave a message for someone to call me?"

"I'll do better than that," Javie smiled. "I'll drive them back to your sandwich shop."

Uh-oh. The nose crinkling again. Followed by a stare. Yep. For sure Twila must have a crush on the guy to the extent she thinks I'm her competition. Yeesh.

I glanced at the large wall clock and announced that I had to get going. I thanked Javie and hightailed it directly to Liam's office. This time I knocked.

Liam's voice was chipper, as usual. "Door's open. Come on in." He motioned for me to grab a chair near his monitoring system, and I did. In spite of having spent the morning scouring over security tapes with law enforcement, he looked relaxed and content, unlike the harried version of him I'd come to know at Chan-Tech.

"I take it those deputies reviewed every bit of footage and then some, huh?"

"Reviewed and dissected."

I bit my lower lip. "Did they find anything?"

Liam shook his head. "It was a cursory review. They took the tape with them."

"Oh no. I was afraid of that. I really needed to have a good look for myself."

"Hey, you're talking to the consummate professional over here. I made backups before they got here. Look, I've got plenty of time, so let's have a look together, okay? I can speed things up or slow them down as needed. And by the way, just because one of your food items was the last thing the victim ingested, doesn't mean you were the one who tampered with it. Or if indeed, that's what did her in."

"Tell that to Deputy Vincent. I was afraid I'd leave here in shackles last night."

"Yeah, some of those guys can be quite intimidating. I think they must have taken a course on it or something."

We both laughed.

"Want any bottled water or anything?"

"Nah, I'm fine. I want to see who milled around the table before Tambra got there as well as a general look-see at the guests." I couldn't very well tell Liam I wanted to find out who Eric's mystery woman was, but I figured if I could spot her on the tape, I'd find a way to ask him if he knew her.

"The video surveillance footage appears in grids. Twelve boxes, each one focusing on a different area in this building. I can enlarge any one of them for a better look. The top row is the main entrance. Good way to see the guests as they arrived. The second row down is the corridor leading to the banquet room. The third row is the banquet room at different angles, and the bottom row is the fashion show runway. Only limited video surveillance in the models' dressing area."

"What about the other monitors? You've got two more of those."

"Outside footage on the monitor to my left and the kitchen area on the one to my right."

"You mean I was being filmed the entire time I prepared those charcuterie boards?"

"I'm afraid so. But don't stress it. I had no idea that was you. I would have had to zoom in."

"Wow. Now I understand why those deputies had to take the tape back with them. I'm not even sure where to ask you to begin."

"How about we back it up ten minutes before the incident? I can do a panoramic sweep of the area, and we'll see what it brings up."

"Didn't you do that with the deputies?"

"Nope. Only a regular run-through. Like I said, they'll be perusing it at their leisure and with a full staff."

"I'm game if you are. Let's go for it."

Chapter Fourteen

For once it was nice concentrating on something without Edith offering her two cents. Still, I had the unsettling feeling she wasn't too far away from Liam and me and wondered just when she'd make an appearance.

Liam focused on the area that encompassed the charcuterie trays and we watched as the guests helped themselves to the cured meats and cheeses. Something caught our attention and surprisingly, we called it out simultaneously.

"Did you see that?" I asked. "It's a server but I can't figure out what she's doing. She's walking past the charcuterie tables with a tray and—wait a sec—oh, I see. She's setting out forks. But a few minutes ago, two servers put forks on either side of the table. In fact, I remember seeing them last night. I guess I didn't notice this one."

Liam cleared his throat. "Watch closely. I don't think she's setting out forks. Hold on. I'll back up the tape and rerun it. Too bad she's not facing us."

I clasped my hands together and held my breath.

"I can't believe we missed this before. Then again, we did a generic sweep, not an in-depth one."

"What am I looking for? What did we miss?"

"The server's holding what looks like a linen hand towel. I can't really tell what she's doing but—oh wait—I see. Looks like she's polishing the forks. Is that something you normally do when they've already been set out on the table?"

"No. That's really strange. Unless someone complained about them. But still, replacements would be brought out from the kitchen. Can you get a close-up of her?"

"Only her back. She's facing the table. Give it a minute. When she leaves, we'll have her profile view."

So much for thinking it would be that easy. Unfortunately, a handful of people clouded our view of the server, and next thing we knew, she was off-screen.

Liam was undaunted. "Let me see if we can zero in on her when she first arrived. Before she went over to polish the forks."

He backed up the tape, but again, we had the same problem. Her face was obscured by guests who made their way to the charcuterie boards.

"Ugh, sorry, Katie. It's like watching a ghost. Nothing to define them."

Too bad I can't introduce you to Edith.

"Her uniform. It must be from Hidden Boulders because it doesn't look like the ones the servers from Randolph's Escapade wore."

"Hey, I know this isn't allowed, but I'll take the chance. I'm going to print out the best shot I can of her. Sit tight."

I took the still-shot image from Liam's hand and perused it. "It's impossible to see her face, but the server's uniform is pretty distinct."

"I'll need some time, but let me see if I can't clear up the image. I can call you when I manage to do that. And frankly, I think you may want that copy. I know it's only speculation, but why would someone monkey around with the cutlery unless they had another motive?"

"You mean like planting a poison or something?"

"Yeah. Only, wouldn't they be more likely to focus on the food?"

"Unless she was buying time until the crowd moved away."

"Good point."

"Can you run the tape to the section where Eric Wright shows up?" I asked. "Our linen-towel server may not be the only one we need to focus on. I watched Eric have a nasty verbal altercation with his wife shortly before she took her last breath and landed on the floor. It's the same spot as our linen-holding server, but later on."

"Can do. Hang in there."

Sure enough, Liam and I watched in slow motion as Eric replayed the fist-banging episode. Now, in slow motion, it appeared as if he opened his fist above the charcuterie board as if he was unleashing something onto my carefully designed food elements. It was certainly a bit more telling than the female server fussing over the forks.

My hands trembled slightly, and I widened my eyes. "Can you zoom in any closer?"

"I can, but the image will be blurry. It won't do you any good. Hey, don't look so disappointed. I'll shoot off a text to the lead deputy who was in here."

"But aren't they under the assumption that they took the only copy?"

"It doesn't matter. I'll tell them we always keep a spare copy of the video and that I had another look for my own edification. Trust me, I'll point them to this very spot on the video with the line, 'Possible suspicious activity.' If that doesn't get them to zero in Eric, nothing will."

"You think he might be the culprit? Or should I say, *killer?*"

Liam shrugged. "I've seen his hot temper from time to time, but Tambra's death wasn't the result of a heated exchange. If she was murdered, it was calculated. Still, that doesn't mean Eric wasn't responsible."

"What do you know about their relationship? Was he seeing someone on the side?"

"Wouldn't know. He and I didn't cross paths that often. Probably a good thing. Lance is my boss, not Eric. And Lance is about as laid back as anyone could get. But he and Eric are tight, so I wager if Eric did have some woman tucked away on the sidelines, Lance would be the one who'd know about it. Look, I'm sure those deputies and marshals will be asking all of the same questions."

"Yeah, I suppose you're right. But as of this moment, I'm the one on the firing line."

"Maybe not for long. The investigation is in its infancy. Wait for the tox screen and the autopsy."

"Funny, but that's what my friend Maddie said. And Lilly-Ann, my assistant at the shop."

"They're right. Think about it. How many things did you worry about in the past year that actually came true?"

"Good point. Still, this is a first for me. I could stand to lose everything. My business, my reputation, my—"

"Slow down. You haven't been charged with anything, and even if the worst thing imaginable happens, you've got a host of friends who'll come to your rescue. Some who even have connections with bail bondsmen."

"You?"

"Uh, no. But Bari's brother-in-law in Phoenix is one. There, isn't that comforting?"

I shook my head. "Not really, but I'll take a business card."

Liam laughed. "Sit back. We've got lots more video to eyeball."

As the footage progressed, I crossed my fingers I'd see the mystery woman with the ombre dot banded-waist maxi dress, but sadly, no such woman appeared. At least not in the last forty-five minutes.

"Are you sure I'm not taking you away from what you're supposed to be doing?" I asked Liam.

"This *is* what I'm supposed to be doing. No worries. We'll keep going."

Just then, a blinding silver haze engulfed the room, but I was the only one who noticed.

"Tell him to swing the video to where the models hang their clothing. Go on. Do it."

I clenched my fists as I tried to figure out how to ask Liam. Especially since he told me, the surveillance was limited in that area.

"I had a funny thought. If someone other than Eric tampered with the food, they wouldn't be likely to return to the kitchen area. They'd sneak out of here past the fashion show runway. Can you do a broad scope between the runway and where the clothing is hung? I know there's an outside door there. I saw it when I first visited this facility. We'd be looking for someone flying out of here like nobody's business."

"Sure thing."

I sat tight and watched, wondering exactly why Edith was so insistent we check out the wardrobe area.

"Sorry, Katie. Doesn't look as if anyone scurried through here. All of the models appear to be dressed and ready to make an entrance."

I noticed the wardrobe rack off to the side and squinted. "Can you zoom in to the racks where the clothes are? I thought I saw something."

"No problem."

As soon as Liam zeroed in, I gasped. "Did you see that? Did you?"

"Holy cow. It was so subtle on the full screen we missed it entirely. I'm giving it a rerun."

I sat, mouth wide open, as I watched a figure in a banded-waist maxi dress push her way through the lineup of models and out the door. But that wasn't what astonished me. It was the clump of white material I noticed on the floor as she made her retreat.

"Can you zoom in on that pile of white fabric?"

"Sure thing."

The clump of white fabric turned out to be two piles, and in that second, I was positive I had my answer. "That's a server's uniform. See? The long sleeves on what looks like a white jacket are really visible. My guess is that the small pile is a white apron. And I know for a fact they make them calf-length."

Liam let out a slow whistle.

"Oh my gosh. Are you thinking what I am?"

"Yep. I've got to clean up that photo of your linen-carrying server and do it pronto."

"How long will that take?"

"At least an hour or so, but I do have other things I need to tackle. How about I work on it and drop it off at your shop on my way in to work tomorrow?"

"Fantastic. Breakfast's on me."

He grinned. "Sounds like I've got the better end of the deal."

I thanked him and made my way out the door. It was almost three, and Stacee was no longer at the fancy receptionist's table. Instead, a short gentleman with a comb over leafed through some papers. I waved and kept walking. Apparently, the second shift had arrived.

As I opened the door to my car, a whirl of silver and white brushed in front of me, gradually taking form in the passenger's seat. "Now, aren't you glad you got those buns of yours moving? What do you think? The fancy-dancy patootie who shed that server's jacket like a snake or the husband? Hurrmuph. Think they worked in tandem? I don't need to wait for your friend to print out a good image. Face it. If the shoe fits, buy three pairs."

"Huh?"

"It had to be her. The woman on Eric's balcony landing. And trust me, she was no Juliet."

"Yeah, I'm ninety-nine percent sure it was her, too, but that won't do any good until we find out who she is, and that will have to wait until tomorrow."

"Fine. I'm bored. What do you say we drive over to The Chanterelle on Parkview so I can see what Imogen is up to?"

"Absolutely not! You know for a fact she wasn't responsible for your premature demise, so why can't you leave it alone?"

"It's an itch I can't scratch."

"Then deal with it."

Imogen Brodeur, the owner of The Chanterelle in Scottsdale, and Edith attended the same culinary school decades ago. Suffice it to say, there was some rather unfinished and unpleasant business regarding Imogen's plagiarism and Edith's razor-sharp response. A response that resulted in a professional feud that apparently is still continuing past the grave. At least for Edith.

"Just a quick look-see?"

"No, Edith. Not now." *Or, hopefully, not ever.*

Chapter Fifteen

I awoke earlier than usual on Monday after a fitful night's sleep. The concern that all eyes were on me regarding Tambra's death morphed into downright dread, not a good place to be.

Speedbump gobbled his kibble in record time and gave me that quizzical "aren't you going to take me for a walk?" look. The sun hadn't yet cleared the horizon, but it was light enough out to meander down our block. Two cars passed by, and both drivers waved. I wasn't sure who they were, but it didn't matter. Drivers in my neighborhood waved at everyone.

Following a quick cup of coffee and a slice of toast, I took a brisk shower—mainly because I didn't feel like waiting for the water to warm up—got dressed, and headed to The Char-Board. Since we opened at 7:00, I usually arrived forty to fifty minutes earlier, but today I'd beat Lilly-Ann and Matt to the door. At least that's what I figured. But I figured wrong.

Lilly-Ann's car was parked directly across the street when I arrived, but that wasn't all. A sheriff's car blocked the view of our entrance, having nabbed the spot in front.

This is SO not good.

My McCafé medium roast mingled with the dry toast, resulting in heartburn, but that was the least of my worries. I clenched my fists and walked inside, expecting to see a deputy or two ready to escort me to their office.

Instead, I saw an ashen-faced Lilly-Ann seated at one of our tables with two deputies on either side of her, both of whom were at Hidden Boulders Saturday night.

"Good morning." I tried to sound chipper. "I'm Katie Aubrey, the owner. Is everything okay?"

Another hour or so, and I expected Liam to breeze in. *Please let those deputies be done before Liam shows up. He'll be here for breakfast in another hour. Geez, what could those deputies want with Lilly-Ann? Unless they're asking her about me.*

"Good Morning," the taller of the two men said. "We needed to have a word with Ms. Wentworth. Shouldn't take much longer. Sorry to disturb you."

Lilly-Ann was a deer in the headlights, but there wasn't much I could do about it.

I nodded. "No problem. I need to get set up for the day. I'll go about my business and leave you alone."

"I won't," a raspy voice grumbled.

I turned, and sure enough, Edith had made herself comfortable at Lilly-Ann's table. This time in a fuchsia kimono. I shuddered. Seconds later, Matt walked in.

He took one look at Lilly-Ann with the deputies and mouthed, "What happened?"

I motioned for him to join me in the kitchen and kept my voice low. "The fashion show director sort of dropped dead after tasting one of our pancetta rosettes Saturday night. Sorry, I should have called you yesterday to let you know."

Matt's eyes resembled golf balls. "Wow. I heard something on the news about a suspicious death at an event, but I didn't pay much attention. That was us? You? Oh geez. Don't tell me they think you or Lilly-Ann had anything to do with it."

"Uh, yeah. That's exactly what I think. But I don't understand why those deputies are questioning her. Right here and now. We all got grilled Saturday night. I'll tell you more about it as we work, but we'd better get moving since there are only two of us. Lilly-Ann's stuck at that table."

"More like plastered to it. Did you notice her hands? If she gripped it any tighter, the wood would crack."

Great. Another expense.

Matt and I moved about the kitchen, preparing salads and chopping veggies, when he suddenly put his knife down and looked up. "'Brioche, Toast and Most'" should be here any second with our deliveries. I'll take care of it. I know what we use and what goes in the freezer."

"Good, because I'm on auto-pilot right now. Hey, before I forget, a friend of mine is coming over for breakfast. He's the security officer at Hidden Boulders and is helping me to identify someone who may have had something to do with that death. Which, by the way, I expect the authorities to label a homicide by tomorrow the latest."

"It wasn't one of our customers, was it?"

"No, but she was in their social circle. More or less. It's that bunco group crowd. Anyway, her name was Tambra Wright, and if it's any consolation, I don't think anyone is grieving her early departure from this world."

"Wow. What a bummer. I mean for you and Lilly-Ann. When will they know for sure what killed Tambra?"

"I imagine they already know something from the preliminary toxicology screening, but that information hasn't been released to the public yet. As for the autopsy, I'd give it a few more days."

Matt stepped away from the sink and cracked open the door to our dining area. "Lilly-Ann's face is the same color as pea soup. Think we should do something?"

"I'm not sure what. If those deputies don't finish questioning her now, they'll be back later."

"Hold on. They're getting up."

With that, he closed the kitchen door, and we both held our breath. A few seconds later, a haggard-looking Lilly-Ann pushed open the door and moved, zombie-like, to the counter. She stared at Matt and me, jaw wide open, until words could form in her mouth.

"I'm officially a person of interest." No tone, no voice inflection. Only words, and if I didn't know better, I would have sworn they came from a ventriloquist and not Lilly-Ann. She pulled out a stool and sat. "Tambra spotted me when we first arrived Saturday evening and wasted no time informing her little entourage that she and I had worked together a number of years ago and that I was not to be trusted."

"That conniving snake," I muttered under my breath. "She must have been near the kitchen area, and we didn't see her." Then I motioned for Lilly-Ann to continue.

"When the deputies and marshals questioned the bunco ladies, they told her what Tambra told them. *That,* in combination with the fact that I helped prepare our charcuterie boards, put me on their person-of-interest list."

I winced. "Some idle gossip? That's what put you on their radar?"

"*That,* and something else. Tambra also told them I said she'd better steer clear of me if she valued her life." Then Lilly-Ann grabbed a napkin from the end of the counter and wiped her eyes. "The trouble is, I *did* say that. But it was years ago. And at the spur-of-the-moment. Right after, she threatened to ruin my reputation and that of an innocent friend who happened to be our councilman."

Matt looked at me. "I'm lost."

"Just as well," I whispered before turning back to Lilly-Ann. "So what happens now?"

"I was told not to leave town and that they'd be in touch."

"Hurump. If that isn't a cliche, I don't know what is. Look, they don't have any real evidence, and until they do, I say we go about our business. Although it might not be such a bad idea to get the name of a good criminal defense attorney. And not just you. Me, too. It's my catering business, and I could be a likely suspect as well. I had a rather unpleasant dealing with Tambra, too. Not the grand scale like you, but still enough for tongues to wag."

"Do you know any criminal defense attorneys?" Lilly-Ann continued to dab her eyes while Matt busied himself with the food prep.

"Offhand, no, but my friend Liam does. His wife's brother-in-law is a bail bondsman. He might know. Good news is that Liam's coming in here for breakfast. He's the security director at Hidden Boulders. I already told Matt. Yesterday, I went over there to see what I could find out, and when I discovered Liam was at the security helm, I was overjoyed. I've known him and his wife, Bari, for years. Liam used to work at Chan-Tech, too."

Matt turned his attention back to us. "Good deal. Those bail bondsmen have lots of connections. If I were you guys, I'd find out and put the lawyer's name on speed dial."

Lilly-Ann gasped, and I shot Matt a look. "I'm sure we'll be fine." *I'm not, but I can't lose it now when we open in a little bit.*

"Brioche, Toast and Most" arrived in time for Matt to make a quick getaway before he could stick his foot further in his mouth. I looked at the clock and grimaced. "We'd better move it. We open in less than ten minutes."

"I'm not sure I can handle anything today," Lilly-Ann said. "My head's a mess. And here I thought I'd get in super early so we'd have time to catch our breath. Sorry, Katie. I'll do what I can."

"You already are."

Minutes later, I put the OPEN sign in the window, turned on all of the dining room lights, and ushered a number of our familiar patrons into the sandwich shop. The aroma from our coffee maker filled the room, and I realized I was desperate for another cup. Unfortunately, I didn't have the time. Not even for a quick gulp.

We usually get a substantial number of diners, plus those who want coffee and sandwiches to go, but for some inexplicable reason, the customers came in non-stop. I found myself hustling from the tables to the lineup for take-out orders when Matt motioned me over.

"Lilly-Ann's not doing so great. She's barely holding it together in the kitchen."

"I know. I asked her if she wanted to go home, but she said no. Said it would be worse. At least she has something to keep her occupied here."

"Hey, are you catching any of the drift from the tables? Everyone's talking about Tambra's death. Only they're all calling it a murder."

"I know. It's like gossip central in here. I'd eavesdrop to see if I could pick up anything substantial, but that's impossible."

"Not for me!" A whirly haze of yellows and greens engulfed the room, and I knew there was no way I could stop Edith.

"Try to be discreet," I mumbled under my breath. "Don't knock anything over. Especially the drinks."

"Huh?" Matt answered. "You want me to snoop around? Is that what you're saying?"

Yes, but to the person who's not inhabiting this world.

"Um, sort of. Don't be obvious, but if you do hear something that points to a possible murderer, let me know."

Matt nodded at the same time Edith put in her two cents. Only she did with a dizzying display of flickering lights that all but gave me a migraine.

Chapter Sixteen

Seconds later, Liam walked in and grinned. I rushed over and gave him a hug. "Were you able to clear up the image?"

"I did, but I didn't recognize the woman from any of the members at Hidden Boulders. Then again, I haven't been working there that long."

"Come on, there's a free table over by the window. I'll join you in a few minutes. Regular or decaf? You can at least start on coffee while you peruse the menu."

"I'm a creature of habit. How about regular coffee and a toasted bagel with cheese? Oh, and I'll take any of your sugary sweets. I'll chalk it up to my carb count for the day."

"Sounds good. Hold on." I walked to the counter, got the coffee, and returned to Liam before shouting out his order to Lilly-Ann. Her response was a methodical "okay," and I worried she'd be a basket case by noon. Still, she was right. At least here, she'd keep busy.

I pulled out the chair across from Liam and plunked my elbows on the table. "I'm ready to check out the mystery woman while your breakfast is being prepared. It's a no-brainer in my book. The woman with the banded-waist maxi dress was the one who impersonated a server."

He took out a large manila envelope and pulled out a glossy 8 x 12. "It's a sharper image than what we saw on the tape, and yeah, I'm with you on this one."

I studied the woman's facial features but didn't recognize her from the bunco crowd and certainly not from the sea of humanity that paid to attend the fashion show. Long Roman nose, dark eyebrows that could have used a trim, and unflattering listless hair that hung to her shoulders.

Liam glanced at the photo again and shrugged. "Unfortunately, the deputies might not buy the impersonator theory. My sense is that once they come up with a theory, or a suspect, they work to find supporting evidence, not broaden the search. I've already pointed them in Eric's direction. This new development might muddy the waters. Especially since Eric is a viable suspect."

"Not that viable. Two deputies were in here this morning to speak with my assistant, Lilly-Ann. They informed her she's a person of interest."

"Huh? How? What did I miss?"

At that moment, Matt arrived with Liam's breakfast, and I asked him to refill the half-empty coffee cup.

"Lilly-Ann and Tambra had a history, and it wasn't a good one. Tambra more or less scammed her years ago but managed to place the blame on Lilly-Ann and used coercion to keep her from going to the police."

"Geez, the more I hear about Tambra, the more I wonder why everyone isn't a suspect."

"Apparently, just Lilly-Ann and me, as far as I know. Which reminds me, can you check with Bari to see if her brother-in-law knows any good defense attorneys. Just in case."

"No problem, but I think you're pushing the panic button way too soon."

A second later, Matt returned with the coffee, said hello, and took off for another table.

"You've got a good crew working here." Liam bit into his cheese sandwich. "Are you usually this slammed in the mornings?"

"We're constantly on our toes with lots of foot traffic, but I think the news of Tambra's death brought out a whole new crew of rumormongers."

"I suppose that's to be expected, considering the only other high-profile homicides took place years ago, and as I recall, there were only two of them. The TV anchors should have been convicted for beating the stories to death."

I laughed. "Yeah, didn't some woman try to poison her husband a while back? Geez, hope this town doesn't get a reputation for that sort of thing. I'd like to think we're jumping the gun and Tambra died from another cause entirely, but the way those deputies acted, my money's on murder."

"That's the scuttlebutt at Hidden Boulders, too, I'm afraid." Liam finished up his sandwich and bit into the cherry-filled pastry. "Hmm, I think Bari and I are going to be frequenting your place when we both have the same days off."

"That would make my day."

"Listen, I'd love to stay and chat, but I've got to get going. I'll keep my ears to the ground and let you know if I find out anything. Hang on to that photo, I printed one for myself."

I took another look at the image and was about to put the paper back in the envelope when a strange thought crossed my mind.

"Liam, not only were the women at that fashion extravaganza decked out in fancy clothes, but they were laden down in jewelry. Chokers, dangling necklaces, earrings of every sort. You get it. Now look at our mystery female. Not as much as a small gold chain or stud earrings. Whoever it was, made sure their jewelry didn't give them away."

"Talk about covering one's tracks. Let me take another gander at the photo." He crinkled his nose and let out a chuckle. "Well, I'll be damned. Her hair is lopsided. It's a wig. Has to be. No one's hair can look that bad. No wonder I didn't recognize her as one of the members. Or staff, for that matter."

I peered over his shoulder and focused on the photo. "I really need to pay more attention to details. I mean, I do, when I'm preparing charcuterie boards, but you know, this is different."

"Hey, take it easy. It's only because I'm in the surveillance business that I've learned to be discerning, but even I missed it on the first round."

"Too bad we can't show this to the deputies, but it probably wouldn't matter anyway. Face it, Lilly-Ann, Eric and I all have past histories, or in my case, a miserable experience, with Tambra. A photo of a woman in a wig isn't about to get us very far."

Liam reached over and gave my wrist a squeeze. "It'll be all right. I'll be banking on the Hidden Boulders gossip trail to pick up where we leave off."

He stood and was about to head out when I remembered something. "You wouldn't happen to know Javie Rivera, who works at your rec center, would you?"

"I've chatted with him a few times, and he seemed like a good guy. From what I've heard, he's a decent worker. Why? New love interest?"

"What? No. Possible new employee. Tambra gave him a boatload of grief about his beard and hair. Said if he didn't cut it, he'd be out of a job. I watched how he interacted with others and thought he was the genuine deal, so I gave him my card and asked him to stop by. Of course, it probably doesn't matter now, considering she's, well, you know."

"Hey, you never know. It's worth a shot to interview him." Then Liam looked around at the ever-growing customers. "And maybe the sooner, the better."

I thanked him for everything as he headed out, barely making contact with two customers who rushed in and spied the empty table.

"I'll be with you in a second," I told the middle-aged women who raced to nab a seat. "Just need to wipe down a table."

From a few feet away, Matt called out, "Got it," and hurried over with Clorox spray and some paper towels.

"I'm going to see how Lilly-Ann's doing in the kitchen. Boy, this is non-stop, huh?"

He nodded. "I think I heard the word 'murder' at least fifty times since I got here. Too bad I couldn't hang around for the rest."

"Well, I can, and I did." The lemon yellow and moss green haze intensified, temporarily gluing me to the floor.

"Not right now."

Matt turned, Clorox bottle in hand. "What's not right now?"

"Um, uh, hanging around to listen."

"Yeah, I'll just pick up what I can."

"Good."

A fast whirlwind of chartreuse engulfed the room, and I rolled my eyes. The second Matt walked away, I muttered, "Tell me what you heard." Then I tried to act nonchalant as I breezed past the customers, waved to Lilly-Ann, who was slicing tomatoes as if they were heads on a guillotine, and grabbed the trash bin so I could speak with Edith in the alley.

"Okay, no one's here. Tell me what you heard. And what happened to the fuchsia kimono?" I put the empty bin down and waited for a response.

Edith materialized a few feet from the bin and made sure to keep a wide berth. I remembered something about her being able to pick up on odors. "Like I would know. Now I'm saddled with this hideous moss green pleated shirt and equally horrific butter yellow cardigan. One measly suggestion to the middle management, and poof! They retaliate with a vengeance."

"Um, well, I'm sure you'll get past it." *I know I already have.* "So, what scuttlebutt did you hear?"

"Two tables of blonde tennis players, complete with those obnoxious HB logos on their tennis tops, talked about a woman who goes by MM. Said it wouldn't surprise them if this MM chickee was behind Tambra's sudden by not surprising passage into the great beyond."

"Did they say why?"

"No, they moved on to designer jewelry and some wellness website toting stress relief. Had to laugh when one of them said shoving Tambra into the next world beat anything on the market."

"MM. Hmm, I wonder if that's Meredith Mason. She's the only one of the bunco ladies with those initials. Good catch, Edith."

"Oh, honey, I'm just warming up. Hope the trash isn't piling up in the small bin inside because we could be awhile."

"Try to give me the Cliffs Notes version, okay? I really need to get back."

"Who are you talking to, Katie?"

I turned and faced my neighbor, Mercedes Alvarez, a sweet middle-aged lady who owned the pottery shop next door. She'd gotten a shorter haircut since we last spoke, and her salt and pepper curls looked tighter and bouncier.

"Um, uh, earbuds. Bad habit." I immediately tossed my hair over my ears and smiled.

Mercedes laughed. "Don't worry about it. We all talk to ourselves. It's when we answer that we have to be concerned."

No, it's when we converse with annoying ghosts that should be reason for concern.

Chapter Seventeen

"Nice lady," Edith said as Mercedes retreated back to her shop, having tossed a bag of trash into our shared receptacle.

"Yes, very nice. Now, be quick and tell me what else you gleaned at those tables."

"Deirdre and Deborah are having face waxing treatments at the spa. I suppose that's why they weren't here for the tongue waging."

"Not the chitchat. The *murder* chitchat."

"Fine. Were you aware Eric was the consummate social gambler? And not very polished at it, from what I heard. Owed beau coup bucks to more than a few people. Maybe his wife found out, and he had to get her out of the way. I told you we should have found an insurance policy. It's not too late."

"Are you nuts? I'm not going back into his house. *Talk about pressing my luck.* What else were you able to find out?"

"Tambra had some side deal going on, but I couldn't tell if it was business or pleasure. The rest of the blabbing was downright boring—Botox treatments and golf."

"What about golf?"

"Some issue with the signage and the conditions. I don't know. It was a snoozer."

I was about to respond to her when I remembered something. Eric had a huge file on his computer for the golf course at Hidden Boulders. What was it? Oh yeah, drainage, tree management, and turf control. Maybe there was an issue with the person who was directly responsible for it. But then again, I wasn't sure how that would link back to Tambra's demise.

"Okay, keep up the surveillance. But do it discreetly, will you?"

"I'm the epitome of discretion."

And I'm the Queen of Sheba.

I returned to the kitchen, empty trash bin in hand, when Matt announced, "Hey, you just missed a phone call from a guy named Ian. I told him you'd be back any minute, and he said he'd try you in a bit."

"Thanks." I put the bin back in its place and swallowed. Either Ian called to tell me what happened with the crew from Randolph's Escapade after Lilly-Ann and I left, or maybe it was a bit more personal. Like asking me out. His signals were kind of hard to miss. Either way, I needed to chat with him. Every glimmer of information I could get my hands on was important. Especially if I intended to get out of this unscathed.

"How are you doing with the breakfast meals?" I asked Lilly-Ann. She looked up and shrugged. "Okay, I guess. I'm not really thinking."

"At least you got the orders up for table three," Matt chuckled as he snatched the plates from her and raced out of the kitchen. Lilly-Ann bent down and sobbed into her hands. At first, small sniffles. Then louder sobs until she all but wailed.

"I'm no good here today. I'm afraid I'll really louse things up and maybe even get us into a worse mess. What if I poison someone?"

"With what? Salt and pepper?"

"Katie, I made a tuna salad earlier and couldn't remember if I added the garlic and onion powders. Had to grab a spoon for a quick taste. I'm really on scatterbrain mode today and terrified I'll be dragged into the sheriff's office for more questioning."

"Listen, I'll shoot off a text to my friend Liam who just left. He's got legal connections. As soon as I hear back, I'll let you know."

"Can you let me know from my home? Seriously, I'm in no shape to keep going. I'm so sorry."

"Hey, it's not a problem. Matt and I can hustle. Go home, make yourself some chamomile tea or whatever it is people do to relax. I'll call you later, and we can go from there. Okay?"

"Thanks. I'll finish this breakfast sandwich and take off."

I looked at her hands, and they were shaking. "I'll take over. Drive home safely. Keep in mind. It's rumors and hearsay, not concrete evidence."

She nodded. "Until there is some. Face it. Those deputies wouldn't have interrogated me if Tambra died from a heart attack or stroke. Any idea when we'll find out?"

"Probably tomorrow. One of the deputies said it would be a day or so."

Lilly-Ann rinsed her hands off in the sink, grabbed her bag, and walked out of the kitchen. I watched as she made a beeline for the front door, pausing for a moment to say something to Matt. With a quick breath, I finished the breakfast sandwich and looked at the order slips that were lined up on the counter. Matt and I could hustle all right, but given today's crowd, I knew it wouldn't be enough.

The instant Matt stepped into the kitchen to retrieve more orders, I told him what happened with Lilly-Ann.

"You don't think those deputies will arrest her, do you?"

I shook my head. "Not unless they have solid and concrete evidence. Still, they can be as intimidating as hell."

"Want to know what's as intimidating as hell? The rest of these breakfast orders. I'll start with the sandwiches and bring them out as soon as I'm done."

"Joining you as we speak."

For the next few minutes, Matt and I worked our buns off. Lamentably, Edith was oblivious to our dilemma, and her raspy voice shook my eardrum. "Is now a good time for me to tell you what else I know?"

"No, it's not."

Matt turned to me. "It's not what?"

"Um, uh, thinking out loud. Not time yet for the lunch crowd."

"No, but if the breakfast crew is any indication of what's coming, the lunch crowd may be on the high side, too."

Edith was undaunted. "I'd like to make a suggestion about the plating. Always add a bright, visual element, even though the customer is not going to eat it. I suggest radishes shaped like flowers with a bit of parsley. Or maybe a few thin carrot stalks and a twisted slice of orange."

Right now, I'll be happy if we get the actual order right.

I ignored her and kept on going, but she was relentless. "Fine. If you're not going to take my suggestions seriously, I'm not going to tell you what else I found out."

"Aargh!"

"Are you all right? Don't tell me you're going to freak out like Lilly-Ann?"

"I'm fine, Matt, but I thought of something. We really should jazz up these orders. Maybe put a bit of parsley on the plates with a few strawberries. It makes a nice presentation."

"Sure. Whatever you think. But it'll slow us down."

So will Edith.

"Yeah, but it will make the customers happy." *And me, too. But not for the same reason.*

Matt and I continued to work non-stop. From breakfast sandwiches to table delivery and cleaning up. I could have sworn I heard Edith say, "Nice job with the little fruits and orange twists," but then again, it might have been my brain on overdrive. Then, at a little past eleven, while I was at the sink rinsing off some bowls, I heard a voice I thought I recognized and jumped.

"Whoa. Sorry to startle you. Your server out front said I could walk directly into the kitchen."

"Javie! Um, nice to see you, but this is an awful time. My other server left a while ago since she felt ill, and there are only two of us scurrying around to get the orders filled, and the tables waited on."

He looked around the room, spied an apron on a hook near our pantry, and walked toward it. "Make that three. That is, if you don't mind. I'm a fast learner."

"Don't mind? I could hug you. Start out in the dining area by taking orders. The little pads are on the counter near the sink, and there's a diagram of the table numbers on fridge. Please tell Matt, the server you spoke with, that I need him in here."

"Got it."

Javie was out of the kitchen and into the dining room in a nanosecond.

What followed was nothing shy of a miracle. He blended into our little production seamlessly, and by the time the noonday rush was over, we were all laughing and joking as if we'd worked as a team for months, not minutes.

"I can't thank you enough," I told him. "Naturally, I'll compensate you for your time."

He grinned. "Consider it my interview. Still interested in a new hire?"

"I think you can give Hidden Boulders your notice."

He walked over, extended his arm, and we shook hands.

"Oh," he said. "I almost forgot the real reason I came today. Well, one of the reasons. The sheriff's office phoned Hidden Boulders this morning to say they no longer needed the 'large wooden platters' and asked us to get them. Usually, I'm not working there Monday mornings, but they needed help with additional clean-up. The area was still a crime scene on Sunday, so nothing could get done."

"I wonder why they didn't call here. The boards belong to us, and they knew that."

Javie shrugged. "Less phone calls that way. I guess they figured we'd return them to your establishment. I've got them in my car and will bring them in once the closed sign goes up. Holy cow- Are you always this busy?"

"Not usually, but news spread quick about Tambra, and every gossip klatch from here to Carefree showed up. Tell me, what happened with your crew Saturday night? The folks from Randolph's Escapade said you were all led off to parts unknown for questioning."

He rolled his eyes. "More like a spin around the merry-go-round. We were spread out in the banquet room, so that it was impossible to speak with each other. Then, one by one, we were questioned. I don't know about the others, but I was asked what I observed and what I recalled about the incident. Apparently, the fact that I was nowhere near the charcuterie table at the time didn't matter." He chucked and continued.

"If that wasn't enough, the marshal who interviewed me had me recount everything I could remember from the minute I arrived at work to the moment when everyone screamed."

"Marshal and not deputy?"

"Marshal. About as amicable as Sergeant Joe Friday from *Dragnet* if you've ever watched those reruns on late-night TV."

"Yeesh. And I thought Deputy Vincent was intimidating."

"You're not the only one. That name was bantered about all morning along with something else—an affair between Tambra and the groundskeeper for the golf course."

"Who's that?"

"Scott Billings."

"As in Deirdre Billings?"

"I don't know. All I do is pick up chatter and dismiss it, but in this case, I may have to store it somewhere in my head. The way things are going, I don't think any of us are in the clear."

Chapter Eighteen

"Y"ou seem to be attracting quite the cadre of gentlemen callers, if you don't mind my saying so. See, it pays to take my advice." The fuchsia kimono was back, only this time brighter for some reason. I tried to brush her away and wound up knocking a glass off of the counter.

"Sorry," Javie said. "Didn't mean to unnerve you. Guess we're all a bit stressed from this. Where's your broom and dustpan? I've got it."

"Pantry." I pointed to the door near the fridge and turned to where Edith had materialized.

"He's not a gentleman caller," I uttered under my breath. "And neither was Liam. You should know that with all the snooping around you do."

I moved away from earshot as Javie continued to clean up the broken glass.

"Not Liam. The phone call from that nippy bit of eye candy."

"Way too young."

"Do not tell me you're one of those uptight, prudish women who never left the nineteenth century. So what if he's young? It's been my experience that younger men have more—"

"Ew! Don't go there."

Javie looked up. "Under the fridge? It's not a problem. I can always pull it out after we close to get any debris that wound up there."

"Uh, sure. Sounds good. Thanks."

"I'll give Hidden Boulders my two-week notice, but I can pitch in here on my days off in-between."

"Great. Just jot them down, and we'll get it sorted out."

"Tomorrow's Tuesday. It may be tight timing, but I imagine a preliminary toxicology report will be issued by then. If nothing else, we'll know whether or not to be chewing on our fingernails. Like I said before, given the scope of the questioning, I don't think any of us are off the hook."

Especially Lilly-Ann and me.

The noonday rush wound down with only a few customers filtering in. Still, it was a steady pace that allowed us to catch our collective breaths. Then, Ian called back. This time I answered the phone, extended the long cord and wedged myself between the back door and the fridge.

His voice was chipper and charismatic. "Hi! Sorry to call you at work, but I didn't have your home number. Glad it was on The Char-Board's website. Which, by the way, really rocks."

OMG. "Rocks." He really is young.

"Hi. I, um, actually planned on calling you as well. I wanted to know what happened with the questioning for Randolph's Escapade. Saturday night was a regular circus."

"One step shy of the Spanish Inquisition, but I don't think it's over."

"Yeah. If yesterday evening was any indication, Sterling's an absolute basket case. He was quite the sight last night when I saw him. Worried his restaurant might somehow be implicated in all of this."

"Why? Why would he think that?"

"The forensic crew took all of our canapes and serving trays for testing on Saturday night. Until those results come back negative, and I don't see why they wouldn't, Sterling may need prescription meds for anxiety. How about you? How are you holding up?"

"I don't need to be medicated, but we're in the same boat. The lab confiscated everything edible from here, plus our charcuterie boards. The good news is that they returned the boards."

"Yeah, that's a plus. I suppose until the tox results are in, all of us will be in limbo."

My phone vibrated for a second, and then—"You call that limbo? If he wants to know what limbo is, he needs to see what I put up with!"

I put my hand over the receiver and mumbled, "Get off the line, Edith." It was one of the few times I was thankful I was on a landline and not a cell phone.

Another vibration and a "harrumph."

"Are you still there?" Ian asked.

"Um, yeah. Sorry. Lots going on here."

"I should let you go. Anyway, I just called to see how you were doing."

"Thanks. That was really thoughtful."

"Oh heck, I'm not really good at any of this, but would you want to get together maybe for coffee, or lunch, or—"

This time the vibration was so strong I almost dropped the phone.

"Coffee would be okay, but I work Monday through Saturday. And I'm sure we're a good distance apart. I live in Cave Creek."

"I know. You mentioned it when we met. Hey, we're not that far. I've got a condo in Carefree, making it an easy commute for me to get to Randolph's for work. Listen, there's a neat coffee shop here—The Roastery. Are you familiar with it?"

And then some.

I thought back to my first and only experience there. Sweet coffee and bitter conversation with Cora Milbrand, Edith's former cleaning lady. "Yeah, it's a great shop."

"What time do you close? Oh wait, it's early, isn't it? I thought I remembered from your website."

"At 2:00, but then we clean up."

"I have this Wednesday off. Would you want to meet there around four?"

"I'll still be in work clothes." *Good grief. What am I saying? I'm making this sound like a fancy date.*

"Fine. I'll dress down if it makes you happy. I'm usually in jeans anyway."

I laughed. "Sure. Four o'clock will be fine. Maybe by then, we should know more about what killed Tambra."

"The *what* is easy. It's the *who* that's going to keep all of us guessing."

"You got that right."

When we ended the call, I stood there like an adolescent schoolgirl, and from the heat I felt on my cheeks, I was positive I blushed.

"You okay?" Matt asked as he opened the fridge. "You look kind of stunned. Please don't tell me you're going to go off the deep end like Lilly-Ann."

"What? Of course not. I'm just running around in circles like the rest of us."

He gave me a quizzical look and smiled. "If you say so."

The pace at The Char-Board wound down until the last forty-five minutes, when it suddenly picked up. An anomaly for us. Three tourists from the West Valley came in, complete with print-off maps of Cave Creek's boutiques. They were immediately followed by two older women that looked somewhat familiar but weren't regulars. Surprisingly, all of them ordered the mini-char boards, and I wondered how quickly Javie would catch on to the prep. As it turned out, I had nothing to fear.

"Ever think of creating a Mexican one?" he asked. I watched as he cubed the Havarti and added a neat little detail into the sides. He smiled and kept cutting. "With chorizo, corn salsa, tortilla chips, cilantro, olives...you get the idea. My mother always made these for family gatherings."

"Consider it done. We'll get the ingredients and add it to our repertoire."

An hour later, after the closed sign was on the door, Javie retrieved our charcuterie boards, and we cleaned up.

"I honestly don't know how we would have managed without you," I told him.

"Yeah," Matt added. "I'm pretty wiped out now. I'd be zonked if you didn't step in."

"Wow. All this time working for Hidden Boulders, and not a single compliment. I can't believe I'm leaving here with two of them." Then he looked at me. "I'll text you my free time in the coming week so you can see where to fit me in."

"Done deal."

By the time I got home and unlocked the door, I was ready to crash on the couch. Speedbump, however, had just awakened from what I imagined was a long day napping. He bounced over to me, tail wagging and slobbery kisses.

"Okay, dog. I'll feed you, and we can go for a walk. But it better be a short one, or you'll be the one dragging me home."

Finally, at a little before five, I nuked a small lasagna dinner and tossed the container into the trash. Then I sank into the couch and grabbed my phone to give Maddie an update but didn't get very far.

"You're not going to spend the night yammering on the phone when you've got to track down a killer, are you?" Edith was in a huff.

"Actually, I figured maybe you could help with that. Can't you poke around the netherworld, find Tambra and see what she says?"

"Oh honey, how many times have I told you it doesn't work that way. There are layers, echelons, and a continuously winding circle of middle managers who are absolutely anal about following the rules."

"So, what do you expect me to do?"

"Get yourself organized, for crying out loud. Where's your murder board? Why haven't you categorized that list of Tambra's? Don't you realize those are suspects? Suspects with motives. All you've got is a photo of a woman in an ombre dot dress. Wig and all. Get off the stick and get cracking."

"Are you sure you weren't a prison warden in your former life and not a food critic?"

"Very funny, missy. And if I have to keep prodding you along, you'll owe me a visit to Imogen's."

I did a double eye roll and winced.

"I saw that, Missy. Come on, let's get moving."

Chapter Nineteen

"I'm exhausted, Edith. I need to unwind for a bit."

"Cry me a river on another day. Unless you plan on unwinding at the Fourth Street Jail in Phoenix, I suggest you snap to it. Where did you put those names? As I recall, it was a laundry list of personal groomers and those bunco women."

"Uh, yeah. I put it in my desk. Hang on, I'll get it." It was a Herculean effort to get myself off the couch, but a few seconds later, I returned, list in hand. I rattled off the names beginning with Kiara, the manicurist, and ending with Deborah, one of the bunco crew. "There are eight names. Where do you want to start?"

A whirl of pinks and mauves engulfed the room before Edith made her official entrance. "Let me look over that list. Hold it in front of me. By the way, good move going out with that cutie from Randolph's."

"It's just coffee."

"Tell me that *after* you've sipped your first cup."

"Aargh. So? What do you think? Tackle it alphabetically or by the seriousness of the offense?"

"Neither. Tackle it by who's got the most to lose if their dirty little secret came out. Start with the ones who have a business. Face it, business owners will stop at nothing to protect their own interests."

"There are only two business owners on this list. Ricardo, who's the co-owner of Up and Running and Alon, from New You."

"Now we're talking. What will it be? Do you want to color your hair first or sign up for physical fitness?"

"Ugh. Neither, but I suppose I'll have to come up with a ruse. Geez, I really like my hair color, although I suppose a few highlights wouldn't hurt."

"Ha! Anything to avoid a treadmill, huh?" Edith moved to one of the chairs and sprawled out.

"I hate exercise. Walking Speedbump is an Olympic feat for me."

"You'll hate an orange jumpsuit more. Trust me, honey, that color doesn't flatter anyone. And if it's Lilly-Ann who gets arrested, you'll probably be implicated too."

"Don't remind me. Okay, better figure out my next step."

"*Our* next step."

"If I only knew for sure what Tambra ingested, I'd know where to begin."

"Alon's a colorist. Lots of nasty toxic chemicals in his shop. I say we get a head start. Then, when the official report is released, all we'll have to do is match them up."

"Oh no. Not another one of your break-ins. That'll get me into the Fourth Avenue Jail faster than the murder."

"Only if we get caught."

I knew I wasn't about to win this argument, so I poured more kibble for the dog, refilled his water bowl, and stood at the door, cell phone and bag in hand. "Now what?"

"Now we find a killer or scratch a name from the list."

New You was located on Hidden Rock Road, diagonal from The Sugary Skull Café on East Cave Creek Road, a stone's throw from The Char-Board. At least I wouldn't be traipsing all over the map to scope it out. I pulled up the website and saw they were closed on Mondays. Not that it mattered. It was past five, and most likely, they would have shut their doors by now.

Edith barked commands like a drill sergeant. "Start with the dumpster. They're bound to have a dumpster out back. They get collected every other week, so evidence might be in there."

"What evidence? And how do you know the dumpsters are collected twice a month?"

"I have to find some way to keep myself entertained."

110

"Oh, brother."

I patted Speedbump and told him I wouldn't be long. After all, how was I to know Edith's little look-and-see plan would result in something far more disastrous?

When I pulled up to New You, there wasn't a single person in sight. Not that I expected to see people milling about. The restaurants and bars were on the main drag with few exceptions, and the street where New You was located, wasn't one of them.

The shop was flanked by a holistic chiropractic office and a nail salon that also offered body waxing. Both places closed as well.

"Not much action, honey," Edith said. "Looks like it's pretty safe for you to park in front."

I nodded, grumbled, and turned the ignition off to the engine. "Fine. Let's get this over with. And I'm only doing a quick look-see. I'm not about to go dumpster diving."

Edith didn't say a word but managed to stir up some small rocks and twigs in what could best be described as a dust devil. Only hers was pinkish.

Sure enough, in the small alley behind the shop, stood a good-sized blue waste removal bin with the red logo for Republic Services. With only a few dents and chips in the paint, my guess was that the bin was fairly new.

"See?" Edith said. "That's not very intimidating."

"Of course not. I haven't lifted the lid yet."

Reaching into my pocket for the food handler gloves I'd taken, I prayed I wouldn't come across anything too gross. At least it wasn't a pet grooming place or, worse yet, a daycare center. I'd be spared smelly diapers and dog poop bags.

The lid was one of those black rubbery ones with an easy grip, and I wasted no time lifting it. "Hmm, that's odd."

Edith materialized and hovered next to me. "What is?"

"The only shops on this small block are salons and a chiropractic office. Why on earth would there be so much confetti from paper shredding? That's all I can see."

"Maybe someone did their taxes. Stick your hand in there and move the papers around."

"I really don't want to touch anything yucky. Even with these gloves on."

"Feel around for bottles and plastic bags. Those colorists tend to use lots of stuff that came from plants. It's the in-thing nowadays. Natural products. Wouldn't surprise me if we find our poison."

It would surprise the daylights out of me.

"How do you know that?"

"Honey, I hadn't seen my natural hair color since Nixon was in office."

I looked at the massive amount of confetti, took a breath, and proceeded to shuffle it around. "This stuff is piled high and deep."

"Keep rooting around. You're moving papers, not rocks."

"This is never-ending. The confetti doesn't want to stay put on the edges of the bin. It keeps falling back."

"Give it a good shove, and keep moving your hands around."

"Arargh."

I bent down, leaned forward, and with both hands, moved the confetti as if I was doing the breaststroke. A small movement at first, but then I plunged my hands deeper into the pile of paper, and that's when I felt a large tube of sorts.

"No bottles, Edith. Feels like a pool noodle. Maybe it's something the chiropractic office discarded." With a fast and furious shove, I slid enough of the confetti out of the way so I could take a good look. Maybe it was my mind trying to blot out exactly what I had uncovered, because it took me a few seconds to realize what I had found. Even when I stared directly at it.

"It's a hand! A human hand! Oh my God! It's a hand, and it's attached to—" And then I let out what best could be described as a primordial scream. So loud it echoed in my own ears.

"Are you sure?"

"Of course, I'm sure. It's cold and hard but trust me, it's no store window manikin. Oh No! It's a dead body."

"Take a good look. Is it a man or a woman?"

"I'm not looking any more than I have to. It's an arm attached to a shoulder and a neck. The head is under the confetti. Oh No! It's a dead body. No!

No! No!"

"Don't you want to know who it is?"

"No, I don't. I mean, yeah, I do, but I don't want to be the one who does it. That's why we have a sheriff's office. And a marshal's office. And a coroner. And—"

"Fine. But enough of the screaming. It's disconcerting."

"Disconcerting? I'm standing over a dead body in an alley dumpster, and you call it *disconcerting*? It's horrific! Downright horrific.*"

I stepped away from the dumpster and took a few deep breaths. Then, for some inexplicable reason, I started shivering. Even in the warm evening heat.

"I need to call 911. What do I tell them? What possible reason could I have for digging through a dumpster behind three places of business?"

Edith materialized in that awful fuchsia outfit and leaned over the dumpster. "Fabricate something believable."

"Like what? What could possibly be feasible?"

"Tell them you inadvertently tossed something of yours in a trash basket in one of those businesses, and you were certain they took it out to the trash. Tell him you didn't realize it until after those places were closed. Pick a place."

"The sheriff's office is going to question all of those business owners. They'll know I wasn't in there."

"Then tell them you thought you heard a meowing sound and went to check."

"From my parked car? Tell them I parked the car on the street and went around back? Honestly, Edith, this is not going to work."

"Well, not if you're going to be that obstinate about it."

"I need to clear my head for a minute and think."

"You mean, come up with a better lie than mine."

"Uh, yeah, more or less. But it's impossible. I'm totally stressed, and the brain virtually shuts down when people are under pressure."

I stepped away from the dumpster and paced back in forth in front of it, hoping to clear my head. That's when Edith's form vanished, and a new whirlwind started. As leaves and paper scraps joined her fuchsia haze, I heard her announce, "Think fast, honey. Someone's coming."

Chapter Twenty

"You're not supposed to go rooting through the dumpsters," a man's voice called out. At first, I didn't see anyone, but a few seconds later, a middle-aged man built like an armored tank emerged from behind the buildings. With him was a mixed brown mutt about the same size as Speedbump.

The dog tugged on his leash in an effort to reach me.

"Is he friendly?"

"Friendlier than I am. What are you doing back here?"

I held out my hand, and the dog sniffed it. Then he nuzzled my arm, and I figured I had beaten at least half of the equation.

"OK. I confess. I had a ton of empty coffee cups in my car and knew there was a dumpster back here since I'm familiar with the hair salon. I figured what difference would it make if I threw them in."

"Well, it does. People pay a hefty fee for those services."

"Yeah. You're right. Only I never threw it in my trash. I walked back here to see if the container lid was open. Some of them have locks on them."

"Sounds like you've done this before."

"No, not really. You must live around here if you're out walking your dog."

"Down the next street. Bosco likes this alleyway, and I like him to do his business and get it over with. We walk this way at least three times a day."

"Good dog, Bosco," I said, petting him on his head. Then I looked directly at the man. Military-type haircut that showed more gray than black. "Um, you wouldn't have happened to notice anyone throwing anything else in there recently, would you?"

"Nope. Not today. Why?"

"Well, I was about to take out my cell phone and call the sheriff's office when you called out to me."

"Why?"

"Because there's a dead body in that dumpster. When I lifted the lid, I saw the arm. And, uh, part of the torso."

"Are you sure? Could be one of those plastic displays. They make 'em quite human-looking."

I shook my head. "It took me at least three or four minutes to catch my breath. It's a dead body, but I don't know if it's a man or woman."

Without wasting a second, the man charged over to the dumpster.

"Wait! Don't get your fingerprints on it. Use a hanky or something."

"Thanks. Good call."

He took out a wad of tissues from his pocket, grasped them in his hand, and proceeded to lift the lid. Then, total silence. At least for twenty seconds. "Hmm, body couldn't have been in here that long. It doesn't smell. Look, I don't want to get caught up in any of this. Those deputies are relentless when it comes to questioning people. Give me a minute or so to get Bosco out of here, okay?"

"But don't you think—"

"Nope. I don't. The Diamondbacks have a game tonight, and I'll be darned if I miss it."

"Uh, sure."

For an older man, the guy blew out of there like an Olympic runner with Bosco at his heels. I watched for a few seconds, then made the call. At least I had practice with my story—trash throwing, blah-blah-blah. Much better than Edith's scenarios.

Funny, but my hands trembled as I hit 911 on the cell. Then, I waited for what seemed like an eternity.

"911. What's the nature of your emergency?"

"I'm in an alleyway behind Hidden Rock Road. I went to dump some trash in the container, and there's a dead body in there. I don't know if it's male or female or how long it's been in there, but there's no smell." *Not yet.*

"I'm sending someone out there right now. Do you have the exact address?"

"Behind New You salon."

"Are you in any danger?"

"No." I looked around. "Not that I know of." *But thank you for bringing that up. Now I'm going to worry that the psycho who dumped the body is watching me.* Given my exchange with Bosco's owner, I seriously doubted he had anything to do with this recent discovery of mine, but then again, I'd been wrong before. I stepped back at least three or four yards and held on to my cell phone as if it was a taser.

"Are you still around, Edith?" I called out.

Her response was swift—a grayish-pink whirl of debris and leaves.

"Good. In case things go haywire before the deputies arrive, you can always create a disturbance."

The whirlwind intensified before morphing into a sludgy haze that lingered over the area. It reminded me of a California smog photo sans the Golden Gate Bridge. With my eyes affixed to the trash bin, I took a few steps back and clenched my wrists. A slight tremor in my hands grew into something more substantial—actual shaking.

With no idea how long it would take for the sheriff's office to respond, I tapped Maddie's cell number and waited for a response. The second she took the call, I said, "I saw a dead body."

"I know. It's been all over the news, and you told me that already. Are you all right? You sound like you're in shock. I know. It must be awful. I've heard it sometimes takes a few people days or weeks for something like that to sink in."

"Another body. In a dumpster. I'm waiting for the sheriff's office to get here."

"Where are you?"

"Behind a hair salon on Hidden Rock Road in Cave Creek. Following a clue. Sort of."

"What clue? From Tambra Wright's murder? Please don't tell me you're playing detective. You could be the next one killed."

"That's not very encouraging."

"It's not meant to be. Tell me what's going on."

"I found out Tambra had a list of people she was intimidating and possibly blackmailing. Had all sorts of private information on them. Anyway, one of them was her colorist, and I thought perhaps he might have been the culprit, so I decided to see if I could find any kind of evidence in the dumpster behind his salon. Evidence of a poison."

"Isn't that something the deputies are supposed to do? Take the clues and find the evidence?"

"Uh, yeah, but the deputies aren't on the firing line like I am. Or my employee, Lilly-Ann, for that matter. When I got to work, two deputies gave her the once over and told her she's a person of interest. Long story. I'm not far behind."

"Holy cannoli, Katie. I didn't realize it was that bad. Still, you shouldn't play detective on your own. You don't suppose the body you found in the dumpster has anything to do with Tambra's murder, do you?"

"You mean, like, her killer?"

"Or another victim from the same murderer. Then again, your new body could be someone totally unrelated to Tambra. Was it a male or female?"

"All I saw was an arm and part of a torso. I didn't look that close. Oh my gosh, Maddie. This is a nightmare. A regular night—got to go. Two sheriff cars are coming down the side street."

"Call me later."

I think I said okay or sure thing before I ended the call, but I honestly don't remember. I didn't realize it at the time, but the rational conversation I had with Maddie would be my last for a while. The shock hadn't hit me yet, but when it did, it really did. I widened my eyes and stood motionless as three deputies walked toward me. Two, having exited from the first car, and the third from the car directly behind it.

"Are you the person who phoned in the 911?" A tall, balding deputy with broad shoulders asked. Behind him stood another deputy. Younger, thinner, and a definite Devin Booker look-alike. He didn't say a word but took out his iPad as if he was ready to record everything.

Then, the nightmare intensified. The third deputy emerged from his vehicle, and my stomach cramped the second I spied him. Deputy Vincent strode toward me. All business and expressionless. "Miss Aubrey, correct?"

I nodded. "Uh-huh."

"I take it you were the one who discovered what you believe to be a deceased body in the dumpster?"

"Oh, it's a body, all right. Deceased. Dead. But not decomposing. I mean, not that I checked it out or anything, but the fleshy parts still looked fleshy, and it didn't reek. Not that I bent down to smell it, but—"

"Miss Aubrey, are you in need of medical assistance? You're rambling, and your face is devoid of color. You may be suffering from the shock of coming across a corpse. Or at least what you believe to be a corpse."

For reasons I couldn't explain, I suddenly got animated and shrieked, "It's a corpse. A corpse. But I need to know if it's male or female."

Deputy Vincent pulled out his phone and placed a call. "Requesting EMT services on Hidden Rock Road, behind the hair salon."

"I'm fine," I said. Unfortunately, he didn't believe me, and next thing I knew, the Devin Booker look-alike approached and insisted I follow him into his sheriff's car to wait to be checked out by the EMTs.

"But I'm fine," I insisted as the deputy opened the rear driver's side door to his car. "The EMTs should be here any second, Miss. Try to remain calm."

I looked back at where Deputy Vincent stood and watched as his counterpart from the first vehicle lifted the lid to the trash bin and made a gesture with his hand. Then I watched as Deputy Vincent peered inside the bin.

"I was right," I called out. "It's a dead body."

The younger deputy nodded. "It would appear that way."

A few minutes later, two more vehicles arrived. The EMTs, who were only too happy to take my blood pressure and my pulse, and an official forensic van from the county. And while my blood pressure was on the low side, it wasn't cause for concern. And neither were my clammy hands or inability to keep from talking. I was told to rest, drink fluids, and, if possible, contact a family member or friend to stay with me once I got home. I almost responded with, "Do they have to be alive, or will an annoying ghost do?"

but I thought better of it.

Deputy Vincent insisted on having someone drive me home, but I was hesitant to leave my car on the street.

"Is there anyone we can call for you, Miss Aubrey?" he asked. "Leave us your keys and we'll have one of the deputies drive it to your residence when we complete our business here. Can't do it sooner."

I nodded, too dumbfounded to utter a word. Maddie was miles away in Chandler, and it would take her an hour to get here. Matt had classes, and I didn't want to upset Lilly-Ann any more than she already was. I also didn't want to start a new employee relationship by having Javie pick me up. Without stopping to think it over, I rattled off Ian Monroe's name and told him Ian lived in Cave Creek.

A few minutes later, I was informed Ian was on his way and that one of the deputies would drop my car off. I handed over the key and remained in the rear passenger seat, somewhat numb but curious as all get out to learn more about the body I discovered.

As luck would have it, I didn't have to wait long.

"It's a woman. Thirty or fortyish. I watched that forensic crew while you played damsel-in-distress."

I hugged myself as if it was the arctic winter. "I wasn't playing, Edith. I'm like, totally unnerved."

"Then pull yourself together because it's a dozy. It's a woman, and I'm ninety-nine percent it's that little chickee from the balcony who got into it with Eric."

"How can you be sure?"

"The last time I saw so much makeup, it was on Alice Cooper."

Chapter Twenty-One

I was about to respond, but at that very moment, Ian approached the deputy's car and leaned in. He flashed a smile, and I could see the dimple on one side of his face. "Hey there. I got here as fast as I could. The deputy explained what happened. Holy crap. No wonder you look so, so—"

"Horrible?"

"I was going to say *dazed*. And maybe a bit ashen, but you'd never look horrible."

Please tell me I'm not about to fall for this guy.

"I'm so sorry to drag you away from whatever it was you were doing, but I didn't know who else to call. I just sort of rattled off your name because I knew you weren't far."

"It's okay. I'm glad you did." He reached over and gave my hands a squeeze. "The deputy said you were checked out for shock, but your hands are like icicles. Give me a second to speak with them, and then I'll drive you home. Okay?"

I nodded. Too stunned to say a word. I was lightheaded and woozy, but still cognizant of what was going on. A minute or so later, Ian returned.

"All set to go. My car's the white Mazda."

When I stood to get out of the sheriff's vehicle, I sort of wobbled, and Ian put his arm around my waist. "Take it easy. My car's not going anywhere without us."

Once seated in his Mazda and buckled up, I took a few slow breaths. "It was awful. Finding that body. I've never seen a corpse up close and personal in daylight. Not that the light mattered, but still. It wasn't like what happened to Tambra. The lighting was dim, and a zillion people were all around. This time it was, well, more intimate. Hmm, I don't know if intimate is the right word, but it was awful, and I can't get that image out of my head."

He reached over and squeezed my arm. "It'll be all right. Just take deep breaths and try to relax. You don't have to say anything."

"I'm rambling, aren't I?"

"That's understandable. Take it slow. And give me directions to your house. Do I make a left or right when I pull up to Cave Creek Road?"

"A left. It's not very far, just a few blocks past The Char-Board on the left-hand side. You'll have to keep your eyes open because it's getting dark already."

Surprisingly, my directions were pretty clear, and Ian had no trouble pulling into my driveway. He got out, opened the door, and reached for my hand.

"If you don't mind," he said, "I'd feel more comfortable hanging out with you for a bit before I take off. Just to make sure you're all right."

"Thanks. I really appreciate it. By the way, I've got a dog. Speedbump. He's really friendly."

Ian smiled. "I love dogs. Just haven't had the time to commit to one with my schedule."

"Not much committing as far as Speedbump is concerned. He kind of came with the territory."

I unlocked the front door and was greeted by slobbery canine kisses. And when the dog was done with my welcome, he did the same with Ian.

"He's not much of a watchdog, but he's great company. Come on in and make yourself comfortable. There's iced tea in the fridge and a few Cokes. I can get you whatever you'd like."

My lightheadedness persisted. So much for thinking I could disguise it. Ian narrowed his eyes at me, took my elbow, and walked me to the couch. "Why don't you sit down first, and I'll bring over some iced tea? You know, sometimes a shock like the one you had, doesn't manifest itself until much later. Not that I'm equating it to that whole PTSD thing, but on a smaller scale, it must be unsettling."

"That's not the worst of it." I clenched my fists and tried not to cry, but it was too late. Here I was, letting loose with my emotions in front of a guy I hardly knew. "I'm so scared I'm going to be rung up the scale from person of interest to much worse. And now, a second body."

"Hey, relax. It's probably a coincidence. That's all. Listen, I don't want to upset you any more than you are already, but the deputy I spoke with said they'd be sending someone over later to get a full statement."

My lower lip quivered, and I grabbed a wadded-up tissue from my pocket to wipe my eyes as I looked at his face. "Yeah, I figured as much."

Ian walked to the fridge and returned with two bottles of Pure Leaf unsweetened tea. "I love this stuff. The sugary drinks don't quench my thirst." He handed me a bottle and sat at the other end of the couch. Speedbump plunked himself on the floor in front of Ian and nudged him. In return, Ian patted his head as he sipped the tea.

"It's none of my business, but I'm going to ask the official question before the deputies do. What were you doing poking around a dumpster a few blocks from your restaurant?"

I opened my mouth, then closed it abruptly. "What I'm going to tell the deputies is not what I'm about to tell you. Are you comfortable with that?"

He nodded. "I'll have to be. If I expect us to, well, get to know each other better."

And then, out of nowhere, a mauve haze settled over the couch. "He's good with words. That's a plus."

I shuddered, and Ian immediately responded. "You may be getting that delayed reaction. Hang on. Do you want me to get you a throw or something?"

"I'll be okay. Here goes." I closed my eyes, took a breath, and told him everything. Everything sans Edith. That would've sent him flying out of here faster than any get-up-and-go. "You've got to believe me. I'm not the kind of person who goes breaking and entering into someone's house. Although, in this case, it was only entering. One of the doors was open. Given the

123

exchange I overheard between Eric and Tambra, I was positive he was the one who did her in. All I needed to find was a hefty insurance policy."

"And did you?" Ian sounded earnest. Not judgmental. I began to relax as I continued.

"No, but I was able to get into their computer and pulled up a file of Tambra's. It was a list of people she blackmailed or intimidated. One of them was the owner of New You, and she had proof he deceived his customers.

"So you thought maybe he could have been the one who poisoned her?"

I nodded. "That's why I decided to check out the dumpster behind his store. You know, to see if anything matched up." I paused for a second to gauge his reaction. Still earnest. "I can't even imagine what thoughts are crossing your mind about me right now."

He grinned. A really wide grin. "I don't know. I never thought I'd meet a real Nancy Drew. Not that I read any of those mysteries, but my younger sisters did."

"So you don't mind hanging out with a, a—"

"Amateur sleuth? Nah. Especially one with charcuterie skills. Hey, I don't blame you for what you did. After that grilling we all took from those deputies, I would've been nervous, too. But whoa. You took a heck of a chance. Especially at Eric's. Who knows what he would have done if he caught you."

OMG. I am falling for him. It's Dustin Hoffman and Ann Bancroft all over again. And that was what? The late 1960s?

"I was lucky. That's for sure. But I did walk away with info that may come to my rescue if I am accused of anything. Same deal with my employee, Lilly-Ann."

I explained Lilly-Ann's history with Tambra to him, and he agreed. She and I were both in a rather precarious situation. Then, to compound it, another dead body.

"What if that body in the dumpster turns out to be someone connected to Tambra or Hidden Boulders?" I gulped. "It would look awfully suspicious for me to be there."

"So, what's your cover story?"

I rattled off the same one I told Bosco's owner, and he gave it a thumbs up. Then, I began to shiver again. This time more pronounced.

"Hang on. I'll grab that throw you've got over there. By the way, when was the last time you ate anything?" He walked across the room, took the throw, and put it over my legs.

"Um, breakfast, I think. I can't even remember. We were so slammed today I never stopped for a sandwich or anything."

"That, plus the shock, could be contributing to why you're so cold, because the temperature in here is fine. Look, I've got plenty of time. I could pick up something for you or make you dinner. Depends what you've got in the kitchen."

"I really hate to bother you. And all I've got are eggs, cheese, and veggies. Plus, some canned stuff. I haven't had time to do a decent food shopping."

"Plenty for an omelet. Hey, if I can't pull off a decent cheese and veggie omelet, I don't deserve a degree in culinary arts."

"Thanks. Really. It's a small kitchen. You should be able to find what you need."

"Relax. I can improvise."

Ian walked to the kitchen, and the second he was out of sight, Edith's raspy voice stung my ear. "Dustin Hoffman and Ann Bancroft, huh? You've got to get over the age thing if you expect any action."

"I wasn't expecting any action."

"You mean from the deputy who comes over to question you?" Ian narrowed his eyes.

I froze. "Um, yeah. That."

"Just stick to your cover story. It's a decent one."

Ian wasn't kidding when he said he could improvise. I don't know what combination of spices he used, but I never tasted a broccoli, onion, and cheese omelet that was so savory.

"You'd better share this with me," I told him, "Or I'll feel terrible."

"Actually, I had a burger before I got the call from that deputy, but if it'll make you feel any better, I'll have a small taste."

We ate at the kitchen table, but the real winner was Speedbump, who managed to procure tidbits from both of us. My body warmed, and I no longer had that queasy, woozy feeling. Not until the sound of cars pulling up gave me a jolt. "Must be the deputy or deputies."

"Deputies," Ian replied. He stood by the front window and watched. "Looks like they returned your car. Both the MCSO vehicle and yours are now parked in front." He walked back to where I sat and narrowed his eyes. "Take deep breaths. You can do this."

"I'm not a very good liar."

"If you plan on prying into Tambra's death, you may have to bone up on those skills."

"Stick around, will you?"

"I'll have to. Someone will need to remind you of what you said. That's the only trouble with cover stories."

"You sound as if you know."

"Not really. I just read a lot."

Chapter Twenty-Two

I opened the door and let the two MCSO deputies inside. The tall balding one and the Devin Booker look-alike. A sudden sense of relief brushed over me when I realized Deputy Vincent wasn't anywhere in sight. Still, facing the other two men was formidable, if nothing else.

"Hi." My voice was more of a squeak than an actual sound.

"We won't take much of your time, Miss Aubrey," the balding one said. "We understand this has been an unsettling experience for you, but we need to ask you a few questions. Is there someplace where we can sit?"

"Um, sure. The kitchen table." I pointed to Ian and motioned them over. "This is my friend, Ian. Is it all right if he joins us?"

The two deputies looked at each other before the bald one spoke. "Only if your friend agrees not to say anything."

Ian nodded, and the four of us sat at the kitchen table. The deputies introduced themselves as Paul Biglow and Jae Ayton, before Deputy Biglow opened his iPad and looked directly at me. "We understand you were the one who phoned 911 having discovered a body in the dumpster behind New You and a chiropractic office."

"That's right." I kept my voice steady and didn't offer any more information than necessary.

"That begs the question, Miss Aubrey, what were you doing at that dumpster? Your place of business, according to my notes, is a mile or so from here."

Ian widened his eyes and bent his head slightly as if to say, "You know what to say."

I went on to explain that I was on my way out to eat when I decided to unload some coffee cup trash into the dumpster since it was on my way to the restaurant. I explained that I wanted to make sure the lid wasn't locked, so that's why I never actually tossed trash inside. Then I saw the corpse and phoned the sheriff's office.

"Was anyone else in the area at the time?" Deputy Ayton asked.

"Actually, yes. A man was walking his dog. A medium-sized brown mix. Maybe had some Boxer in it."

"And the man?"

"Middle-aged and heavy set." I was about to tell the deputies that we had no contact but thought better of it. Especially if someone else in a nearby house noticed Bosco and his owner.

"Right before I phoned your office, he walked over to inform me not to put trash in the container since it wasn't mine. Then I told him I was about to call 911 since there was a body inside. He didn't believe me, so he looked for himself."

Deputy Biglow frantically tapped on his iPad. "And then?"

"And then he said he didn't want to get caught up in anything and took off with the dog."

"Anyone else in the area?" the deputy asked.

"No. That was it."

Deputy Biglow pushed his chair back and stood. He was immediately followed by the younger deputy.

"I know you can't tell me whose body it was until he or she is identified by next of kin, but can you tell me if it was a he or she?" I widened my eyes and tried to look as earnest as possible.

"This goes no further," Deputy Biglow said. "Although I'm certain the news will be all over it by morning. It was a woman. That's all I can disclose."

"Well, hell's bells! I can disclose more!"

I jumped and nearly knocked my chair to the ground. A canary yellow film settled around the table, and I tried to act as if it wasn't there. Of course, as far as everyone else was concerned, it wasn't. But I knew Edith had returned from her latest sojourn and, most likely, had no intention of leaving anytime soon.

"Can you imagine the indignation? They gave the Jean Harlow gown to some fly-by-night floozy but trust me. She won't be wearing it much longer."

Dear God. If Edith keeps this up, she'll never move on, and I'll be stuck with her forever.

The deputies thanked me for my time and informed me that if they had further questions, they'd contact me. *Terrific.*

Once they were out the door, Ian smiled and told me I should take up poker playing. "What's your next step?" he asked.

"I'm that transparent, huh?"

"Hey, anyone who goes dumpster diving for murder clues isn't about to quit even if they discover something unpleasant."

"Nice euphemism. Geez, I really hope those deputies don't return to ask more questions. I've seen enough of those crime shows. They ask the same questions with little twists to see if they can trip you up."

"Isn't that only for suspects?"

I winced, and Ian returned the same look. "Oops. Sorry. But seriously, you can't possibly be a suspect. Even if that's what they hinted at. Having words with someone doesn't automatically point a finger. And face it, Tambra had words with everyone."

"True, but—" In that second, two things happened simultaneously. Speed-bump rushed to the door and barked frantically while the entire house went black. No lights. No hum from the refrigerator. And no bluish timer on the TV cable.

"Power outage?" Ian took a step toward me and grasped my arm.

"Maybe. I haven't lived here for that long, so I don't know if that kind of thing happens in this neighborhood."

"Uh, I think it's just your house. Look outside. The streetlights are on, and the other houses have their lights on. Do you have a flashlight? Never mind, I'll use the one on my phone. Which side of your house is the electrical box located?"

"On the left when you go out the front door. Wait. I'm going with you. Think something tripped?"

"It happens. Come on, and grab your phone, too."

As we approached the front door, every single Halloween fright movie I'd ever seen came to mind. Someone throwing the house into pitch darkness so they could take an ax to the occupants. I cringed. *Stupid imagination.*

Then I had another thought. Edith! Was she trying to create the kind of situation that would force me into Ian's arms? I wouldn't put it past her. Unfortunately, I couldn't very well ask her, so the best I could do was follow Ian outside.

Speedbump walked alongside us, lifting his head occasionally to growl. Ian turned my way. "Does he do that often?"

"Never. This is creeping me out. What if someone's out here?"

He panned the flashlight around us and shook his head. "Not anyone. Wait. Don't freak out. What I meant was, that *if* someone was here, they're not anymore."

"That's comforting."

We walked past the front porch and rounded the house until we reached the electrical box and watering system. Ian pulled the door open and shone the light. "Your master power switch is off. Hmm, those things don't go off by themselves."

When he pulled the metal door open, I thought I saw something fall to the ground. I pointed my cell phone's flashlight down and saw a legal-size envelope. "Something dropped out." I bent down, retrieved it, and lifted the flap. Inside was a single piece of paper with a message scrawled with a black marker. "Stop poking around. Next time the power will be cut for good—at your restaurant. Keep it up, and it will get worse for you."

I thrust the envelope at Ian and, with shaking hands, aimed my flashlight beam on it.

"Holy crap. I already flipped the switch back. If anyone dusts for prints, they'll find mine on the breaker."

"You're saying I need to call those deputies again?" I asked.

"Yes. If either of us expects to get any sleep tonight. And speaking of that, do you have an extra toothbrush?"

"Huh? What?"

"If you think I'm walking out, think again. I'll stay on your couch, but right now, you need to make that call. Who knows what the person who wrote that threat is capable of?"

And then—Edith. In her full glory. Yellow haze and whirlwinds. "Tell him your bed is more comfortable."

I gasped and didn't say a word. Ian took my elbow, and we walked back inside. "I'll make us some tea, and you can call the sheriff's office. Deal?"

"Yeah. It's a deal."

Twenty minutes later, Ian and I found ourselves across the table with the same two deputies who had vacated the house earlier. I handed the envelope to Deputy Ayton, who pulled out disposable gloves from his pocket and read the note before holding it up for Deputy Biglow to eye.

"My fingerprints are on it," I said. "And Ian's are on the master switch in the breaker box."

Deputy Biglow sighed. "I'm not putting any great hope into securing prints, but maybe the forensic team will be able to glean something else from the note. You never know."

I looked directly at him. "Like what?"

"Handwriting, for one thing. We may have something similar on file. And substances. Food, toxins, whatever."

Then Deputy Ayton leaned back and looked at his partner before speaking. "I see you have security doors, but you may want to invest in one of those home surveillance systems or maybe even contract with an alarm company."

I turned to Ian. "The security doors were installed recently by the property owner. Thank goodness for that. I suppose I'll call ADT or Brinks."

"Not a bad idea," Deputy Biglow said. "And if I were you, I'd do the same at your place of business. Now, if you don't mind, I've got another question for you."

Here it comes.

"The note demanded you stop poking around. What I'd like to know is if the author meant your episode with the dumpster or if there's anything more you'd like to tell us."

I froze for a split second and hoped they hadn't noticed. "Must be the dumpster because all I've done is cater the event at Hidden Boulders and work in my sandwich shop."

"All right, but if you think of anything else, let us know. We've got two suspicious deaths on our hands, and we don't want a third."

Geez, talk about bedside manner.

When the deputies left, I was more unnerved than before and definitely didn't want to be alone in the house.

"Um," I said to Ian. "You mentioned a toothbrush. I can do better. I can give you an entire dental hygiene kit. Two, if you want. My father and brother are periodontists. It's a family thing. So was my grandfather."

"I take it you're comfortable with me spending the night on your couch. I wasn't sure if I overstepped my bounds, but honestly, I'm worried about you."

"I'd offer you the guest room, but I never really set it up."

He laughed. "The couch is fine."

"I don't know about you, but I'm way too wound up to even think of sleeping. Want to watch a late-night movie? My brain's too foggy to play cards or anything."

"Same here."

I grabbed an extra pillow and blanket and put them on the coffee table before we settled on the couch to see what Turner Classic Movies had in store for us. "If I fall asleep here, you can—"

"Don't worry. I'll let you sleep. I don't have to be at work until tomorrow afternoon. But what about you? Should you set an alarm or something?"

"Don't worry, honey," I'll wake you up. You want ice cubes or an annoying static sound from your TV?"

Ugh. Edith. I wondered how long she'd been lingering.

"I'll set an alarm on my cell phone. It should be enough. Then, for Edith's sake, I added, "Definitely enough."

With that, I grabbed the remote and turned the TV on. Then I put the remote on the coffee table, leaned my head back into the couch, and closed my eyes. It was the last thing I remembered until waking up at three with my head against Ian's shoulders and *The Dirty Dozen* playing on Turner Classic.

Chapter Twenty-Three

"You spent the night with a strange guy? In your house? On your couch? Yikes, Katie. He could have been a serial killer, for all you know." Maddie's voice was a five-alarm for sure. "You should have called me back. I would have raced right over. You sounded so normal when you told me about the dumpster body. Must be one of those post-traumatic-shock things."

"Yeah, that's what Ian said." I looked over at Lilly-Ann and Matt, who were fast at work, and continued my call to Maddie. I told her how he stayed with me until the morning and even made us breakfast before I rushed off to The Char-Board.

"Just be careful, will you?"

"Sure thing. Catch you later."

Then I glanced back at my two workers. I hadn't yet told them about what I discovered yesterday and figured it could wait until after the morning rush. But as things turned out, I mentioned it the second Lilly-Ann spoke.

"Thanks for understanding about yesterday," she said. "I was in no shape to work. I would have chopped my fingers off or something. I'm hoping your friend can get me the name of a good lawyer."

"I plan on calling Liam this afternoon. I may need that lawyer more than you do."

"Are the two of you still worried about needing an attorney?" Matt asked as he brushed past us to refill the condiments.

"I know I will. I found another body yesterday."

As soon as I said that, the room went still. Seconds later, Matt spoke again.

This time emphatically. "What body? At the Hidden Boulders?"

I shook my head. "Nope. In a dumpster." I then went on to give them the salient details, excluding the one that involved Ian spending the night with me on my couch. When I finished, the two of them stood motionless for a good five or six seconds.

"Let me get this straight," Lilly-Ann said. "You thought there was some connection between Tambra and her colorist, so you decided to look for evidence behind his shop?"

"Uh-huh. Pretty much. I was acting on some scuttlebutt I overheard."

Last thing I need is to tell more people the truth about breaking into Eric's place.

She brushed a strand of hair from her forehead and crinkled her eyes. "That was pretty chancy."

Matt took a step toward us. "Forget chancy. Was it someone from Hidden Boulders? Male? Female? Did you recognize them, or was the corpse too, well, you know. Messed up?"

"Ew!" Lilly-Ann blurted out.

I shook my head and remembered what Deputy Biglow told me about keeping my mouth shut. "All I saw was an arm and a torso. The shoulder, I think. I couldn't tell."

"It'll be on the noonday news for sure," Matt continued. "I'll keep checking the local apps on my phone."

If I could have set up an alert on my iPhone with the headlines, I would have. Instead, I opted for the same thing Matt did—look and see.

The breakfast crowd rivaled the one from the day before, and lunch was no different. The three of us scurried from table to kitchen so many times we could have done it in our sleep. Many of the same patrons from yesterday were back. This time with more rumor mongering. Unfortunately, we were pressed to prepare meals, so there was no time to mill about and catch the chatter.

At a little before noon, Ian sent me a text, hoping I was doing okay, and said he'd call later. Didn't want to bother me at work. When I paused to read it, an all-too-familiar voice rattled in my ear. "He may be a keeper if you don't muck it up."

Thanks, Edith.

Then, at a few minutes past twelve, a woman I didn't recognize, who was seated by the window, announced to the man across from her, "It's officially been ruled a homicide. It just came across my phone on the news app. Tambra Wright was poisoned. Oh, and another body cropped up a block or so away. And here we thought Cave Creek would be a lovely place to retire."

I stood a few feet away and spun around. "Sorry, but I couldn't help but hear you. Did the news mention what kind of poison?"

The woman looked up and went back to her phone. "It doesn't say, but I'm sure the TV news will have more details. I suppose one poison's as good, or bad, as the others. Funny, but I've always avoided buffets for health reasons, but now I've got another one."

"Quit being so dramatic, Corissa," the man said. "Obviously, the woman's murder was intentional, or the whole lot of folks at that event would have followed suit."

I gulped. "Does it say anything about the other death?"

The woman shook her head. "Only that a middle-aged white female was found in a dumpster near here. Behind some businesses. Whoever took out their trash must have had some surprise."

"Yeah. Some surprise."

By the time I walked back to the kitchen, Lilly-Ann and Matt received the same news compliments of Matt's phone.

"If we could only find out *what* poison was used on Tambra," I told them, "we'd have a better idea of who could have done it. Some poisons, like plant-based ones, are easy to come by."

Lilly-Ann pursed her lips. "That's a comforting thought. What if it's something we have here? In our own kitchen?'

"It would be hard to prove."

Really? What makes me think that?

"As soon as the lunch rush is over, I'll call Liam and see what he knows."

At that very moment, the door opened, and Deputy Vincent walked in.

Please tell me he doesn't have a warrant to search our kitchen.

"Miss Aubrey? I'm sorry to disturb you at your place of business, but I need a word or two with you. Privately."

"It's a small sandwich shop, and my employees are in and out of the kitchen. How about we talk out back?"

"Fine with me. Lead the way."

I looked down the alley and didn't see Mercedes. "We can chat right here by the door. Tell me, should I be putting a lawyer on retainer?"

"Only if *you* deem it necessary."

Terrific.

"I need to know. Am I a suspect? A person-of-interest?"

He narrowed his eyes and looked directly at me. "As you know, we are looking into a number of people whose interactions with Tambra are cause for concern. As for the discovery you made yesterday, *that,* I'm afraid, is in its infancy as far as our investigations are concerned. What I can disclose is that the deceased female in the dumpster was an acquaintance of Ms. Wright's."

"Oh my gosh. Then the murders were related, weren't they?"

"We don't know that. Not at the moment. That's the reason for my visit. I'd like to revisit your interaction with Ms. Wright and the other women at Hidden Boulders prior to the fashion show."

"Okay. We met to discuss catering the event. I wanted the business."

"Expound on the tension between the two of you. I know you gave a statement Saturday night, but I'd like more detail if possible."

"I don't know what other details I can provide. A few snipes went back and forth. Truth is, Tambra was rude and offensive. But no threats were made, and certainly nothing of a physical nature."

"What about Ms. Wright's interactions with the other women at the table?" He pulled out his iPad and looked at his notes. "In attendance were Cherie Simms, Meredith Mason, and Deirdre Billings. Is that correct?"

"Yes."

"For lack of a better way to ask this, I'll use your words. Were they sniping too?"

I shook my head. "No, they were too intimidated by her. She bulldozed them. Cut them off when they spoke and gave them 'the look.' You know, like the kind all of us got from our teachers."

Again, with the narrowing of his eyes. "Not all of us. But I understand what you're saying."

Oh, brother.

"You said the body I found was an acquaintance of Tambra's. It was one of them, wasn't it? Which one? This is a small town. Really small. Before we close for the day, one of our customers will blurt it out. I mean, being an acquaintance and all, it's not as if there's far to look. Tell me it wasn't Deirdre. She's the nicest one in that group". *And the one who got me lots of bookings.* "Look, I won't say a word. Besides, it'll be on the news by the time I get home from work. Who was it?"

He took a deep breath and rubbed the back of his neck. "The unfortunate victim was a Cherie Lynn Simms. And before you say a word, need I remind you *not* to be the one blurting it out to customers."

"Cherie. That's awful." I flashed back to when I first met her, and she wasn't wearing heavy make-up. Certainly not what Edith described. Then again, I had no idea what Cherie could have been up to or why the heavy face paint? I widened my eyes at the deputy. "What was the cause of death? It's been over twenty-four hours. The coroner must have rendered a preliminary cause of death. Or a good guess. Oh my gosh! Do they think Cherie was poisoned too? Is that why you're really here? To present me with a search warrant? I guarantee, all we have are normal foods and spices."

Deputy Vincent rubbed his temples. "The second homicide does not appear to be from poisoning, however we are awaiting results from the preliminary tox screen. Does that answer all of your questions, Miss Aubrey?"

"Uh, yeah. For now."

"Good. If anything comes to mind regarding Tambra Wright and Cherie Simms, contact my office immediately. And this conversation goes no further. Understood?"

I nodded. "So I'm off the hook?"

He shook his head. "That's not what I said. As we garner new evidence, everyone who came in contact with our victims will be under scrutiny."

Wonderful.

He opened the door to the kitchen and proceeded to walk straight through past the dining area. I followed him like a puppy, hoping no one would be alarmed to see him exit our kitchen. To be on the safe side, I rushed to his side and, in a voice that was clearly audible, I said, "Thanks for stopping by. It's always a pleasure to see you, Uncle Travis."

He turned, rolled his eyes, and moved like a jackrabbit to his vehicle. I turned to re-enter the shop when a sickening puce haze obscured my view.

"Good for you. You're getting quite brazen. Always a formidable trait. Especially since we've got more poking around to do." I jumped and looked around. No one on the street.

"What poking around? Haven't we had enough? Or should I say, 'haven't *I* had enough?'"

"You heard the man. You are *not* off the hook. And what about Lilly-Ann? She's one step away from wiping out your Kleenex supply."

"What did you have in mind?"

"A bit of reconnaissance, that's all. And some old-fashioned detective work."

Just then, the door swung open, and a customer walked out, barely bumping into me. When the coast was clear, I whispered, "What reconnaissance?"

I was met with a swirling array of horrible yellow, puce, and brown colors. In that second, I knew the dumpster incident would pale compared to what Edith had in store for us.

Chapter Twenty-Four

"What was that all about?" Matt asked when I walked back into the kitchen. Lilly-Ann, who stood a few feet away, salad bowl in hand, chimed in. "Are they going to search the restaurant?"

"No, he wanted some information about yesterday. That's all."

"Did he mention me?" Lilly-Ann's hand shook, and I worried she'd drop the salad bowl and its contents. "He saw me but walked right by."

"No, he didn't. Look, I'm going to call Liam right now. No sense putting it off."

Matt winked. "Want me to put out a jar asking for legal fee donations?"

"That's not funny," Lilly-Ann shot him a look and returned the salad to the fridge.

"I'm going to make this call, so I'll be tied up for a few minutes."

Matt nodded. "No problem. We've got it." Then he approached Lilly-Ann. "Sorry. Didn't mean to upset you." Then to me. "Or you either."

I walked outside again, cell phone in hand, and dialed Liam's number. He picked up on the second ring. "Hey Katie, I was about to call you. It's been a regular circus around here. That body they found in a dumpster was one of our members—Cherie Simms. The bunco ladies found out from her housekeeper, who was questioned by the deputies and had to identify the body. Seemed the housekeeper's card was in Cherie's pocket. The woman was also Deirdre Billings' housekeeper. Do I need to say more? Anyway, the news is spreading like manure around here. At least it wasn't on our premises, so I didn't have to sift through the video surveillance. Although I do expect to be questioned by the sheriff's deputies. Some news, huh?"

"Actually, I already know about Cherie. Only I didn't know it was her. I was the one who opened that dumpster. Long story."

"What? Hold on. I'll close the door."

For the next few minutes, I described what happened in detail and waited for Liam's reaction.

"Good call in tracking down who could have had it in for Tambra but holy geez, finding a body? And Cherie's no less. My take is that the deaths were connected. Be careful, will you? Maybe let the sheriff's office and the marshals do their jobs. This kind of changes things a bit."

"Not where Deputy Vincent is concerned. Lilly-Ann and I are still dangling on the hook. Any chance Bari was able to give you a name of a good defense attorney?"

"Yep. That's why I was about to call you. Got a pencil?"

"I will. I've got to go back inside. I'm standing in our alleyway."

"I'll wait."

Liam gave me two names. A man and a woman. Both with stellar recommendations. He also told me he thought I was jumping the gun, but if it made me feel better, then sure. Call one of them. I desperately wanted to tell him that Cherie was the person who was with Eric on his balcony the night I snooped around. However, there was no way I could have done that without mentioning Edith's keen observation at the dumpster.

"Listen, Katie, I'll let you know what I hear, okay? Meanwhile, I'm serious. For all we know, we could be dealing with a seriously deranged individual. One murder might be revenge or the like, but two? And so closely related? FYI, We're beefing up security around here. Not just surveillance."

"Did you know anything about Cherie?"

"No, only the name and member information. Single membership. Lived here four years."

"Any chance you were able to get the name of the housekeeper?" *I'm one step ahead of you, Edith.*

"Sorry, no, but if you were to call Deirdre, I'm sure she'd tell you. I watched her on video surveillance today, buzzing about from person to person before she left. Guess no card or bunco games today. Only reports from gossip central."

Thanks, Liam. I will. And thank Bari. I really appreciate it."

"Any time. Remember, no risks? Okay?"

Define risk.

"I'll be careful. Let's keep in touch."

"For sure."

As much as I wanted to phone Deirdre immediately, I couldn't. We had customers, and we were also behind on preparing the mini-char boards that were so popular. I'd be glad when Javie could join our crew full-time in the next two weeks. I had visions of an expanded char board repertoire and smiled as I returned to the kitchen to prepare them.

Unfortunately, Edith wiped that smile off my face seconds later. She had materialized this time in a khaki outfit that looked as if her last venture was on a wild animal hunt somewhere in Africa.

"What now?" I whispered, head bent down as I cubed the salami.

"The deputies are going to be all over her house looking for clues, but nothing's stopping us from peeking into that locker of hers at the golf course."

"She has a locker at the golf course?"

"Who has a locker at the golf course?" Matt asked as he walked past me to put some dishes in the sink.

"Huh? Nothing. Only thinking out loud."

"No worries. I do that too when I'm prepping for an exam." He spun around and returned to the dining area.

"I didn't know Cherie golfed. How do you know?"

Edith plopped herself on the edge of the counter and stretched her translucent legs. "I listen. She mentioned issues on the fourth hole when you met with Tambra and the bunco women."

"What kind of issues?"

"Does it matter? Drainage. Forget the golf course. We need to get into that locker. It's probably a combination locker. I can upset the tumbler. If it's keyed, you'll need to get your hands on one of those mini bolt cutters. You can stick it in your bag."

"I'm not about to get caught at the golf clubhouse breaking into a locker.

Besides, you have to be a member to get inside."

"Really? You're following the rules now? When you close for the day, go into a hardware store and buy one of those things. It may come in handy later on. I'll wait in your car. Don't dilly-dally. It won't take those deputies long to figure out she's got a locker at the golf course."

I looked around to make sure Lilly-Ann and Matt were out of sight. "What makes you so sure Cherie was hiding something in her locker?"

"Because houses are the first places people search. Hells bells. You read enough of those mysteries. You should know that."

I did a mental eye roll. "Fine. The hardware store and the golf course. Anything else on your playlist?"

"Yes. Snag that little cutie from last night. He's good eye candy."

"You watched us?"

"Not much to watch unless you enjoy the sound of snoring."

"He snores?"

"No. You do."

I watched as Edith gradually faded, leaving a haze of beige that dissipated seconds later. It was now twenty to two, and the lunch rush was over. Only a handful of customers remained, and I went back to the mini boards that needed finishing.

Matt flipped the closed sign on the door at five past two, and he and Lilly-Ann tackled the clean-up. I added a few final touches to my boards, wrapped them, and put them in the fridge for tomorrow. Then I approached Lilly-Ann.

"Liam gave me the phone numbers of two attorneys. I'll pass them on, but I'd hold off for a day or two. It's still early in the official investigation, and things might change. Still, at least we know where to turn. I'm going to google both of them and let you know what I think tomorrow. Of course, it might be a good idea if each of us had a different one. Conflict of interest and all that."

"Yeah, that makes sense. Uh, what did you mean when you said things might change? How?" Her voice was as shaky as it was earlier.

"The deputies are gathering evidence, and Liam's keeping his eyes and ears open, too. If they get another, more substantial lead, like a link between those two deaths, they might leave us alone. We don't have any grudges or history with the person in the dumpster."

Lilly-Ann responded before I realized what I had said.

"We don't know whose body was in that dumpster, so we don't know about grudges or history."

"Um, think back. Other than Tambra, is there anyone else in your past who'd pose a problem?"

She shook her head. "No, I guess not. I'm just being silly, I guess. It's nerves. What about you?"

"The only person in my past was my ex-boyfriend, Evan, and we all know how that turned out. Not my problem. Payback's a you-know-what."

Lilly-Ann chuckled, "Karma, for sure. Say, have you given Ian any thought? He's awfully nice, even if he *is* younger."

Just then, the phone rang, sparing me from answering her. Frankly, I wasn't quite sure of what to say. I'd be lying if I didn't admit I felt some attraction for him, but it was too soon to open my mouth. I lifted the receiver, and it was Liam again.

"You can thank me now or later. Deirdre's cleaning lady is a woman by the name of Cora Milbrand."

"Cora Milbrand? Oh my gosh! She's my cleaning lady, too."

"Where have I heard that name before?"

"She was the person who found the deceased body of the woman whose house I'm renting. The nephew owns it now. It was in the papers."

"That's probably why it sounded familiar."

"How'd you find out about Cora?"

"I took a break, and while I was at the vending machine in our break room, Scott Billings popped in. He's in charge of the grounds keeping for the golf course. He came from a meeting with a few of the board members and needed a Coke. Actually, something stronger, but it's still work hours. Anyway, we got to talking, and he mentioned Cora's name. Said his wife pitched a fit because the cleaning lady had to cancel this week due to the emotional stress of identifying a dead body."

"Oh, brother. I didn't think anything could upset Cora. Maybe she needed a break from Deirdre. Hmm, if she canceled, then she has an opening and golly, my house needs a freshening up."

"You're in the wrong career, lady."

"Sleuthing's a necessary sideline. Food artistry is right where I want to be."

"Yeah, from what I saw, you got that right. Keep me in your loop."

"For sure. And thanks. Your info may not be a break in the case, but it's one step closer to getting there."

"Okay, guys," I said to Lilly-Ann and Matt when I finished my conversation with Liam. "Hang tight until tomorrow."

"And if you don't get your derriere moving, you'll be hanging." A nasty puff of wind blew in my face, but no one noticed. I grabbed my bag, made sure everything was set for the next day, and followed Lilly-Ann and Matt out the door.

"Hurry up." Edith was relentless.

Once on the street, I looked at both of them and shrugged. "Maybe we'll have good news tomorrow."

Lilly-Ann shrugged. "It can't get much worse, can it?"

And then some.

Chapter Twenty-Five

"I'll wait in the car while you run inside the hardware store for a bolt cutter." Edith stared at her nails and hummed. "They've even given me a horrible shade of mauve. No taste whatsoever. Oh, and if anyone asks about the bolt cutter, tell them you lost the key to the lock on your fence."

"No one's going to ask. I'll be in and out."

Ha! That woman must have an extra sensory sense because the minute I took the bolt cutter to the checkout line, the man at the register asked why I needed it since he wanted to make sure I bought an appropriate one.

"Yep. The Pittsburgh 12-inch should do the job," he said. "Wouldn't want to use it for anything much bigger, though."

I nodded. "Uh, yeah. It should be fine."

Back in the car, I glanced at Edith, who had a big smirk on her face. "I was right, wasn't I? You need to trust me."

"You followed me in, didn't you?"

"I got tired of looking at my nails. Come on. We haven't got all day if we're going to get to that golf course before it gets dark."

"We've got plenty of time."

"Not with what I have in mind."

"No shenanigans, Edith. This is reconnaissance, not a Broadway production."

"Sometimes a little fanfare gets you the results you need."

And the price tag that goes along with it.

The clubhouse for the Hidden Boulders golf courses was as equally formidable as their recreation and performing arts center, only a tailored-down version. The same design with floor-to-ceiling windows and impressive greenery surrounding the entrance.

The parking lot was sectioned into two areas—one for cars and the other for golf carts. Both full.

"This isn't going to be as easy as we thought," I said under my breath in case someone was in earshot.

"Stop being a pessimist. The trick is to act like you know what you're doing. Hold your head up. And don't walk inside. Stride. Act like you own the place."

"Oh, brother."

I locked the car and walked straight ahead toward the building before I lost my nerve. At least I had a bona fide reason to be in their rec center. But their clubhouse? Who was I kidding? I had *imposter* written all over me. Or worse yet, *intruder with a bolt cutter. Since when did I become the kind of girl who carried a bolt cutter in her pants pocket? Ugh.*

I felt that thing in my front pocket and was thankful I didn't get talked into purchasing a larger-sized one. Then I took a breath and headed inside the building.

The lobby was similar to the main structure but no reception area. Instead, small seating clusters hugged the corners of the room. A credenza with iced tea and lemon water stood against the wall to the left, while another credenza with literature and brochures graced the right of the room.

Ornate metal signs indicated the separate areas for the men and women, but I needn't have bothered to look. Four women exited from the left and brushed past me as if I was as invisible as Edith.

I resorted to my infamous mental eye roll and walked straight ahead into the ladies' locker room. Thankfully, I was the only one in there, but I couldn't guarantee it would stay that way for long.

"Now what?" I whispered. I had no idea where Edith hovered, but I knew she couldn't be far. "How am I supposed to figure out which locker is Cherie's?"

"Open your eyes. They all have gold engraved name tags fastened on them. Pretty hoity-toity if you ask me. Start looking."

The bank of single lockers covered three walls, leaving the fourth wide open for an elliptical machine, two recumbent bicycles, and five treadmills. Not to mention two water coolers in a small alcove.

"Got it," I said. I started for the closest wall when the door flung open, and I heard a woman's laugh. I charged toward the treadmill, clipped the safety clasp to my top, and pushed Go. The thing took off slowly, but it must have been pre-programmed because an instant later, I found myself moving at a fast clip. I stared directly ahead at the wall, refusing to turn my head for fear of being recognized should that woman turn out to be one of the bunco ladies.

Meanwhile, I pushed the speed setting down to a tolerable pace and kept going. The woman with the laugh, like the others I encountered in the lobby, ignored me and kept talking. I hadn't seen anyone else enter, but then again, I had been too afraid to look. I pushed the speed setting further down and caught a sideways glance as the woman approached one of the water coolers. That's when I realized she was on her cell phone.

Her voice was crisp with a slight edge to it. "No, I don't think it's funny, Merry. It was a nervous laugh. I've been a mess. I only played nine holes. Who can relax with two of our members murdered? What? Yes, they were murdered. Tambra's been all over the news, and Cherie was found in a damn dumpster. If that's not foul play, I don't know what is. We're sitting ducks. Face it, we've all been privy to what's been going on. It's a regular *Peyton Place* as of late. Look, I can't talk here. Someone's on one of the treadmills. Huh? No, I can't tell who. I'll call you later."

I continued to stare straight ahead, and when I finally mustered up the courage to turn my head, all I caught was the woman's rearview. A poster child for Jazzercize. Long chestnut hair and fast, fluid movements toward the exit.

"Do you know who that was, Edith?" I asked. I pushed the "cool down" button and looked around. No, Edith. At least not for a few seconds. Then, she slowly materialized, still sporting her safari outfit.

"Nope, but we need to find out. Now! Didn't you catch what she said? About being privy to what's going on? Get off the treadmill and go after her. Cherie's locker can wait."

"What am I supposed to do? Tackle her in the lobby? I don't even know what to say."

"Act like you know who she is. Trust me. She'll be too embarrassed to admit she doesn't know you. Ask her what the course conditions were like. Golfers always yammer on and on about the course conditions. Hurry up. Before she gets into her car."

I stumbled off the treadmill and made a beeline for the lobby. The woman had just reached for the front door when I shouted, "Hi! I thought that was you. I was under the impression you'd be playing eighteen holes this afternoon." Then I remembered her reference to Merry. "That's what Merry told me, anyway."

The woman spun around and looked directly at me. Expressionless at first. "Um, hi. Yeah, only nine holes. I've got an early dinner engagement. What about you? Did you play, or do you have a later tee time?"

"Not today. I stopped by to use the treadmill. I always like to—"

"Enough with the babbling." *Crap. Edith cannot keep still.* "Go for the jugular. See what she knows."

"What I meant was, I like to stay in shape, but I'm nervous using the clubhouse right now. What with Tambra poisoned and Cherie, well, you know. Who does that sort of thing? Putting a body into a dumpster."

"That's exactly what I told Meredith. It has to be someone we know. And someone who knows what we know. Face it, there aren't many secrets around here."

An ice-cold draft hit me in the back of my neck. "Get her to tell you what she knows. But don't be obvious. Act like you know, too."

"But I don't."

The woman narrowed her eyes. "You *don't* what?"

"I don't believe what's been going on."

"Good," Edith bellowed into my ear. "Use a frame of reference."

Wonderful. I'm back in tenth grade English.

I lowered my voice. "You mean the affair with Tambra and Scott? Don't tell me you think Deirdre is responsible?"

"Over an affair? She's been keeping her sheets warm, too. No one murders for cheating anymore. What's the point? Besides, sweet little Cherie Simms didn't have a keeper. And look where she wound up. If you ask me, it's about the money. The payoffs."

"Money? Payoffs?"

And just as the woman opened up her mouth to speak, a car pulled up to the front door. A sapphire blue Lincoln Navigator. And suddenly, something clicked. I'd seen that woman before. Getting out of the same Lincoln. It was the day of my meeting with Tambra at the Mountain View Recreation and Performing Arts Center.

"That's my husband. Putting in another long day at the bar."

She walked to the driver's side of the car, and although she kept her voice low, I heard every word. "Get out and let me drive. Last thing you need is another DUI. And I don't want to be late for that dinner party tonight."

"Nice talking with you," I announced as I approached the car. Seconds later, the husband exited, giving her a cold stare. "Why don't you broadcast it on national radio, Sharla?"

The man looked vaguely familiar, but I couldn't place him. Tall, well-built, slightly receding hairline. We were face-to-face as Sharla slid into the driver's seat, and although I couldn't place him, he had no trouble calling me out.

"The Char-Board, right?" It was more of an announcement than a question. "Thought you looked familiar. Had breakfast there not too long ago. Decent pastries. I take it you're a member here as well?"

Good grief. What lie can I fabricate now?

"We need to get a move on, Phil." Sharla leaned out the window, saving me from blowing it all together. She motioned for her husband to walk around the car and get in before turning her attention back to me. "Like I said before, it's beginning to read like Agatha Christie's *Ten Little Indians*."

He spun his head around and shouted, "Stop scaring people off, Sharla. Tambra got what was coming, and who the heck knew what Cherie did in her spare time?"

Try theft.

"Um, it was nice chatting with you," I muttered.

Sharla nodded. "We'll have to play nine holes sometime."

Then the husband spoke. "You'll never guess who took a long work break at the bar before coming up with some excuse to scope something out at the clubhouse. No wonder we have issues with the drainage. Talk about being asleep at the switch."

She ignored his comment and, instead, looked directly at me before speaking. "Remember, honey. It's all about the money, but I think all of us should be on high alert."

With that, she gunned the engine before I could offer up a response.

Chapter Twenty-Six

A dusty dirt devil nipped at my feet, followed by Edith's voice. "Nothing ventured. Nothing gained. Make a note of it. Money. Payoffs. Now hustle your little butt back into that locker room and snap off that lock. For a snotty place like this, one would think they'd have recessed combination locks, but nope. BYO."

I rolled my neck and walked, wordless, back into the clubhouse. Thankfully the women's locker room was empty, and Edith had already located Cherie's Master lock. She wasted no time with the fanfare and made the thing clang against the metal door.

"I see it. I see it. The thing is huge."

"It only looks intimidating, but trust me, honey, it'll snap like a peapod. Get moving, and if anyone shows up, tell them you lost your key."

"If someone *does* show up, don't leave me in the lurch and wander off to see if that Jean Harlow gown became available."

A quick flick of the lights and I knew Edith wasn't thrilled with my attitude. Too bad. She wouldn't be the one in the Fourth Avenue Jail.

The bolt cutter felt larger in my pocket, as if it had morphed to the next size up. I pulled it out, stood in front of Cherie's locker, and grasped the lock with my free hand. Then I gave the cutter a good squeeze and closed my eyes. The sound was sudden and sharper than I had expected. SNAP! In an instant, the lock fell apart, and I pulled the door open, making sure to put the two broken pieces in my pocket.

"My food handler gloves. I forgot them. I can't let my fingerprints get all over the locker."

"Grab one of those towels from behind the treadmill and improvise. And thank you, Missy, for mentioning the Jean Harlow gown. Now I'm tempted to see which bimbo they bestowed it upon."

"Not now! This was your idea in the first place."

In a flash, I grabbed two hand towels, tossing one over my shoulder and wrapping the other around my hand. Then, I took a good look at the locker's contents.

"Ugh. Not much. A white sweater on the hook, one of those metal coffee canisters with a Hidden Boulders logo, a business card for some waste management/construction company, and a pile of hand towels. Wait! There's a small fabric clutch bag in here, too. Maybe we did hit the jackpot after all."

I made sure the treadmill towel was still wrapped around my hand and proceeded to open the bag. "Drat. Just her jewelry. She must have taken it off when she played her last round of golf." Then, I looked closer and couldn't believe what I saw. "It's a Byzantine gold chain, and the last time I saw it, it was on Meredith's neck. Hold on, there's more." I eyeballed a small silver and gold tennis bracelet as well as a gold charm in the shape of a ladybug.

"Edith, I don't think any of this stuff belonged to Cherie. In fact, she may very well have been the club's kleptomaniac in addition to having gambling debts. Hmm, maybe Tambra found out about that, too, and Cherie stopped in her tracks. For good. Now what? I can't very well call Deputy Vincent with my latest discovery. Bad enough, he questioned what I was doing at that dumpster."

"No, but you can drop a little hint that maybe they should check her locker out."

"Hmm, *that*, and take a photo or two for my own reference."

"Smart cookie. Now you're thinking like a woman who's one step ahead of the game."

"Huh? One step ahead? I'm being dragged all over the place, thanks to you."

"You're welcome. And while that mind of yours is busy spinning around, ask yourself this, "If Cherie killed Tambra, who killed Cherie? And why?"

"Are you saying it wasn't a strong enough motive?"

"Motives for murder don't always top the Richters Scale."

I snapped the photo and returned everything to the locker, sans the broken Master Lock that I shoved into my pocket next to the bolt cutter. Then, I tossed the treadmill towels into the receptacle marked Towels and breezed out of the locker room as if I really did have a pass to preview the place.

No sooner did I unlock my car door when my cell phone beeped—Ian. A regular call, not a text. "Privacy, Edith," I said. "Please?"

A whirl of dust inched up to my waist and disappeared.

"Hi!" I said. "I got your text around lunchtime. Thanks for checking on me."

"I wanted to call sooner, but this is the first real break I've had. You doing okay?"

"Uh-huh. Um, thanks for staying the night. It was nice."

"It was nice?" What am I? In fifth grade?

"It was a first for me. Falling asleep with someone on the couch. Yeah, it was nice. Listen, I know we agreed to meet for coffee tomorrow, but I think we've moved past that. What I mean is, I wanted us to get to know each other better, and well, that kind of happened. So can we skip coffee and I'll make you a real dinner at my place. If you'd like."

Edith materialized in front of me with the same hideous outfit. "Tell him yes before he changes his mind."

I brushed her away or at least made the motions.

"That sounds wonderful. What can I bring?"

"Yourself and an update on your amateur sleuthing. Deal?"

"Deal."

"I'll text you the directions. Hope you like seafood."

"Love it."

"If you want, you can bring Speedbump along. No sense having him stay home alone."

"You know what that means, don't you?" Edith hovered out of arm's reach. "It means he wants you to spend the night and not have to go home to the dog."

"Shh, stop reading into things."

"What?" Ian sounded off-guard.

"Sorry. I meant I should stop reading my texts while I'm talking. Bad habit. And yeah, thanks. Speedbump will enjoy seeing you again."

Edith's voice was even more authoritarian. "If you're under the sheets before dessert, don't say I didn't warn you."

This time, I kept still and ended the call. The sun started to fade, but there was still enough daylight left, so I didn't need to turn on my lights. I pulled out of the parking lot and started for the drive that would take us out of Hidden Boulders.

A beige Chevy Equinox rolled past me on the opposite side of the road, but other than that, there was no traffic. I supposed that would make sense, considering there were no tee times once dusk was imminent. I kept driving but had a hard time focusing. Here I was, intent on solving a murder, yet thinking instead about Ian's dimples and wondering if what Edith said about the dog had any merit.

It had been months since I'd had any sort of physical contact with a guy. And the physical contact I did have, was with a self-centered louse. But in the end, he got what he deserved, and that chapter in my life was gone for good. But did I want to start another relationship right away? Especially one with someone who was younger.

I kept driving, trying to push Ian further and further from my mind, and having no success. The sun gradually sank in the sky, and I reached for the knob that turned on my headlights. That's the second a dark-colored sedan I hadn't noticed behind me pulled past me with barely a foot between us. No accident. Not with a clear opposite lane for the driver to use.

No signal, no lights. No nothing. It was intentional. And downright scary. I held my breath as the car passed and watched as the driver picked up speed, disappearing before my eyes.

"Stupid driver," I said out loud. "Probably thought I was going too slow for him. Or her. Geez."

I shrugged and continued to head down the long drive. I passed hedge rows and the turnoff for the Mountain View Recreation Center when another car appeared in my rearview mirror. Also dark colored.

"Wake up, Missy. You're being followed."

I spun my head to the passenger seat, and Edith was sprawled out, still in khakis.

"How can you be sure?"

"Because it's the same car. I, for one, paid attention. The driver must have pulled off to the side so he could get behind you again. And yes, it's a he. Unless women are sporting facial hair."

"You could see facial hair?"

"It's a gift."

"Okay. I know what to do." *At least, I hope I've watched enough TV dramas to do what they do in these situations.*

"Slow it down, Steve McQueen. If you wind up where I am, I'll never get those brownie points to prove how humble I've become."

"Great. And here I thought you were concerned about me."

"I'm concerned. Why else would I be trekking around on these murder cases with you?"

"You don't have a choice."

"Well, you've got one right now. Watch out!"

The sedan hugged the side of my car, this time by inches, not feet. My hands shook on the steering wheel, but when the driver blasted his horn, I automatically swerved to the right, narrowly avoiding a row of jacarandas. Worse yet, by the time I realized what I had done, the sedan was further down the road, and I had made track marks in the recently mowed lawn.

"Think that jerk made his point?" I asked.

"He's not making a point. We're not talking road rage. Whoever Mr. Facial Hair is, he's obviously figured out what you've been up to and wants to put a stop to it."

"What am I supposed to do? I can't very well notify the sheriff's office about an intimidating driver."

"No, but you can play his game as well. You're young with good reflexes."

"You just told me to slow down. Now you want me to gun it and hug his car?"

"That was before he showed up for round two. I say turnabout is fair play."

"I hope you're right, Edith. I really do. Because I don't want to find myself bartering for a Jean Harlow gown."

Chapter Twenty-Seven

T his is so against my better judgment, but what the heck? I pulled back onto the driveway, gripped the steering wheel, and pressed on the gas. Seconds later, I could see the dark-colored sedan a few yards away from the intersection onto the main drag.

"If I press it now, we'll both career into the intersection, Edith. The plan's not going to work."

"Then change it. Follow that car!"

"Follow that car." Talk about a TV trope.

I signaled to the left and remained a good six or seven yards from the vehicle when all of a sudden, the driver pulled the fastest three-point turn on record and flew back up the drive to Hidden Boulders.

Two can play that game.

I executed my turn as if I was taking a road test, but just as I was about to turn into the Hidden Boulders drive, a large black Amazon delivery truck beat me to it.

"Why do they have to make those things so tall?" I bellowed. "I can't see ahead of me. Can't you do anything, Edith? Like hover overhead or something?"

"I'm not superwoman. And I can't hover at breakneck speeds. Besides, I need to be anchored to your presence."

"Fine. Fine. Anchor yourself."

With that, I followed the Amazon truck, making sure to stay at least a few car lengths back. A few minutes later, the driver turned right onto one of the residential streets, but all I saw in front of me was a wide-open driveway with no dark-colored sedan in sight.

"Drat." I pulled off to the side of the road, put the car in park, and rested my head against the steering wheel. "Well, that was useful. Now I'll never know who I was up against. I didn't even get a make or model of that car. Let alone a license." Then I glanced at Edith. "What about you? Were you able to do any reconnaissance?"

"I got you the facial hair."

"Wonderful. Look, I might as well head home. It's late. I'm hungry, and I'm not about to get any further with this chase. Besides, I need to concoct a reason for me to pester Deputy Vincent about scoping out Cherie's locker at the golf course."

"Don't sweat it. Call and tell him you had a thought. He already knows you're a snoop. Now he knows you're a snoop who thinks a lot."

"Nice description, Edith. Maybe I can put it on my dating profile."

"You don't need a dating profile. You have Ian if you play your cards right."

"Uh, yeah. About that, please do not appear at his house tomorrow. I don't care what's going on with you. Boundaries. Remember?"

"I can't help it if I get bored."

"Then work on some of the charcuterie designs you were itching to do. If I'm not mistaken, I've got a small event coming up at Randolph's Escapade."

"And a nephew to dodge, remember? Wasn't Sterling Moss intent on having you meet the nephew from Colorado?"

"He was. And I wasn't. Enough about my dating life."

I was now on Cave Creek Road, headed back to my house, when I realized something. The headlights from the car behind me had been tailing me for at least two miles. I shook it off, telling myself that there's lots of road traffic and it's not unusual for someone to take the same route as the one I took. Still, it gave me the creeps.

I turned and faced Edith for a second. "I think it's that same sedan. Following me. I'm not going directly home. I'll weave in and out of some of the side streets and see what happens."

"The only thing that will happen is you wasting gas. The marshal's office is a few blocks away. You can drive over there, but I guarantee your stalker will lurk somewhere on the street and pick up where he left off. I say, drive as if you're going home and then stop short."

"Are you nuts? He'll slam into me."

"Fine. Pull off to the side and then stop short. Blast your horn and get out of the car. Fling some profanity at him."

"I'm not flinging anything. Especially profanity."

"Fine. I'll compensate."

I never thought the words "I'll compensate" sounded intimidating, but that was before Edith uttered them. For the life of me, I couldn't imagine what she had in mind, and that was probably a good thing. I drove a few yards ahead and pulled off on Rancho Manana Boulevard, where I veered to the right, slammed on the brakes, and narrowly missed colliding with a parked Jeep Cherokee.

My stalker slowed and inched forward, giving me plenty of time to exit the car and wave my hands in the air. I fully expected him to take off as if nothing happened, but suddenly, his car stalled. Not only that, but a plume of noxious brown smoke came out of his exhaust pipe and engulfed the car.

"You did that?" I shouted to a billowy whisp of white smoke that materialized in front of me.

"Not done yet," was the response. "You've got him by the neck. When he gets out of the car, get a photo of him. Wait! I'll make it really easy for you. That phone has night mode, doesn't it?"

I don't know what it has. I just snap and shoot.

"I'm not sure. "I'll just—"

"Hurry up. Aim your camera low."

Low? What on earth for?

And then, I realized why. As I approached the sedan, I watched the driver fling open his car door and stand, but only for a second. He slid, landing on his rear, and I wondered if Edith had somehow managed to bridge the tangible and intangible gap, resulting in giving him a shove.

Another look at the driver and I had my answer. Edith's affinity for water-related mischief didn't stop with Eric's plumbing. Water puddled up under the driver, and I imagined the hoses under the car's hood had come undone.

Way to go, Edith!

The driver struggled to stand, affording me the perfect opportunity to hone in with my cell phone, first for the license and then for the man with the facial hair. Lamentably, that's as far as I got. A Chrysler van pulled up next to the driver, and the good Samaritan who jumped out of the van offered to help.

"Oh, brother," I muttered to myself.

A gust of air blew my hair all over my face. "You've got what you need. No sense getting tangled up now. Retreat. Retreat."

"This isn't a battlefield," I said under my breath.

"It will be if that driver eyeballs you. Angry people are irrational."

You think?

I turned away and got back in my car. Seconds later, I tapped the signal light and pulled out, putting as much distance as I could between my car and the vehicle mess Edith left in the road. And yeah, she was right. I did have what I needed. A full-blown photo ID. Even if I didn't get the license. But who was the guy? And why was he after me? That was the million-dollar question.

I trudged into the house at twenty minutes of eight, and it felt like midnight, but at least Edith had retired for the night. Or whatever it was she did. Her nagging was the worst, especially when I pulled into my driveway, and she recited a laundry list of what I should do. Thankfully she took off after that. But not before I caught the words "snoop report" and "Liam."

My stomach rumbled, and food shot to the top of my list. An open box of Oreos was inches away in the pantry, along with pretzels and chips, but I knew I'd feel bloated and miserable if I went that route. Instead, I forced myself to nuke two eggs with sliced tomato and Swiss, sharing some of it with Speedbump. The thought of a seafood dinner tomorrow with Ian was the only saving grace as I rinsed my used dish in the sink and headed for the couch.

And while I didn't want to call Deputy Vincent this late in the day for fear he'd know I'd been up to something, I had no qualms about pestering Liam. In a quick text, I sent him the photo of the driver who ran me off the road and asked if he recognized the guy.

Five minutes later, he phoned me, the alarm evident in his voice. "That man ran you off the road? When? Where? Or should I ask, did you do anything to provoke it?"

"Not with my driving skills. More with my poking around. In the ladies' locker room at the golf course. Cherie Simm's locker, to be specific."

"I thought you weren't going to take any chances."

"Not so much a chance as an opportunity. I knew the sheriff's office would be searching her house, but I thought I'd get one step ahead and see if there were any clues to her demise in her locker at the golf course."

"And?"

"Stolen jewelry. I'm pretty sure."

I paused for a second to catch my breath, then gave him the full rundown. "I think someone somehow found out what I was up to and tried to send me a message. Do you have any idea who that man is? A member of Hidden Boulders?"

"Not a member. The golf course manager and groundskeeper."

"Scott Billings? Deirdre's husband? The possible affair with Tambra?"

"In a nutshell."

"I wonder how he knew what I was up to?" Then I remembered the conversation between Sharla and her husband. Something about someone taking a long work break at the bar before scoping out the clubhouse. It had to be Scott. "Oh my gosh. He must have seen me go inside and knew I wasn't a member. Maybe I should notify the sheriff's office."

"He'd only deny it was him. And without any actual proof, there's not much you can do. Hey, from what I've heard, Scott has ways of getting even. Let it ride for now, but be on your guard. I'll see if I can pry into his dealings around here. And if you ask me, he should be on the suspect list, not you or Lilly-Ann."

"Tell that to Deputy Vincent."

Chapter Twenty-Eight

"Hmm," I mumbled to the dog, "do I take Edith's advice about planting a seed in Deputy Vincent's mind about Cherie's locker or let it ride for a few more days? I mean, he's bound to scope it out eventually. After all, she was a club member, and all of them golf. Duh? It would be a no-brainer."

The dog cocked his head for an instant and then retreated to his rug by the sink.

"That's a big help. Guess I'll let it ride for tonight and deal with it tomorrow. Besides, I'm too wiped to hold any kind of coherent conversation. All I want to do is plunk down and channel surf."

I grabbed the remote and adjusted the cushions on the couch before settling in. Then, I turned the power on to the TV, expecting to see something mind-numbing and boring. Instead, I caught the tail end of the local news and heard the words "Tansy oil," along with "indisputable evidence it was the poison that killed local resident Tambra Wright at the Hidden Boulders fashion show recently."

Tansy oil. Clueless, I immediately googled it on my phone. Seemed it was an oil derived from the tansy plant that could be used with caution to treat digestive issues and a host of other stuff. But the caveat was enough to scare the daylights out of me. As little as ten drops could kill someone. Tambra was sure proof of that.

I went on to find out where it could be purchased and learned that there were two varieties – blue oil that was non-toxic and available online from lots of legitimate sites, including Walmart, and the pure tansy oil that wasn't as easily obtainable. That variety could result in convulsions, violent spasms, and, ultimately, death. Yeesh. The question was, where did Tambra's killer acquire it, and how did they get her to ingest it at the fashion show. Seemed it could be cultivated and used by herbalists, so that left the field wide open.

The killer could have drizzled it on the pancetta rosette that Tambra bit into, but how did they know she'd select *that* particular food item from the charcuterie tray? Then again, they could have been bold enough to drizzle it while Tambra was making her selection and then quickly remove the adjacent meats and cheeses as if they were putting them on their own plate.

It was late, and I didn't want to bother Liam again with a phone call, so I shot him off a quick text—NEWS SAYS TANSY OIL KILLED TAMBRA. NEED ANOTHER LOOK AT THE TAPE.

The return text came quicker than I expected—ONE STEP AHEAD OF YOU. WILL CHECK IT OUT TOMORROW AM AND CALL YOU.

I sent back a thumbs-up emoji, got up from the couch, and grabbed the list I had written that detailed the people Tambra intimidated or even blackmailed. Edith had been pretty certain Alon, the colorist, was the best place to start since he had access to all sorts of chemicals, but now that we had definitive proof the culprit was an herb, the list needed revisiting. Was there anyone on there who could have had access to tansy oil?

As far as her so-called girlfriends went, other than Tambra's little "holds" over them, there was no information regarding what on earth those women were into other than bunco and golf. I glanced at the other three names—her personal trainer, her masseuse, and her manicurist. The only possibility I could come up with was the masseuse since they use oils when massaging clients. But tansy oil? I seriously doubted that would be her go-to choice. However, given the nature of her profession, she might know where such an oil could be acquired. I put a huge Asterix next to her name and contemplated planting another seed in Deputy Vincent's head. Unfortunately, I contemplated it out loud, resulting in a visit from Edith. She materialized a few feet from the TV, sporting a hideous denim jumpsuit that accentuated all of the wrong places. Even for a ghost. She took the opposite side of the couch and leaned toward me.

"If you're waiting for those seeds of yours to grow a garden in that deputy's head, forget it. I say we give that masseuse a little visit. What was her name? Julie?"

"Judi. And no more visits. Look what the last one got us—Cherie's dead body in a dumpster. I'm surprised I can even function after discovering her corpse."

"Deal with it, Missy. You're the one who needs to keep out of that jail. Don't just sit there staring at the TV. Google that woman's place of business and make an appointment."

"Not at this hour."

"Good. You're on board."

"I didn't say that. Oh, never mind. You'll only pester the daylights out of me. Look, I'll find the address for Pressure Points Plus, but I'm not about to do anything until after tomorrow. I'll be working, and then I have dinner at Ian's place."

"With or without the dog?"

"Honestly, Edith. You're incorrigible."

In a flash, Edith was on her feet. She spun away from me, hands on her hips, and huffed, "How dare you! And flaunting it right in front of me! I had dibs on that Jean Harlow gown, and you knew it, Rosaline. Don't think it's going to remain draped over your body for much longer."

I jumped from the couch and tried to see who Edith was talking to but no luck. "Is there another ghost in here? Please don't tell me there's another ghost in here." My voice wobbled between a whine and a directive, if there was such a thing.

Suddenly, a puff of creamy yellow haze, and Edith turned her attention back to me. "That horrible Rosaline is gone for now. She's worse than Imogen."

"What do you mean, 'for now'? Don't tell me she's going to hang around here, too. This isn't a hotel."

What am I saying?

"Relax, I doubt she'll be back. That wrench simply enjoys throwing it in my face. The gowns, that is. But I'll get even."

"Um, maybe you can let it go. Remember, humility and all? Besides, you're the one who's adamant we get moving on these murders."

Edith let out a breath of ghostly air and stood still for a second before she spoke. "Fine. Get that Pressure Point address, and we'll take it from there."

"*After* tomorrow. I don't get to dine on fine seafood every day."

"Or have a hot date. Dog or no dog with you."

"Enough with the dog. And my—" But it was too late. Edith had already vanished, leaving behind some foul-smelling bluish smoke. I returned to the couch and watched as Channel 10's Stephanie Olmo pointed to the map of Arizona and indicated, "zero chance of precipitation in the valley for the next week." *Big surprise there.*

"Well, dog, that's about as exciting as it gets. I'm googling Pressure Points Plus, and from there, it's off to bed. Maybe tomorrow will get me one step closer to figuring this out."

Sadly, it didn't. In fact, all tomorrow got me was one step closer to a full-blown panic attack.

I arrived at the Char Board early the next morning to find Deputy Vincent standing at the front entrance, search warrant in hand. The only saving grace was that it was too early for customers, and Lilly-Ann and Matt hadn't yet arrived.

"Good Morning, Miss Aubrey," he said, "our office has obtained a search warrant for your premises. I hate spoiling your morning."

Sure you do.

"You're here twice in a row? For what? And why?"

"If you'll kindly let me inside, I'll explain."

I unlocked the door and made sure to lock it behind me. "Let me guess. You're hoping to discover some tansy oil. It's not exactly the kind of thing we'd add to our salad dressings."

He handed me the warrant and took a breath. "The local news doesn't waste any time, does it? And apparently, neither do our silent witnesses. Listen, I'm just following protocol. So if you don't mind, all I need is a look-see at your pantry and other storage areas."

I waved to the kitchen. "Knock yourself out."

The deputy opened the pantry, scanned the food items, and moved to the refrigerator. Then, to the cabinets below the sink and a small broom closet. "Thank you for your time, Miss Aubrey. Have a good day."

"That's it? 'Thank you for your time'?" What's really going on?"

"That *is* what's going on. Simply put, our office received an anonymous call claiming they overheard you on the phone at this establishment discussing how thujone, the main element in the oil, can be used to cause respiratory distress. And when they saw yesterday's news, they immediately felt obligated to contact our office."

"And you believed them? What a concocted lie!"

"I didn't say I believed them, Miss Aubrey. I said I was following up."

"So you know this whole thing is bogus, right?"

"I know I'm obligated to follow protocol. Again, thank you for your time. We'll be in touch."

He left minutes before Lilly-Ann breezed in. One look at me, and she cocked her head. "What's up? I've never seen you with a scowl like that on your face. Matt, yes, when it's exam time, but you're always so chipper."

"Can you believe this? Deputy Vincent was in here with a search warrant. Someone tipped him off that we had tansy oil, or thujone, in here. You know, it was on last night's news. The stuff that killed Tambra."

"I take it he didn't find anything." She walked to the kitchen and put her bag on the counter while I trailed behind her. "Someone's trying to set us up. Or make you nervous. Maybe they figured you were looking into those murders. Not that we know what killed Cherie, but still..."

Her voice drifted off as Matt walked in the door and shouted. "Morning! Caught the news. What the heck is tansy oil? I've heard of vegetable, olive, and motor, but not tansy."

"Come on," Lilly-Ann said, returning to the front area. "I'll explain while we chop vegetables. You can start by getting them out of the fridge. Let's get a move-on into the kitchen."

I meandered back to the dining area and began to set up the tables when I noticed a slip of paper that had been slid under the door. It wasn't there when Deputy Vincent and I entered, and Lilly-Ann or Matt would have seen it when they came in. Most likely an advertisement for some local service.

The black scrawl burned through me as if the paper was on fire. "Second warning, Katie. Drop it NOW!"

Chapter Twenty-Nine

I crumpled the paper and tossed it in the trash. As if that would matter. Someone didn't want me poking around, and it didn't take a genius to figure out it was most likely the person or persons responsible for giving Tambra and Cherie their sendoffs. Not only that, but I was convinced it had to be the same "silent witness" who sent Deputy Vincent on his little social call. Liam said he'd get back to me today, and I kept my fingers crossed he'd be able to glean something more from that tape. Something we'd missed the prior times.

Not wanting to keep Lilly-Ann and Matt in the dark about my poking around at the Hidden Boulders clubhouse, especially since their proximity to me put them at risk, too, I gave them the rundown about my escapade. Matt thought it was a hoot, but Lilly-Ann equated it to bungee-jumping off a high bridge. I assured both of them I'd be cautious, but given the expressions on their faces, I don't think they believed me. It was worse when I mentioned the threatening notes. So much so I had to put my best face on to convince them there was no reason to worry.

Funny, but in spite of non-stop customers and hustling orders, the day dragged. So much so that I kept looking at our kitchen clock when I wasn't glancing at my iPhone. Then, at a little past noon, Liam called.

"It may not be much, Katie," he said, "but it might be something. Remember the server who appeared to be polishing the forks?"

"Uh-huh."

"I tried to pan out the view to see where she headed, but it blurred. However, I did catch something interesting. I could be wrong, but the number of forks dwindled substantially from when that area was first filmed."

"There were lots of guests. That could explain it."

"Hmm, you're probably right. Never mind. Sorry, but the footage didn't yield any more information than we already had."

"Bummer. But we're on the right track, Liam. I got another threatening note early this morning. It was slipped under the door to the sandwich shop, and it was personal. They said to drop it. Now."

"Or?"

I gulped. "That's the part I don't want to think about. If whoever wrote it killed Tambra and Cherie, then they wouldn't have any qualms about adding a third party to the list in order to prevent me from further snooping."

"Look, I'd be really careful if I were you. Don't go anywhere out of the ordinary, and lay low for a while. Meanwhile, I'll be on high alert for anything I see or hear at this end."

"Understood. And thanks."

Not that Speedbump was in any sense a guard dog, but he did have sharp teeth, and I'd heard him growl at birds and rabbits when he was in the yard. I rationalized that, in order for my own safety, I'd take him with me to Ian's when it came time to leave for Carefree.

Lilly-Ann, Matt, and I moved seamlessly through the remainder of the day when Javie appeared at a little before two. I ushered him into the kitchen, and he waved to Lilly-Ann and Matt as they wrapped up the salads and put them in the fridge.

"Need any clean-up help?" he asked. "I popped in to let you know I gave Hidden Boulders my official notice. The tension there is beyond palpable. It's like a tinderbox about to explode."

"Can you be more specific?"

Javie moved closer to the counter and leaned on it. "Eric Wright and Lance Baker had a 'behind the doors' knockdown and drag-out fight that could be heard all the way down the corridor from Eric's office. Unfortunately, those of us in earshot couldn't figure out what it was about. If that wasn't bad enough, Scott Billings and Eric got into, making the situation between

Eric and Lance look like child's play. I'll say one thing – I can't wait to get started here."

I grabbed the order notebook I kept near the fridge and opened it. "We've got orders for charcuterie trays that need to be done for the weekend. Two house parties on Friday and one sweet sixteen on Saturday. Any chance you can put in an evening with Lilly-Ann and me at the end of the week?"

Javie nodded. "I'm off tomorrow if that helps."

"It sure does. Especially since everything needs to be rolled out at the same time."

"What time do you want me?"

"How about at three? That'll give us more than enough time, and Lilly-Ann and I won't be stressing so much."

"Great. I'll be here. So, you guys need anything done right now?"

"We'll be fine, but there is one thing, and it has nothing to do with clean up here. Let me know if you find out more about the verbal altercations between those parties."

Javie chuckled. "I'll get the gossip, that's for sure. Trouble is, it's hard to weed out the truth from the exaggeration. Still, I'll give it a shot."

"Thanks. Guess we'll see you tomorrow. Oh, and remind me to have you fill out an employee withholding certificate. You know, the W-4."

"Sure thing."

Javie smiled as I walked him to the door. When he turned the knob, someone out front gunned their engine loud enough to make the few remaining customers take notice.

"Road idiots," a woman said. "They think Cave Creek Road is a dragstrip." Her dining companion shook her head. "That sounded more like a take-off, Alice. They started up real fast and kept going. Like they were angry or something."

I turned to the women and shrugged. "Won't be the first time, I suppose." Then, I bolted back to the kitchen to finish up before we closed for the day. Thoughts of Ian and my gourmet seafood dinner wafted in and out of my mind as I wiped down tables and helped Lilly-Ann with the remaining dishes. Matt returned from having taken out the trash and looked around.

"Anything else we need?"

"Nope," I said. "Let's call it quits and lock up."

We dispersed two or three minutes later, and I raced to my car. In the back of my mind, I wondered if I'd made an excuse about needing protection in order to take Speedbump with me to Ian's. It was a lot easier than having to admit I really did want to spend another night with the guy. Even if it meant sleeping on the couch.

When I approached my car, something was off. From a few yards away, it looked as if it was angled funny. Then, as I got closer, I realized why. All four of my tires had been slashed. Stunned, I remained motionless until I finally reached for my phone and dialed the sheriff's office. Then, I pulled out my AAA card and phoned them.

Forty-five minutes later, having watched the deputy-on-duty complete a grueling report, I stood silently as the tow company AAA sent loaded my car onto a flatbed headed to Wilhelm Automotive on the same road. Wilhelm was an automotive business that I was familiar with, having used it in Chandler. I didn't bother with my insurance company since I would have paid the deductible anyway. At least my Visa credit was good.

As the tow truck pulled away from the curb, the deputy, a man in his mid to late fifties with a haircut that looked as if he just came out of boot camp, shook his head. "I've never seen anything like this in Cave Creek, and I've worked this area for the last seven years. No doubt it was deliberate."

No kidding.

"Tell me, have you received any threats?"

I gulped. "Sort of."

He crinkled his nose. "Maybe you should explain."

"Um, Deputy Vincent is somewhat familiar with the situation. It involves the deaths of Tambra Wright and Cherie Simms. I was the person who discovered Cherie's body in that dumpster near here. Maybe someone thinks I know too much. But I don't. Know anything, that is."

The deputy looked up from his iPad. "What kind of threats?"

"A written note slid under the door of my sandwich shop right across the street. The Char-Board. I'm Katie Aubrey. I tore it up and threw it in the trash. All it said was, "Drop it."

And, of course, my name, in full black ink.

"Hmm," the deputy rubbed his chin. "You could be right. About someone thinking you know more than you do about one of those deaths, at least. My advice is to keep your house locked tight when you get home and don't go anywhere alone. I'll send word to Deputy Vincent. And try to retrieve the remnants of that note, will you?"

I called Uber and waited only ten more minutes for someone to take me home. I wasn't particularly worried about getting to work since Lilly-Ann could take me, but as far as driving to Carefree, all bets were off. I wasn't sure an Uber would be available late at night, and I didn't want to put Ian out.

Upset and disappointed, I phoned Ian once I got in the door and explained.

"Oh my gosh." His voice sounded concerned. "You should have called me. I would have been right over."

"You've already rescued this damsel in distress. Don't want to make it habit. Listen, about tonight, I don't have a car and—"

"Do you have an appetite?"

"Uh-huh."

"Okay, then. How about I bring the trappings to your place and cook up my seafood surprise there?"

"Really? Won't it be too much trouble?"

"Trouble? No. All I need to do is put things in a cooler. I think I can handle that. How about I get there at six?"

"Six it is. And hey, thanks."

"Don't thank me until you've tasted my cooking."

I called Lilly-Ann as soon as I got off the phone with Ian and explained what happened. A few seconds of silence, and then, "Of course, I can pick you up and take you home from work tomorrow, but oh my gosh, Katie! What if whoever did that is gearing up for much worse?"

"Uh, yeah. I kind of thought of that myself, but the positive spin is that I'm on the right track as far as my snooping around."

"That's what scares me."

CHAPTER TWENTY-NINE

"It'll be fine. Honest."

When I lie, I lie.

With Ian coming over at six, I immediately jumped into house-cleaning mode, vacuuming, wiping, and tidying up the bathrooms. At least I was one of those people who made her bed every day and didn't clutter up the bathroom and kitchen counters with all sorts of stuff.

Satisfied all was well with the house, I plunked myself on the couch and took out a scribbled list of suspects. That's when a cloyingly sweet aroma drifted through the house, and I nearly gagged.

Edith! She knows Ian is coming and will hover around here like a fly at a picnic.

Chapter Thirty

"Now you show up?" I dropped my list of suspects and looked around, waiting for her form to materialize. "Where were you when I got those flat tires?"

Edith gradually morphed from the haze and smoke into her usual form, this time donning a beige trench coat and brown boots. "Shh, keep it to yourself. I intend to rectify this unseemly choice of attire as soon as I can."

"Rectify the odor in this room first. It smells like a French bordello."

"For your information, Missy, I went to great lengths to create a romantic atmosphere."

"Then go to even greater lengths to get rid of it."

"If that's what you want, but keep in mind, the aroma of cooked fish is not conducive to lip locking."

"Who said—?" And with that, she was gone. Thankfully with the cloying fragrance.

Bending down, I picked up the list of suspects I had hastily written and reread it when it occurred to me, it was Tambra's list, not mine. And while it made perfectly good sense to follow through on the people she had blackmailed and/or intimidated, I had a nagging feeling I was missing something.

Then, that annoying raspy voice. "Don't you retain anything you read? I mentioned this before, you know. Draw a murder map. Get a murder notebook. Do something while you wait for Sir Lancelot to walk through your door. Oh, and take a shower, will you? No one wants to smooch with a partner who reeks of deli meats."

"What? I don't reek of anything!" Then, I did something I hadn't done since college. I lifted my arms and took a sniff. Hard to tell, but why take a chance? I got up from the couch and ran the water in the shower, figuring that if nothing else, Edith might leave me alone. Then I put on a decent top and fairly new jeans.

Speedbump gave me that familiar sad-eyed doggie look that all canines must have been taught from birth. "I've got less than a half hour before Ian gets here," I said, "but I suppose we can hurry. Come on, dog, let's make it a quick walk."

As if on high command, Speedbump charged to the door and waited. Seconds later, we were on the street and heading south, only to run into Colleen Wexby, the eyes and ears of our neighborhood. She waved and rushed toward us. "Katie, I haven't seen you in ages. Of course, in this heat, it's impossible to see anyone. By the way, were you expecting company last night? I saw someone drive past your house twice and figured maybe they were checking for the right address."

I stood still and let it sink in. "Um, no. What kind of car?"

"A dark sedan. Maybe blue or even dark burgundy. Hard to tell."

"Is that all they did? Drive past?"

"Uh-huh. Why? Is something wrong?"

I really didn't want to get into it with her, but then again, given her penchant for watching our street, I needed every prior warning if Tambra or Cherie's killer was stalking me.

"Actually," I began, "it may be a stalker." With that, I gave Colleen the details about getting run off the road but neglected to mention my snooping around in the Hidden Boulders murders.

"Oh heavens, Katie. That's horrible. Did you notify the sheriff's office?"

I nodded. "Anyway, if you see or hear anything, please let me know, okay?"

"Absolutely. You'd be amazed at how many unhinged people are out there." Then she bent down and gave Speedbump a pat. "He's not a rottweiler, but still, he can bark."

"Yeah, and he's turned out to be great company. Anyway, I need to get going. Nice running into you."

Colleen smiled. "Likewise. And don't worry. I've got my antennae up."

I hustled Speedbump home, and no sooner did I unleash him when I heard a car pull into the drive. "Stay here," I said to the dog, "I'll be right back."

Funny how the sight of Ian's white Mazda made me smile as I approached the vehicle.

"Hey," he said as he opened the driver's side door, "sorry about your tires, but I'm glad you agreed to a change of venue." Then, he stepped toward me and gave me a hug. For some inexplicable reason, not only did I hang tight, but I think I actually kissed his shoulder as I moved away. I felt a slight rush of heat on my face and hoped it wasn't a visible blush. "Um, do you need a hand bringing stuff inside?"

"I think I've got it. It's only a cooler, a frying pan, and a large skillet. I know your kitchen has everything else from the last time I was here."

I held the front door open as Ian came inside with a giant cooler and placed it on the kitchen counter. "Be right back with the rest of the stuff. Hope you're hungry, but not too hungry since this will take about an hour and a half, but don't worry, we'll eat the salad first before we starve."

"Good." I waited while he brought the remaining items inside, and then, not only did I close the door, but I used two locks to bolt it shut.

"Can I get you something to drink before you get started? Iced tea, water, Coke..."

"Iced tea. Thanks. And I can get it. Please, sit down. Relax. All I really want is your company. We're having creamy shrimp risotto with mascarpone, but I've got to confess—I made the stock ahead of time. Same deal with the ingredients for brussels sprout Caesar salad."

"My mouth's watering already."

"Great. I'm hoping to dazzle you."

You are already.

For the next few minutes, I watched as Ian skillfully heated oil in a saucepan and added the shrimp, occasionally mashing them with a potato masher to release the juices. From there, he let them cook before combining tomato paste, some wine, and then the other ingredients—carrots, celery, peppercorns, onion, garlic, and some thyme sprigs. Once the stock was in, all it needed to do was simmer. Then it was on to the risotto, a process in and of itself. I watched, wordless, as Ian added garlic and onion to the arborio rice, pausing every now and then to chat.

"Listen," he said, "the warnings were one thing, but the tire slashing had to be intentional. I'll be honest. I'm worried. After we eat, what do you say we take a look at the viable suspects and see if we can come up with connections."

I chuckled. "Before you got here, I was about to put together a murder map, or at the very least, some sort of graphic. I can't keep all of this in my head for much longer."

"Terrific. By the end of the night, you will have seen my culinary skills and my attempt at sleuthing."

"Good, because there's something else. My neighbor from down the street saw a car scooping my house out last night."

"Geez. This is getting scarier by the minute. I've got to pay attention to what I'm doing at the stove, but after dinner, we really need to get down to business and figure out what's going on. This has got to be scary for you."

"*We*, huh?"

"Yeah, we. Okay with you?"

And then, a voice I dreaded, even though I half expected her to stick her ghostly nose in. "Don't stand there tongue-tied. Say yes. Y E S. Tell him you're fine with it."

"I *am* fine with it."

Ian looked startled. "Well, good. Glad you were so emphatic."

Emphatic. That's one word for it.

When he turned his attention back to the stove, I motioned for Edith to disappear. Then quickly disguised that motion as if I was dusting off lint from my top. "I suppose I should set the table. It's just so much fun watching you."

Ian flashed a smile as I stood to get the dishes and utensils. "Any scuttlebutt at Randolph's Escapade about Tambra's murder?" I asked.

He shook his head. "Only the usual rumblings. The servers who were there were shaken up, but all of us are clueless. The MCSO deputies returned for further questioning, but all of us got the sense it was only part of their protocol. I think we're off the hook as far as suspects."

"What do you think about the poison? Tansy oil of all things."

"Interesting, for sure. Not the usual take, but when I heard it mentioned on the news, I remembered reading about herbalists who cultivate it for one reason or another. Did you know they used to use it to line coffins to preserve the bodies?"

"You don't think...?"

"Nope. Morticians today have other alternatives, I'm sure."

"But why grow it in the first place?"

Ian shrugged. "Medicinal purposes? Hard to say. Well, the moment of truth's upon us. Let's start with the salad while we wait for the shrimp risotto."

What followed was a full-course culinary masterpiece that I never expected. I wiped the sides of my mouth with a napkin and let the playful flavors of tomato and shrimp linger on my palate. "I'm stunned. You're amazing. *This* is amazing. Is it one of your signature dishes?"

Ian shook his head. "No, just something fun. Come on, let's clean up, and then we can try to get a handle on who's got it in for you. Like I said, it's scary." He bent down and petted Speedbump, who was otherwise occupied with a rawhide bone I'd gotten him a few days ago.

Minutes later, with a clean kitchen and a small bowl of leftovers in the fridge, we settled on the couch to peruse the scant notes I had. For an instant, I thought I caught a whiff of that obnoxious cloying odor Edith insisted on infusing into the house. When Ian wasn't looking, I moved my thumb across my neck to indicate a "no-go" for Edith and closed my eyes, hoping she'd get the message.

Seconds later, the odor disappeared, simultaneous with the sound of ice cubes hitting the kitchen floor. "It's a glitch with the ice cube maker," I said to Ian. "No worries. Speedbump will get them." Then, to be on the safe side, I repeated my original gesture to Edith.

Chapter Thirty-One

I pointed to a few sheets of construction paper and a new marbled composition book on the coffee table. "First and foremost, Scott Billings is going to take center stage. He's the person who ran me off the road. I have a good contact, Liam, who's in charge of surveillance at Hidden Boulders. He was an IT specialist where I used to work. Anyway, when I showed him the photos I snapped, he recognized my perpetrator as Scott Billings. Unfortunately, if I were to call the sheriff's office, I wouldn't have hard proof. Just after-the-fact snapshots."

"Don't worry. We'll keep prodding. And putting this down on paper will help our thought process. I mean, something has to, right?"

"I take it you've never completed a murder map either." Then I laughed. "Neither have I, but we've probably watched enough crime shows to come up with something."

Ian moved closer to me and opened the notebook. "Maybe we should start here. I mean, it's not as if we're going to plaster the walls with our notes. Want me to do the writing, or do you want the honors?"

"Go for it. Your handwriting's bound to beat mine any day."

Ian picked up a pen and leaned back. "Read me the other suspects you mentioned. The ones Tambra threatened. I'll get all the names in one place, and then we'll add more. Then maybe go old-school with motive, means, and opportunity. In columns."

"I thought you never did this."

"I'm a big Columbo fan."

A full hour flew by, and when our preliminary list was completed, we studied it as if we were prepping for the LSATS. Then, I read it out loud as if that would somehow point us in the right direction.

"Other than Scott, we've got Tambra's personal image specialists, the colorist, the masseuse, the trainer, and the manicurist. Then the bunco women—Eulodie, Deirdre, and Deborah. We can cross off Cherie, unless... whoa. Could she have killed Tambra and then, well, suffered the same fate? I know for sure she was the woman on Eric Wright's balcony the night I snooped around in there. She was into something with him."

"Anything's possible at this point. I'll keep her on the list with a sidenote. Keep reading."

"Okay. Eric, the husband. Husbands are always numero uno where the police are concerned. And given what we know, his relationship with Tambra was on the rocks. If he did carry a large insurance policy on her, it would be a no-brainer. Plus, the Cherie thing."

"I'd give him points for motive and opportunity, but means?"

"Means are going to be a problem for everyone. Who on earth has access to tansy oil?"

"Yeah, we'll have to look into that for sure. Go on."

"Back to Scott Billings. He's Deirdre's husband, and I learned he was having an affair with Tambra. Maybe that hit the skids, and he wanted Tambra out of the way. Then there's Lance Baker, the assistant manager at Hidden Boulders. And for no other reason than the fact he and Eric had a knockdown verbal altercation recently."

"How did you find out so much?"

"Javie overheard them."

Ian widened his eyes and moved an inch or two away before laughing. "Guess I'd better keep things on the straight and narrow, huh? Who knows what other contacts you'll pull out of your hat?"

I gave him a playful poke which he retaliated by pulling me closer and planting a kiss on my neck before turning back to the notebook. "We need to stay focused. Any other entries?"

"That's it. Quite the list, huh? And you know what the awful thing is? I'm convinced the top two on Deputy Vincent's list are me and Lilly-Ann.

Lilly-Ann, due to her past relationship with Tambra, and me, because of one very sharp, very observable interaction prior to the fashion show. At least I don't think he has me pegged for Cherie's murder. He knew how distraught I was."

"True. But dangling on a list for one murder is more than enough." Ian took the list from me and gave it another look. "Tambra was a real beaut, that's for sure. And I can understand why someone might have wanted her out of the way. Face it, who wants to live under the fear that she could destroy their reputations and their lives? But what about Cherie? Think Eric got her out of the way? Maybe she knew too much about whatever he was into. I'm afraid unless we can figure that out, we're stuck. And here's something else to make our stomachs twist around. What if we're talking two killers, not one? I mean, there's nothing definitive leading to a connection between those murders."

"Nothing that we know of, true, but given both victims were members of Hidden Boulders, and in the same social circle, it seemed logical to me. Except, I can't explain Scott."

"What did you say his position was?"

"The golf course manager."

Ian pinched his shoulder blades together and bit his lower lip. As if he didn't look sexy enough. "That might be worth looking into. That is, if anything odd was going on regarding course management."

"That may be the easy part, given what Liam can find out. It's everything else that's staggering."

"For sure. The only definitive thing we know is Tambra was poisoned. Cherie's cause of death, as of the last news report, is still undetermined. *That,* or determined but not available to the public right now. Not that I want you to revisit something that's going to make you uncomfortable, but do you remember anything out of the ordinary about her body when you found it?"

"Other than the fact she was dead? No. Of course, I didn't look too closely." *And apparently, neither did Edith.* "I guess I wasn't thinking. I should have looked for ligature marks or bruises."

Ian reached over and squeezed my arm. "You're not a detective, although you seem to be a pretty darned good sleuth. I just thought maybe you noticed something that you didn't think of before."

I shook my head. "Nope. Just your everyday corpse."

"All right then. Back to the murder map. Let's see if we can figure out any connections between the players. It's a start, if nothing else."

Forty-five minutes later, with lots of scribbles in an old notebook, we agreed on the following connections: Eric and Cherie, Eric and any of the women in that bunco group according to that note of Tambra's I uncovered, Eric and Scott, since Scott had an affair with Tambra, and finally Eric and Lance, given their blowup. But where *I* fit in regarding Scott's behavior was anyone's guess, and lamentably, we couldn't link him to the other players. Worse yet, none of that explained his behavior behind the wheel when I left the clubhouse.

"Looks like the common denominator is Eric," I said. "Although Scott runs a close second as far as I'm concerned. Too bad he wasn't the one seen on that surveillance video acting suspiciously at the charcuterie table. That honor belongs to our number one contender. But that doesn't negate Scott from murdering Cherie. Aargh. I suppose we should take it one corpse at a time, huh?"

"Yep. Want to flip a coin?"

"Nah. Given the connections, Eric's the one we should focus on for now."

"Good. You said *we*." He flashed me a smile and continued. "Guess we should find out what Eric and Cherie were into. You mentioned overhearing her say something about 'that other little matter' he put off. All we need to do is find out what that minuscule matter is, and bingo! We may be staring into the face of a killer."

"Whoa. Sounds like you've been reading one thriller too many, but don't get me wrong. I want this over with more than anything, but I have no idea where to begin. The one thing I do know is that Tambra's list called out Cherie for owning gambling money, but somehow I don't think that's it. I found stolen jewelry in Cherie's locker at the Hidden Boulders clubhouse. Meredith's gold bracelet, as well as two other pieces. I wanted to point

Deputy Vincent in that direction but couldn't very well do that without implicating myself."

Ian reached a hand over and rubbed my shoulder. "He's a detective. Checking out Cherie's locker is probably next on his list. I think they work with a tight circumference and gradually expand."

"And you know this, *how?*"

"Told you I was a fan of mysteries and crime shows, which brings us back to our starting point. If we can get ahold of Eric's planner, I think it will be obvious what he was into. Trouble is, no one uses a paper planner anymore. Well, except for my mother. And computer planners are becoming passé. Face it, whatever he was up to, I guarantee it's on his phone under the notes or reminders app."

"That explains why I couldn't glean too much from his computer, but—Holy Cow—his phone? If Eric is like everyone else in the 21st century, that little piece of hardware is probably attached to his hip. Yeesh. And here I thought Dorothy had it tough when she needed to get that broomstick. But I may have an idea. That is, if Liam's willing to take the risk. And knowing him, he will."

"Uh-oh. Tell me, and please say it's not another break-in."

"Nope. All Liam will need to do is monitor Eric, and when that cell phone of Eric's lands on any surface other than Eric's pocket, Liam rushes over to chat with him and coincidently puts his cell phone next to Eric's. The classic bait and switch. Then Liam rushes out, checks the reminders app on the phone, and then notifies Eric that their phones got switched."

"I think that's a whole lot easier said than done."

Not if Edith creates a disturbance. But how would I ever explain that to Ian?

"Hmm, there's always sleight of hand."

"Is Liam pretty adroit with card tricks? If not, it may be something best left to the Artful Dodger."

"Liam can use technology to manipulate the lighting and all sorts of stuff. It may be our only option right now."

Just then, my landline rang. "I'd better take this. My mother has an uncanny knack of calling at all the wrong times. Give me a sec."

I walked to the kitchen and picked up the receiver. Colleen Wexby's voice was fast and shrill. "Katie! That dark sedan drove past your house a few minutes ago. I was taking the garbage out and watched the driver slow down in front. Then they did a three-point turn and watched your place from the opposite side of the street before taking off."

"Were you able to get a license?"

"No, but it was light enough for me to see the color – dark blue, not burgundy."

Yeah, that narrows it down.

"Um, thanks, Colleen."

"Wait! That's not why I called. When the driver was opposite your house, he or she extended an arm, and I could see a cell phone. Whoever they were, your place was the subject of that photo shoot. And I don't think they were interested in real estate."

Chapter Thirty-Two

"Everything okay?" Ian asked when I stepped back into the room. "Uh, not exactly. That was my neighbor a few doors down. She watched someone scope out my house a few minutes ago from their car and take a picture with their phone. The description of the car matched the one that ran me off the road and drove by my house last night. It had to be Scott. But what does he think I know?"

"Listen, I may really be overstepping my bounds right now, but I'd feel better camping out on your couch again. I don't have to be at work until later tomorrow. I'll swing by Walmart or Best Buy in the morning and pick up a Ring doorbell system. I installed one at my own place. Not a problem."

"I did call ADT, by the way. After that first incident with the breaker but they can't install a system until next week. I'm on the schedule."

"At least the Ring device is a start. What do you say?"

I smiled. "Yes to both—you and the Ring device."

An ice cube fell from the icemaker and rolled onto the floor. "Tell him he doesn't have to sleep on the couch. That bed of yours has plenty of room."

Oh no. Edith. How long does she intend to hang around?

"I'm not telling—" And then I caught myself. "What I mean is, I'm not telling you anything you don't already know. Um, about me feeling more comfortable with you staying here tonight."

"Good. Because I wouldn't have felt comfortable driving home and worrying about some loco groundskeeper with who-knows-what on his agenda. Too bad there's nothing definitive, or I would have insisted on calling the sheriff's office. Maybe we should rethink Eric and move directly to Scott."

"I know. Look, I'll give Liam a call in the morning and see what he says. He sees both men, and if Eric's cell phone is filled with notes, Scott's must be too. It's a start if nothing else."

"Think you can make it a head start and phone him now? I don't think this can wait."

I saw the look of concern in Ian's eyes and reached for my phone. "Sure." Three minutes later I had divulged everything to Liam, who was more than shocked about the tire incident and the drive-by stalker. He agreed to give his sleight of hand a try but made no guarantees. "Scott usually stops in here around eleven. Likes to check the comings and goings from the clubhouse. I'll see if I can work my magic. Either way, I'll let you know." Then, a voice that wasn't totally unexpected after I thanked Liam and ended the call.

"If you want him to work your magic, I need to do mine. I can get Scott so flummoxed, he'll forget he even owns a cell phone, but you have to be in that office too, Missy."

Ian raised an eyebrow. "Everything okay? You look stunned."

"Um, fine. He'll do it." *But that means I'll need to leave work mid-morning and scoot over there.*

"Great. It's a start for sure."

As if her voice wasn't enough, a white haze filled the room, but thankfully it was only for my eyes. "If *you* want a start, do more than talk. And I'm not referring to your little information-gathering plan."

Arragh. It never ends with her.

I nodded. "I don't know about you, but my brain's too popped to do much more tonight."

"Ditto. It's not late. Want to watch a movie or something? Who knows, we may both wind up falling asleep on the couch again."

"A movie sounds good, but you don't have to sleep on the couch."

Ian's eyes widened, and I kept talking before I'd lose my nerve. "What I mean is, we can share my bed. To sleep. Just sleep. I'm not inviting you to…well, you know."

If I thought Ian was cute before this moment, he surpassed it when a slow blush covered his face. He reached for my hand and grasped it. "It's early in our relationship. I get that. Don't worry, sleep it is. Unless you don't mind snuggling. I suppose I'm one of those few men who actually like cuddling."

I'm doomed. Really doomed.

Ian was right about the cuddling. When I woke up the next morning, my head was nestled under his shoulder, and his arm was draped around mine. I gave him a quick kiss on the cheek, then dashed into the shower. "Give me a warning if you come in here, or use the guest bathroom. There are plenty of towels in there."

"Guest bathroom it is," he mumbled, and I breathed the proverbial sigh of relief.

I rushed through a quick breakfast—English muffin and coffee—so I wouldn't keep Lilly-Ann waiting.

"Did Wilhelm give you any idea when your car would be ready?"

"Early. Lilly-Ann will drop me off there, and then we'll meet at The Char Board in time to open."

"Sounds good. I'll clean up and head over to Best Buy for a Ring device."

"Oh my gosh. You'll need a key. Hang on. I had extras made."

I opened one of the drawers near the refrigerator and handed him a key.

"I'll lock the bottom lock and leave the key on your counter when I'm done ."

"Actually, I'd feel better if you kept it. I mean, I know we haven't known each other long but I trust you like nobody's business."

In that second, Ian gave me a hug, followed by a kiss on the neck. "You won't be disappointed. I'll call you later today."

"Sorry to drop this on you," I said to Lilly-Ann and Matt after we had caught our collective breaths from the morning rush, "but I need to drive to Hidden Boulders to check on something. Good news is that I called Javie, and he should be here any minute to help."

Lilly-Ann took a step toward me and nearly bumped into Matt, who just returned with an armload of dishes from the dining area. "You're not getting yourself in too deep, are you?"

"I need to go over some clues with Liam." *And play magician at the same time.*

"Javie should be in here any second," Matt announced. "I saw him coming up the block while I was clearing tables. Seems like a nice guy."

I nodded. "Yeah, I think he'll fit in just fine."

Five minutes later, with everything squared away for the lunch hour, I left the sandwich shop and started up my car. I had taken the advice from the mechanic at Wilhelm and had them install a car alarm so if anyone approached, the whole world would know. Much cheaper than having to replace tires.

Stacee, the receptionist at Hidden Boulders, was at her usual spot when I walked inside the building. I smiled, waved, and approached her. "I'm meeting with Liam for a few minutes this morning. He's not exactly expecting me, but I'm sure he won't mind."

"Funny, you should say that. Liam buzzed the desk a few minutes ago and said you might be in. Not definitive, just a hunch he had. Boy, you two sure are on the same wavelength."

"Yeah, we go way back."

"Don't tell me – You're commiserating on those two murders."

"Guilty as charged. Since my establishment was involved, I can't afford to sit idly by."

"I get it. By the way, my news app flashed the latest on Cherie's cause of death. The coroner found ligature marks on her neck, but they are not discounting poison either. Gee, you think her killer poisoned her and then decided to make it definitive by strangling her?"

I gulped. "Um, guess that's one way to take care of things."

A cold breath blew across my neck, and I winced. At least Edith didn't pull anything outrageous, and I braced myself for the commentary I knew was coming—her netherworld. "I told you so." Sure enough, she wasted no time.

"Didn't I tell you that you should have looked at the body? You would have seen those strangulation marks days ago. Don't stand here dilly-dallying. Look behind you. That's Scott Billings, isn't it? Better hightail it into that security office if you expect to get some answers. And might I add—"

"Don't add anything."

"Huh?" Stacee looked perplexed.

"Uh, what I mean is, please don't give me the details; it's gruesome enough."

"I know. And imagine, right here in our own Hidden Boulders community."

"Well, I'd better see Liam. Catch you later."

"Sounds good."

I took off for Liam's office, thankful Scott had turned in the opposite direction. Restroom maybe? Or the kitchen? No matter. I was relieved I could get there before he showed up."

No surprise Liam had the grin of the Cheshire Cat on his face when I rapped on the door and walked inside. "I had a hunch you'd show up. But what about The Char-Board? You were pretty slammed when I was last there."

"Javie's on board, and we're all set. Talk about a stroke of luck. So, how do you want to work this? Scott's here but at the other end of the building."

"Oh, he'll stop in. He always does. I'll tell him you remembered something about the night Tambra succumbed and pull up the tape to the section where Eric leans over the charcuterie table. When he does, I'll grab my cell phone and pretend I forgot to charge it. Then I'll ask to use his and somehow do the switcharoo."

"You're ingenious."

"Tell me that after our plan works."

The light in the room flickered for a nanosecond, and then, "Oh, it'll work all right. It has to. I'm on a tight schedule."

"Lucky for me, I'm not."

Good, because this could turn into a real humdinger.

Chapter Thirty-Three

"We'll have to work fast," I said, "and check his notes app ASAP. Same deal with his text messages and emails, although I doubt whoever he's dealing with used email. No one does these days. It's all text messages. Still, we can't afford to let anything slip by us."

"Agreed, and *fast* is the pivotal word. Once Scott realized he snagged the wrong phone, he'll be in here lickety-split."

"Lickety-split? Haven't heard that expression in ages."

Liam laughed. "What can I say? My mother used that expression whenever she wanted me to hurry up. Guess it just stayed."

Just then, there was a quick rap on the door, and sure enough, Scott breezed in. "Morning." Then he glanced my way, and for a split second, he recoiled. Hardly noticeable to the untrained eye, but I was already on high alert. "You look familiar," he said.

"Katie Aubrey, charcuterie chef. I remembered something from the night of Tambra's death and thought what I saw was on the video."

Scott furrowed his brow. "Must be important for you to trek in here. What was it?"

I bit my lower lip and took a breath. "Eric Wright acting oddly around the charcuterie table."

Scott took a few steps closer to Liam and the monitors. "Did you review the footage already?"

"We were just about to when you walked in. Pull up a chair. Plenty of room for you on my right since Katie already commandeered the chair on the left."

Scott wasted no time seating himself next to Liam. He leaned into the screen and watched the footage while I seriously wondered how this would play out. Then, true to plan, Liam took out his phone and turned to Scott. "Sorry, but I need to make a call. Trying to get an appointment with my optometrist and was told to call after eleven."

I held my breath and hoped Edith's intervention wouldn't be called for. Liam took out his phone and delivered the best groan I'd heard in years. "Darn. Forgot to charge the blasted thing. Hey, Scott, mind if I borrow your phone? Don't want to tie up the house phone."

Scott reached into his back pocket and handed Liam the phone. "Do you need to stop the tape?"

"Nah, I can walk and chew gum."

"Hang on," Scott said. "I'll turn the lights up a bit in here. My keypad is impossible. Need to update the phone, but I've been putting it off." Without another word, he walked to the dimmer switch and upped the lighting. Crap! So much for a switcheroo.

I caught the deer-in-the-headlights expression on Liam's face as he started to place the bogus call and crossed my fingers Edith noticed it as well. In a flash, the fire alarm went off. Loud, sharp, and shrill. Liam crotched forward, cradling the phones on his chest, and announced, "Nothing registering on camera, but that doesn't mean we don't have an issue. Better exit now!"

With that, he stood and ushered us out the door before Scott had time to react.

"Good going, Edith," I whispered under my breath. "And thanks for not blurting out your usual commentary."

"That wasn't me. I was about to make the monitor flicker on and off like 1950s static on a three-channel TV."

By now, the four of us, if I counted Edith, were in the corridor making a beeline for the main entrance when Stacee charged toward us, hands waving. "Some mishap in the kitchen. Probably burnt toast. I could hear Twila cussing like mad all the way down here. The call went in to the fire department, and they have to respond, even though I phoned them with the update."

Thank you, kitchen staff, for messing this up. Liam will have to return Scott's phone, and we'll be back to square one.

Edith must have realized the same thing, or, worse yet, developed some new skill that enabled her to read my mind. Perish that awful thought. In any case, she immediately jumped into action by doing something I never saw her do before, and I hope I never do again.

She ran straight through Scott's body, causing him to wobble and hyperventilate. One minute she was hovering in front of me, and the next, darting through him like a linebacker, sporting a vintage tennis outfit that best belonged on a teenager. Scott sank to the ground and choked out a few words, "I think I'm having a heart attack."

Way to go, Edith!

"Take it easy, buddy," Liam said. "Sit on the ground. The paramedics should be here any second."

Stacee rushed over to Scott, joined by a few of the maintenance workers. Off to my left, I could see the kitchen staff clustered about but only recognized Twila. Layered blond bob and all.

"Stop staring," Edith hissed. "You're not *that* much older than she is. So what if she has a figure that makes men turn heads. You have experience."

I recoiled and hoped no one noticed. "Thanks a heap."

As if on cue, the kitchen staff walked toward Scott, and I took that opportunity to get Liam's attention. "We can stand behind those columns and check out the phone."

"Let's go for it."

Seconds later, a fire truck and an ambulance arrived. Talk about a stroke of luck. Liam tapped the phone and smiled. "Thank goodness Scott unlocked it. I forgot all about the password issue. Here goes. Notes."

I stood still as he studied the first app, but from the look on his face, I knew it was a bust.

"No go, huh?"

"I'll try Reminders."

Again, I held my breath, and again a look of misery on Liam's face. "Just an appointment with his broker. Bummer."

CHAPTER THIRTY-THREE

"What else is there?"

"Emails and text messages. I'll start with the texts."

This time a wide-eyed expression flashed across Liam's face, and I knew we were in business. "I can't believe this. Must be he never moved from this thread. Check it out." He handed me the phone, and I read the most recent message. THAT CHEESE PLATTER WOMAN BEAT ME TO CHERIE'S LOCKER. RELAX. SHE DIDN'T SEE ME BUT SHE'S ON THE RUN. DO SOMETHING. YOU'RE ONE LUCKY SOB—SHE DIDN'T FIND WHAT YOU WERE LOOKING FOR. I STILL WANT TO BE PAID FOR THIS FAVOR.

"Who sent it? Does it give a name?" *And that explains the cat and mouse game. As if bumper cars would scare me away.*

Liam shook his head. "Nope. Only a phone number. I can run it across the Hidden Boulders database when I get back to the office, but it'll take time. Meanwhile, I'll go further back on these threads. I wonder what he was looking for. Cherie might have been blackmailing people, too, for all we know."

I tapped my foot and looked to my right, where a gathering crowd prevented me from seeing what went on with Scott. I did, however, see four firefighters, one woman, and three men, race into the building. Liam was glued to Scott's phone, and I tried to take a peek. "Hopefully, this miraculous diversion will give us the time we need. What did you find?"

"A text that goes back five days ago. Get this—TELL THE SHE-WITCH YOU'RE SEEING THAT SHE SHOULD QUIT MESSING WITH PERSON-NEL. I take it the 'she-witch' is Tambra, but I wonder what the caller meant by 'messing with personnel.'"

"Can you go back to more messages?"

Liam scrolled for a few seconds and then spoke. "Only one more text. Equally cryptic. HEARD CHERIE'S CALLING IN HER MARKERS.

"I know what that is. I've watched a zillion 1940s noir films. Boy, are you a boy scout! It's demanding payment for gambling debts. Sounds like Cherie was on the path to collecting money, and someone didn't like it. Maybe enough to do her in. Geez, Liam, you really need to find out who sent those text messages to Scott."

"No kidding. That text was sent two days before the one about messing with personnel. Uh-oh. Looks like the paramedics gave Scott the all-clear. I'd better get over there and return his phone, but not before one of us takes a screenshot of those messages."

I grabbed my iPhone and tapped the camera app. "On it." Seconds later, I had added three photos to my collection of dog pics and sample charcuterie trays. "Looks like the firefighters have left the building."

"Let's get a move on."

By the time we walked over to Scott, the crowd had started to return to the building. I could hear Stacee's voice even a few yards away, "I told them it was probably burnt toast."

Liam wasted no time rushing over and handing Scott his cell phone. "Holy cow, buddy, you gave us a scare. I'm assuming everything's all right or —"

"They said it was an anxiety attack. Not a heart attack. I guess the symptoms are similar. An anxiety attack. I only thought that happened to women."

I did a mental eye roll when I heard him and didn't say a word. Liam, however, did it for me. "Whoa. Only women? Really? I'm sure you weren't being sexist, but honestly…Fear's an equal-opportunity player. What's going on?"

Scott glanced my way, and Liam gave a nod as if to say, "It's okay."

"This doesn't go any further, understood?" Scott's voice was tenuous, and I wasn't sure whether to attribute it to his earlier anxiety attack (aka Edith run-through) or something else. Seconds later, I had my answer, but it only opened a wider door as far as two murders, possible blackmail, and not-so-petty thefts were concerned. To delve deeper, I only had one recourse—I needed to speak with Cora Milbrand. And the sooner, the better.

Chapter Thirty-Four

"Okay, Scott," Liam said. "I'm listening."

"Drainage. I'm sure you've been privy to the complaints and back-handed comments around the recreation center."

Liam nodded as I tried to recall where I had heard the word *drainage* recently. Then it hit me—Sharla's husband mentioned it the day I located Cherie's locker and snapped the lock off to appease Edith. Then, something else came to mind. It was Eric's files. I didn't pay much attention to the file he had on golf course management or the subsequent mini-files on drainage because, well...drainage. How does that ever point to murder?

Scott rubbed his hands together as if it was fifty degrees and not ninety-five. "The only explanation I can think of for the ongoing issues every time it rains is that someone sabotaged our golf course when it was initially built, but I can't prove it without incurring a tremendous expense, and the operating board would never go for it without definitive proof."

"Sabotaged how?" Liam furrowed his brow.

"Drainage pipes are corrugated. They're either double or single-walled. Today's standard is double-walled since they're stronger. But that doesn't mean single-walled pipes aren't used, provided they're installed with at least twenty inches of backfill."

Liam pressed on. "Are you saying you think our install was with single-walled pipes and not the required inches of backfill?"

"Something like that. I think corners were cut, and someone's going to great lengths to keep that from the general public knowledge."

Just then, I felt an annoying breeze on the nape of my neck and heard

Edith's unmistakable voice. "Ask him why they can't dig a tiny hole and check it out. You don't have to unearth the entire golf course to get an answer."

I rubbed my neck and ignored her. That resulted in the annoying breeze again, only this time in my right ear.

"Okay! I'll ask!"

Liam and Scott were immediately taken back. I had no choice but to explain. "Um, sorry. I was thinking out loud. I don't understand why a teeny-tiny hole can't be drilled somewhere on the golf course, preferably not a noticeable spot, to find out if Scott's theory is right."

Then I looked Scott in the eye and waited for a response.

"There's no such thing as an unnoticeable spot on the course. And even the tiniest disruption would cause tongues to wag, rumors to spread, and complaints to be registered. In the back of my mind, I wondered if Eric didn't have something to do with it, especially since he was on the planning board committee and worked closely with the developers."

"I can see where that's going if you can't, Missy." This time Edith let the breeze hit me straight in the face.

"Not now," I blurted out before I knew it.

Scott shook his head and sighed. "It'll come out sooner or later. Might as well ante up, but it stays here."

I had no idea what he was talking about, but apparently, Edith did. I kept still, along with Liam, and let Scott continue.

"I needed to find out if my assumption was correct, and I knew my best bet was to cozy up to Tambra and see if I could pry information out of her."

Oh my gosh. The affair. Not romance. Just kiss and tell. Ew!

Liam brushed a strand of hair from his forehead. "I take it you didn't get very far."

"She was dead before anything got heated up. Probably just as well, but it does put me in a rather precarious situation. As of now, however, I'm not sure the deputies are aware of my involvement with her."

Guess again. And if Sharla knows, it might as well get posted to Instagram and Facebook.

I was aching to ask about the text messages but couldn't let on. My gut told me Scott used the drainage problem as a foil to hide the real issue, but I had no way to pry it out of him. Not without some behind-the-scenes information from Cora Milbrand. After all, she cleaned their house and had to have picked up some choice tidbits from Deirdre. I knew what I had to do, but it would need to wait. Getting time with Cora was like setting up a visitation with the Pope. Still, I had to make that call.

Eric took a step closer to Scott. "Are you thinking someone killed Tambra because she had undeniable proof about the original drainage installation and could set off a lawsuit like nobody's business."

"It sounds awful when you say it out loud, but yeah. That's exactly what I thought. Why do you think I keep checking the comings and goings from the clubhouse? I've been looking for anything suspicious. You know, conversations from unlikely parties."

"Okay, buddy," Liam said. "So now what?"

"Now I get back to my office and keep digging. If you notice anything out of the ordinary, give me a shout-out, okay? Meanwhile, I'll leave you to the footage on Eric."

"Sure thing."

Scott gave me a quick nod and walked toward the entrance. When he was out of earshot, I spoke up. "Is it possible Tambra found out Eric had a part in a shady development deal regarding that golf course and used that knowledge to leverage an advantageous divorce settlement? I heard Cherie say their marriage was on the rocks. It was the night Tambra dropped dead at the fashion show, and I snuck into Eric's house. It would have given Eric a prime motive to do away with her."

"Quite possible. But difficult to prove. At least we found out one thing—Scott paid some woman to get into Cherie's locker. Now all I need to do is see if I can match up that phone number. How about I give you a call later today?"

"Thanks. I'm going to take my prying one step further and see what I can find out from Cora Milbrand. Gee, what are the odds? The woman cleans my house, too, when she's not complaining or grousing. Anyway, I really should get back to The Char-Board."

"It's a strange mess of things, isn't it? I mean, the drainage issue, stolen jewelry in Cherie's locker, two dead women, and who knows what else. Trouble is, how does any of this fit together?"

I shrugged. "All I know is that Scott tried to give me the not-so-subtle warning on the road, and for all I know, maybe those cryptic black marker messages, too. Eric may have motive, but that groundskeeper sure has action."

"Be careful, Katie. None of us have any idea what he's really like."

It was a few minutes past two, and I texted Lilly-Ann that I was on my way back. Seconds later, she responded, "Everything's fine. Javie's a real pro. Take your time. We'll be cleaning up."

In spite of the convoluted mess going on, coupled with an unsettling feeling someone had it in for me, I was glad of one thing—I made the right hire with Javie. When I got back to The Char-Board, the closed sign was on the door, but the lights were on, and my three employees were fast at work tidying up and preparing for the next day.

"Should Nancy Drew be worried you're replacing her?" Matt asked as soon as I got in the door. He had just finished wiping down a table and turned when he heard me walk in.

"She's way ahead of me, but I'm gaining ground. I think."

Javie, who stood a few feet away, broom in hand, walked toward me. "I'd be careful if I were you. Nothing is as it seems over there. In the back of my mind, I kept thinking the real operation wasn't Hidden Boulders as much as it was manipulating the monies that came into Hidden Boulders."

"I'm not sure I understand. Do you mean two sets of books? One for the IRS and one for Hidden Boulders? That kind of thing probably goes on more times than any of us can imagine."

Javie shook his head. "No, not two sets of books. Look, this is only a thought that keeps crossing my mind, but here goes: Lance Baker and Cherie Simms were pretty darn tight. I'm not saying romantically, but something. On more than one occasion, I overheard them discussing things like "odds, spread, and exposure." All gambling terms. I think they found a way to tap into the money and use it for gambling purposes."

"But how? It's not as if people pay in cash anymore. It's all automatic deductions and credit cards."

By now, Lilly-Ann and Matt had inched closer, neither of them saying a word as Javie continued.

"Lance's office handles the bookkeeping, and Lance oversees it. Money doesn't have to travel in paper form anymore. Look, I'm not accusing anyone of anything, but I'd be a fool to say I didn't have my suspicions."

I immediately thought back to Tambra's little blackmail list. It called Cherie out for gambling debts but did Tambra have any idea those debts might have involved Hidden Boulders? And if so, did she confront Cherie and pay the price?

I bit my lip and let out a slow breath. "Do you think the sheriff's office and the marshals are aware of this?"

Javie shook his head. "If so, it wasn't from anything the kitchen staff at Hidden Boulders disclosed. All of us commiserated after that grueling process, and we all reached the conclusion that, well, frankly, none of us knew what was going on. So, to answer your question, I'd say no, unless they had better luck with other sources."

Terrific. Now I can add "sticking one's fingers into the proverbial pot" as another motive in my never-ending list.

"What about Cherie's relationship with Eric?" I asked Javie. "Have you heard any rumblings about that?"

"No, but for my remaining time there, I'll keep my ears open." He smiled and proceeded to sweep the floor. "Until I'm officially cut loose from there, I'll text when I'm available to help here."

"Sounds good. And don't worry. I'll be careful."

Behind me, the sound of a car gunning its engine as it cruised past our shop caused me to flinch.

"That's the second time today," Lilly-Ann said. "And the same thing happened yesterday. Either there's one crazy driver out there, or revving an engine has now become a thing."

"Probably some teenager who's got the keys to the car and wants to make the most of it," I said. "If it becomes a nuisance, then I suppose we can always alert the deputies, but right now, they've got more on their hands than dealing with a noise complaint."

The rest of the crew agreed as we finished with the clean-up and headed out the door. Thanks to the car alarm I had Wilhelm's install, complete with a sticker warning on the dashboard window, my tires and everything else appeared to be intact.

Between Hidden Boulders and then The Char-Board, I hadn't taken out my phone to check any text messages. Not until I got into the car and put the key in the ignition. Sure enough, there was one from Ian—RING DEVICE IS INSTALLED. I'LL CALL LATER TO SET IT UP ON YOUR PHONE. GAVE SPEEDBUMP TWO TREATS. HE BEGS. STAY SAFE.

I read the last two words again and had to admit I felt a bit more secure knowing Ian had come into my life.

"Are you going to sit there daydreaming like a ninny or get cracking on those murders? If you're out in La-La Land, I suggest we pay a visit to Imogen."

In a flash, I was jolted from my reverie and staring at Edith, who had made herself comfortable in the passenger seat. This time with a crimson caftan draped around her.

"We're not visiting Imogen. Case closed." I rolled my eyes when Edith wasn't looking.

"Then tap in Cora's number and set up that tête-à-tête. You can't afford to waste time."

"What do you mean?"

"That car with the revved-up engine came from Hidden Boulders."

"How do you know? I thought you couldn't gravitate away from my presence."

"I can't. But I was in your presence a few minutes ago and looked out the shop window at the street."

"And?"

"I saw the same car parked in the employee area at Hidden Boulders when you went there the day after Tambra bit the dust. Guess what, Missy? If you ask me, someone's got it in for you."

Chapter Thirty-Five

With the cell phone still in my hand, I tapped Cora's number before Edith could utter another word. Five rings later and Cora picked up.

"This is Cora Milbrand's cleaning service. What can I do for you?"

Oh great. Now she's calling it a cleaning service. Must be her prices are going up.

"Uh, Hi Cora! It's Katie Aubrey. Boy, those dust bunnies are certainly accumulating around my house, even though you cleaned it two weeks ago. Any chance you could get in sooner?"

"Can't be that dirty. It's only you and the dog. Unless you've started entertaining gentleman callers. They can be downright slobs."

Holy cannoli! The woman's worse than Edith.

"Yeah, well, any chance you have an afternoon free this week? Like tomorrow or Saturday?"

"Hmm, you're in luck. My four o'clock canceled tomorrow. Some lame excuse. Hey, I think you might know them. The woman mentioned getting one of those char-cute-see trays from you for a bunco party a while back."

Deirdre. It has to be Deirdre.

"Deirdre Billings?"

"Yeah, that's her. Anyway, you can take her slot. I'll be there at four."

"Great. Thanks, Cora. I really—" But she had already ended the call.

"See?" Edith smiled. "That wasn't so bad, was it? And since we have to wait until tomorrow, I thought we could mosey over to Scottsdale."

"Nice try. No Imogen."

"Well, if you're going to be like that, I *do* have other things to deal with." And with that, she vanished. Poof! No whirling colors, no bizarre scents, only a puff of air and one less ghost.

I turned on my directional signal and pulled onto Cave Creek Road. A few minutes later, I was in my own driveway, glancing at the front door. Sure enough, I spied the new feature and was relieved Ian had installed the Ring device. Then, I sent him a text: THANK YOU FOR THE RING. WHEN DO YOU WANT TO SET IT UP? Then I opened the garage door and drove straight inside.

Speedbump was at the utility room door, tail wagging like crazy. I bent down, petted him, and went inside, wasting no time getting him a biscuit and checking his water and kibble supply. Seconds later, Ian returned the text: I CAN HEAD OVER NOW AND SET IT UP. NEED TO BE AT WORK BY FIVE. It was followed by a smiley emoji, and I sent him a thumbs-up one as well as a smiley when I texted back. *Good grief. This is like middle school all over again.*

Then, once I changed into capris and a decent top, I phoned Maddie. I'd meant to keep her in the loop but had gotten sidetracked so many times I wondered exactly *what* I had told her and when. It didn't matter. Maddie could connect the dots if she had to. After all, it had only been what? Three days?

"Hey Maddie, how's it going? Hope I'm not interrupting anything spellbinding."

"Not unless you're enamored with paperwork. I picked up a few new listings and finally closed on that Tudor nightmare in Chandler. You're the one with all the excitement going on. I figured you were off the hook regarding those murders, or you would have called me by now. You *are* off the hook, aren't you?"

"Let's just say I'm dangling next to it like an angleworm."

"Ew!"

"Seriously, since we last spoke, I scoped out Cherie's locker. That's the dumpster body I came across, in case you forgot."

"I didn't. Go on."

SLICED, DICED AND DEAD

"I discovered stolen jewelry but had to leave it there. Nothing as far as clues regarding her death. Then someone tried to run me off the road. I'm convinced it was Scott Billings, the groundskeeper at Hidden Boulders. Oh, and my tires were slashed."

"All on the same day?"

"Uh, no. A day or so later. I was supposed to have dinner at Ian's house, but obviously, I couldn't drive there, so he came over here and prepared the most amazing seafood dish I ever had."

"From the sound of your voice, it wasn't the seafood that was so amazing. What's going on? And don't brush me off."

"I like him. I mean, I *really* like him."

"*Like* as in love interest?"

"I know. Right? I mean, he's younger and all, but he doesn't act it. And when I'm with him, I feel safe and secure."

"Then forget his age and yours. Those are insignificant in the realm of things."

"Good. Because he stayed over another night. We reviewed the list of suspects and possible motives. Did I mention Tambra's cause of death was tansy oil? Not the Walmart stuff. The poison. Who can get their hands on that? And honestly, I don't know who was more freaked out over the tires and that car trying to run me off the road. Me or Ian? Did I mention he installed a Ring device on my door? Oh, guess not, because he just did that. In fact, he's on his way over to set it up on my phone."

"Whoa, Katie. I haven't heard you ramble so much since you found out Evan cheated on you."

"That wasn't rambling. That was venting. And I really need to get going, but there's one more thing, and you'll be all caught up."

"One more thing? What you've told me isn't enough?"

"Very funny. You remember Liam, my friend from Chan-Tech, who's now the director of security at Hidden Boulders?"

"Uh-huh."

"Well, he and I devised a scheme to find out what Scott is up to. We put it into play this morning, and guess what? That sneaky groundskeeper had text messages from some woman who watched me break into Cherie's locker. And that's not all. According to the texts, Scott is looking for something. Whatever it is, it could give us the motive for the murders. I mean, why else would that guy try to intimidate me?"

"Katie, if you keep this up, you'll need more than a Ring device on your door. Leave it to the sheriff's office. We pay enough in taxes so that we don't have to do their job."

"I wish I could. Honest, I do. But someone's got it in for me, and I need to find out who and why."

"Then don't take any reckless chances, okay?"

"You sound like Liam."

"I guess that's better than sounding like your mother."

I laughed and told her I'd keep her posted.

For the next few minutes, I checked my makeup and ran a brush through my hair.

"That sexy bit of eye candy has gotten to you, hasn't he?"

"Edith! Not now. And could you please give me a warning when you show up?"

"Would you like an intriguing sulfur smell or maybe a faucet that won't shut off?"

"Not cute. Stick to whirling colors and soothing scents."

"I'm more than a spa experience."

"Oh, trust me. You're an experience, all right. Now go! Ian will be here any second."

"Look out your window. He's already here and is about to ring your doorbell."

With that, I charged to the door and prayed Edith would take a hike. Unfortunately, I knew better.

I opened the door, and as Ian stepped inside, I gave him a hug. It was like inhaling crisp linen, and I almost didn't want to stop.

"Hey, I missed you. Even though it wasn't that long," he said. At that moment, Speedbump ambled over and rubbed his nose against Ian's knee.

"Wow. He doesn't even do that with me. Looks like I've got competition."

"Only the four-legged kind. Hey, I'd better get that device set up. Wish I could stay longer, but I need to be at work. Thomas texted me a few minutes ago. Said the sheriff's office paid our kitchen a surprise visit, and Sterling is a wreck."

"Looking for tansy oil?"

Ian nodded and shrugged. "Thomas said they came up empty, but you know Sterling. If he's not nervous or anxious, then he's fidgety and agitated."

"Sounds like the same thing."

"Nope. Fidgety and agitated means more work for us."

I laughed and handed him my iPhone as we walked to the kitchen. It didn't take him that long to download the Ring app and have me set up an account. From there, he set up the device by scanning the QR code on the doorbell. A far cry easier than what I had expected. Then it was miscellaneous stuff like specifying my location and naming my device.

"Why do I have to name it? That's kind of weird."

"To distinguish it from other Ring devices if you add them."

"Oh my gosh. I can barely handle one."

"Hey, you never know. Meanwhile, we have to connect it to your WIFI and test it out."

That took another few minutes, and by the time Ian finished, he had to leave. Speedbump must have sensed it because he nuzzled Ian and leaned against him as Ian headed to the door.

"I'm working for the next few nights," he said, "but how about breakfast on Sunday? If you drive over, I promise to make you something spectacular."

"You already made me something spectacular."

"Fine. Then I'll make something ordinary. What do you say?"

"I'm fine with buttered toast."

"I can do better than that. How about nine-thirty or ten? It can morph into brunch."

Just then, a hideous green plume filled the room but only for my eyes. "I'll tell you what it'll morph into."

"That's…" I was about to say "Enough" for Edith but caught myself. "That's fine. I mean, great. Sounds good." *Oh my gosh, I am totally babbling.* "Do you want me to bring anything?"

"Speedbump if he's up for a ride." Ian reached down and patted the dog's head. "See you then. And try to stay out of trouble. At least until I'm around."

"I'll work at it."

He pulled me toward him, brushed the hair from my brow, and kissed me. And not a short "see-you-later" kiss. A genuine on-the-lips-I-can-almost-taste-the-moisture-in-your-mouth kiss. When I stepped back, I still felt the heat in my cheeks.

Ian then gave my hand a squeeze and walked to the door. "Talk to you soon."

I stood, motionless, as he closed the door behind him.

"Well, Missy, you can stand there all afternoon in a stupor, or you can get down to business and fill in the blanks on that murder map of yours. Must I do all the work?"

"Huh? What?" It took me a second to realize Edith was standing directly behind me, same outfit as before.

"You might not have been paying attention, but I was. Grab that notebook of yours. I'll wait."

"I'm grabbing an apple and some pretzels, if you don't mind. I haven't eaten."

"You just *have* to rub it in, don't you?"

"It's an apple and pretzels, Edith, not a savory five-course dinner."

"It's food. Eat fast."

Chapter Thirty-Six

"Okay, Edith, what's so pressing?" I tossed my apple core into the wastepaper basket and bit the tip off of a pretzel before plunking down on the couch with my murder notebook.

"Those text messages you and Liam found on Scott's phone. Open up your eyes. Think. Maybe Cherie didn't steal those jewelry items after all. Maybe they were gambling debt payoffs."

"Wow. I hadn't thought of that."

"Well, I have. Those women might not have expendable cash on hand, but they sure have jewelry."

"The women…Okay, I know the Byzantine necklace belonged to Meredith. But I have no idea who gave her the ladybug charm or the silver and gold tennis bracelet, and those items are so small that they wouldn't even turn up on one of Liam's surveillance tapes."

"Not the tapes, but what about those website photos from Hidden Boulders? You know, that PR stuff meant to attract buyers to the community. Those bunco gals are regular features. Boot up that laptop, Missy, and let's surf Hidden Boulders."

"For once, you may be on to something. Hang on."

I took the laptop from the kitchen table and moved it to the coffee table. Then, I started it and kept my fingers crossed we'd hit paydirt. Page after page featuring smiling, happy people on the golf course, poolside, and in the dining area. Unfortunately, none of them were the bunco ladies. In fact, I had the strange feeling they were all paid models. No one can look that perfect.

"Keep scrolling," Edith demanded.

"That's all there is on the promo page."

"What other pages do they have?"

"Golf Memberships, Realtors, and Banquets and Weddings."

"Pick one."

I clicked the page on golf memberships, fully expecting to come up empty-handed but instead, found myself staring at a photo of Meredith at a putting green, and if I wasn't mistaken, her left hand clearly had that tennis bracelet on it.

"Maybe we don't have to look any further, Edith. Could be that jewelry all came from Meredith. My take is she owed Cherie big time."

"My take is she did away with Cherie before her entire collection bit the dust."

"So now what? I can't very well phone her and tell her I discovered her gambling secret without confessing to the locker break-in."

"You're a smart woman. You'll figure it out. Meanwhile, I have a bone to pick with that snarky Rosaline."

And in a flash, Edith was gone. No fanfare. No nothing. Just an unsettling silence. I picked up my murder notebook and looked over my notes again, focusing on the original suspect list I gleaned from Tambra's little blackmail/intimidation plan. That's when I noticed one name was missing—Meredith's. All of the other women in that bunco klatch were named loud and clear, but not her.

"I may be on to something," I said to Speedbump, who was otherwise occupied cleaning a front paw. Just then, my cell phone vibrated, and I took the call.

"Hi Katie, it's Javie. Sorry for the background noise, but I called with good news. When I left The Char-Board this afternoon, I drove straight to Hidden Boulders for my second bout of work tonight, and guess what? Eric informed me they made a new hire, and tonight would be my last night working here. He called me into his office as soon as I arrived."

Just then, I heard what sounded like a giant pot hitting the floor and, for an instant, wondered if Edith was up to something in the kitchen. I must have gasped because I heard Javie say, "I'll help you in a minute Twila." Then to me, "Twila dropped one of those huge boiler pots. Good thing it was empty."

"Hey, that's wonderful news for us. I really need you to make charcuterie boards for a number of events that are coming up. Plus, we need you during regular hours. The place is getting slammed."

"I'll be there bright and early tomorrow. And again, thanks."

"I'm the one who should be thanking you. You've saved us at least twice. See you in the morning." *And with any luck, I might be able to track down Meredith at the club and find a way to eke a confession out of her. Or, at the very least, get Deputy Vincent to do it.*

Next thing I knew, I heard something else hit the floor at Hidden Boulders just as Javie said, "thanks" and "see you tomorrow." Either Twila was a klutz or maybe having a bad day. I shuddered. Better Hidden Boulders than The Char-Board.

I looked at the dog, who was now gnawing on his other paw. "What I am about to do goes against my better judgment but what the heck? This investigation is taking forever."

I pulled out Deputy Vincent's card from my wallet and called his direct line. Seconds later, I heard his familiar gruff voice. "Good afternoon, Miss Aubrey. What can I do for you?"

"How did you know it was me?"

"Caller ID. Now, how can I help you?"

"Okay, fine. I know you're not allowed to disclose information on an active investigation, and in this case, two of them, but I've been listening to lots of scuttlebutt, and well, I heard Cherie was into gambling and may have collected jewelry for payoffs. Just rumors, but I thought I'd share it with you."

"If I didn't know any better, Miss Aubrey, I'd be inclined to think you know more than you're saying. And for the record, my office is aware of unauthorized betting that seemed to be prevalent at Hidden Boulders."

"Does that mean you have suspects for Cherie's murder?"

"If nothing else, you are persistent. Rest assured, we are conducting a thorough investigation, and until that time when it is completed, everyone, and I repeat, *everyone,* is under suspicion for those murders."

The way he said *everyone* assured me I was still on his list. "Can you tell me if you think they're related?"

"No, I cannot. Now, if there's nothing else, I need to keep this line free. Have a nice afternoon."

"Wait. About that jewelry. If my rumor mill is on target, Cherie might have stashed some of it in her locker at the Hidden Boulders clubhouse."

"Your rumor mill? Or something more substantial?"

"I'm not sure I know what you mean."

"Trust me, Miss Aubrey, our office conducts thorough investigations, and surprise of surprises, we did have authorization to check Ms. Simms locker. I found it rather odd that it was the only one in use without a lock. And yes, we did find jewelry in there, and if it turns out the jewelry did not belong to her, it leaves our office with two possibilities—either your rumor mill was correct in its assumptions, or someone planted that jewelry there. Rest assured, our forensics team is on it."

Wonderful. The forensics team.

And with that, the call ended, and my stomach churned. I knew I was careful in that locker room, but honestly, I used one of those equipment towels to cover my fingerprints. And up until that point, I didn't know how careful I was. *Terrific. I may need that bail bondsman after all.*

Convinced that time was literally "of the essence," I grabbed a scrap paper from the counter along with a pen and placed another call. This time to the receptionist at Hidden Boulders. I kept my fingers crossed it would be Stacee and not the guy with the comb-over. At least Stacee was talkative.

"Hi!" I said, relieved to hear her voice at the other end. "This is Katie Aubrey, the charcuterie chef."

"Hi! Hey, I heard you've scooped up one of our best employees. We're sure going to miss Javie. Nice guy."

"I know. Nice guy and a great worker. Say, the reason I called is because I wanted to get in touch with Meredith Mason but can't seem to find her number. I should have put it on my phone when she gave it to me." *Okay, so what's a little white lie?*

I held my breath she'd give me the number because I knew Liam had already left for the day, and Stacee was my only recourse.

"Here it is. I'll speak slowly."

I thanked her and asked how things were going at Hidden Boulders.

"The tension is palpable, and I don't think those deputies are any closer to making an arrest than they were a few days ago."

"Yeah, I kind of thought the same thing. Anyway, thanks for Meredith's number. I appreciate it."

"Anytime."

I hadn't realized that I was all but holding my breath until I got off the phone and exhaled for what seemed like minutes, not seconds. "Okay, Speedbump, no time like the present." With that, I tapped Meredith's number on my phone and once again held my breath until she took the call.

"Hi! This is Merry."

"Hi. It's Katie Aubrey from The Char-Board. Hope I'm not catching you at a bad time."

"Nope. What's up?"

And now, another great lie.

"I've got a list of catering orders, and one of them might be yours. Someone got water on it, and it's hard to read. Were you planning to host a bunco event?"

"Sorry, but it's not me. Ever since Tambra's murder and then Cherie's, no one is in the mood to host anything. In fact, all of us are kind of hunkering down, wondering who's next."

"Who's next? What do you mean?"

"Tambra had a hold on all of us, but Cherie was worse. I was stupid to ever get involved with the two of them, but what's done is done. And if you breathe a word of this to the deputies, I'll deny everything. Look, I suppose you'll figure it out anyway because those women talk like anyone's business. Especially Eulodie and Deirdre. Cherie had a nifty little gambling deal going on until it wasn't so nifty."

"What do you mean?"

"She'd let us pawn our jewelry with her until we could ante up. But something must have gone terribly wrong because, well, you know where she wound up. Frankly, I'm out a necklace and two other smaller pieces, but at least I didn't wind up face down in a dumpster."

"Do you have any idea who wanted Cherie out of the way?"

"Someone who was probably in so deep, they didn't have any recourse. Anyway, when things settle down, I definitely want you to make a charcuterie board for my next hosting date. Maybe in a few weeks."

"Sounds good. And thanks."

I glanced at the dog, who stood directly behind me. "Well, Speedbump, at least we know more about Cherie's unofficial pawnshop. Now if we can only find out who the key player was, we might be able to point Deputy Vincent in that direction. And the sooner, the better."

Chapter Thirty-Seven

I shot off a text to Ian before going to bed, explaining what I garnered from Meredith as well as letting him know I planned to extricate information from Cora tomorrow. He responded with a thumbs-up emoji and a text that read NANCY DREW HAS NOTHING ON YOU. CAN'T WAIT UNTIL SUNDAY.

Two seconds later, I texted back a smiley face, same as I did the last time. If Maddie knew, she'd say I was re-living my teenage years sans the technology. It didn't matter. Middle school, junior high, high school…who cared? And as long as she didn't mention the word *cougar*, I'd be okay.

Speedbump jumped to the foot of the bed at the same time I pulled the lightweight blanket down and crept in. I read a chapter and a half from Linda Reilly's new Grilled Cheese Mysteries and then pulled the cord on my bedside lamp. With the exception of the hum from the air-conditioner, and Speedbump cleaning a rear paw, the room was still. I closed my eyes and sunk into my new mattress and cushy pillow. Right in time for Speedbump to pass gas like nobody's business.

"Ugh, dog. Are you trying to asphyxiate me?" I got up and opened the bedroom window. As much as I hate wasting AC money, I really hated noxious odors at bedtime even more. "This should clear out the room in ten or fifteen minutes," I told the dog. "Then I'm closing it, so you better be done for the night."

Once again, I crept into bed and pulled the lamp cord shut. I had started to drift off, losing all sense of how much time had really elapsed since I opened the window. That's when something hit the wall behind my bed and jolted me awake. It must have been fairly loud because Speedbump had jumped down from the bed and stood facing the wall, a soft growl emanating from him.

"Edith! Is this one of your attention-getting things? Because it's not funny, and I'm not in the mood."

Nothing. I pulled the lamp cord and looked around the room from the safety of my bed. Other than a lopsided abstract painting that I had gotten used to, nothing looked out of place.

"Something hit that wall," I announced to the dog. "And please don't let it be a bat. Then again, they have an amazing sense of touch, so I doubt it's a bat. Then what?"

I got out of the bed, closed the bedroom window, and looked at the floor. Whatever it was, it had to have landed there. By now, Speedbump had lost interest and returned to the foot of the bed. I, on the other hand, crept around as if someone had tossed a Molotov Cocktail my way. Scenes from every *Godfather* movie flashed through my mind, and I tried to dismiss them.

"It's on the floor by the left-hand side of the dresser," Edith announced. "And don't get fingerprints on it."

"On what? Should I be ducking for cover?"

"If it was going to explode, it would have. Looks like one of those river rocks with a note rubber banded to it. Grab a pair of those food service gloves and see what it says. I can't be expected to figure everything out."

It wasn't as if I had many options. I traipsed into the kitchen and returned with the lightweight rubber gloves on both hands. Edith had made herself comfortable on my bed, leaning on one side as if she was about to take in a feature film. "Go ahead. Undo the rubber band and see what the note says."

I rolled my eyes and removed the rubber band. Whoever had sent the little missive my way hadn't used regular printer paper. Instead, they had written their unwelcome message on what appeared to be butcher wrap or maybe even the lightweight paper florists use. Same black marker as before but somehow, larger and angrier as if there was such a thing.

"Find someone your own age, if you know what's good for you. And don't you dare call MCSO, or you'll really be sorry. Next time, it won't be a rock.

Walk away. NOW!"

My hands trembled, and I read the note at least three times before I let the message sink in. *Someone doesn't want me to get involved with Ian.*

Was this what it was all about? Jealousy? But what would that have to do with Tambra's murder, or Cherie's for that matter? And how would that explain Scott's actions? Whoever wrote that note was right about one thing, though. I wasn't about to call Deputy Vincent or anyone else on his staff, for that matter. Last thing I needed was to call attention to Ian. Especially if there was some unhinged ex-girlfriend or worse floating around out there.

"So, what do you think, Edith?" I rewrapped the stone and placed it on my dresser.

"Oh, so now, all of a sudden, my opinion has become invaluable? Hold on. I want to announce that to the powers that be."

"Very funny. I'm just trying to get a handle on things."

"If you're concerned about being in emanant danger, forget it. Whoever wrote it obviously enjoys pitching little hissy fits. It's a distractor if you ask me. I don't think it has anything to do with those murders. The sender obviously figured out how to get under your skin."

"And all this time, I thought those notes were warnings to quit snooping around."

"Just goes to show you how clever and diabolical the little minx is when it comes to latching her claws on your latest love interest."

"You mean my *only* love interest?"

"You said it."

"This is awful. The only viable clues I thought I had were from those threatening notes. It's as if I'm starting from scratch."

"Not necessarily. If I'm not mistaken, 'the voice of Greater Phoenix' will be ferreting out your imaginary dust bunnies at four tomorrow. Grill her like a tuna on a hibachi. She's bound to know something. Start with Deirdre. Revisit that murder map of yours. If you can't put any clues together from Cora, then I say we take a breather and pay a visit to—"

"Nice try. No Imogen. But I like your idea of connecting the dots."

"One more thing. Just because you don't want to mess things up with Ian

216

doesn't mean you can't let Liam know about that little surprise message tonight. Of course, Ian works for Randolph's Escapade and not Hidden Boulders, but who knows if some little flirt didn't have her eyes on him the night of the fashion show. You and Liam were looking for a murderer, not a vamp."

"There were like a zillion servers that night, Edith."

"But only one of them is intent on keeping you away from Ian."

"Point well taken."

"Good, because I have other business to attend to. Ta-ta, for now, Missy. And if you can't fall asleep, connect the dots. Better than counting sheep."

No sooner did she say the word *sheep* when she vanished without another word, leaving me wide awake and anxious with too many thoughts crashing through my head at once.

Did the rock-heaving lunatic know my bedroom window was open? Had she been spying on the house all night up until she tossed the rock? Aarugh! Too bad the Ring device only zeroed in on the front door because that was the one place she avoided. *My gosh! She's been watching me all along.*

I made sure to lock the bedroom window and make sure all of the other windows were equally secured before grabbing my murder-map notes and re-reading what I had written. If nothing else, it would give my mind something to do while waiting for sleep to return. Or a major breakthrough to surface. Whichever came first.

Lamentably, neither did. I woke up at a little past four, clutching my notebook with my arm dangling from the bed. Not exactly the epitome of a restful night's sleep or a successful venture in sleuthing, but at least I could start with a clean slate regarding who dealt the final blows to Tambra and Cherie. But boy, was I sadly mistaken.

A quick rinse-off in the shower, followed by one of the fastest cups of coffee on record, and I was pretty much on my way out the door. Speedbump had devoured his kibble and used the doggie door while I threw on some clothes and dabbed a bit of tinted sunblock on my face.

"We'll walk the neighborhood tonight, boy," I said to the dog who by now had mastered the wide-eyed sullen look dogs apparently are taught from birth. "Besides, it's a beautiful morning, and you've got the run of the yard. Enjoy! Meanwhile, I've got charcuterie trays lined up and two murders to solve before things really get dicey."

Then I looked around and continued my conversation with the dog. "Edith must be skulking around over that gown issue with Rosaline, or she decided to give me a break. Either way, I'm not about to push the odds."

With that, I headed to the car, having made sure all the windows in the house were closed and locked. ADT couldn't arrive fast enough as far as I was concerned.

It was barely sunrise, and the turquoise hues on the horizon began to morph into pinks and blues as I approached The Char-Board. I spied a decent parking spot directly across the road and k-turned my way into it as if I were taking my road test.

"That's a two-thumbs up," Javie announced from across the street. I hadn't realized he'd been standing by the doorway to our sandwich shop and wondered how long he'd been there.

"Sorry," I said as I charged toward him. "Usually, I'm here much earlier."

"No worries. Didn't want to be late on my first full day. Um, if you don't mind my asking, you look as if you didn't sleep at all last night. I mean, not that you look *bad,* but you usually look—"

"More put together? You can say it. That's fine. And you're right, it wasn't my best night. Someone tossed a rock through my open bedroom window. And not a prank. It was one of those river rocks with a nasty little threat rubber banded to it."

Javie stood, mouth agape for a few seconds. "Did you notify the sheriff's office? What kind of threat?"

"At first, I thought it might have to do with the murders since, well, I have been poking around. But given what the note said, I think it was just some disgruntled neighbor. No big deal."

"I'd still clue the deputies in if I were you."

"Listen, please don't say a word of this to Lilly-Ann or Matt. She's freaked out as it is, and the last thing I need is to have her distracted. Especially with all the charcuterie orders coming up."

"Understood. And, speak of the devil, here they come now."

I immediately put the key in the door and greeted Lilly-Ann and Matt with so much enthusiasm they both gave each other strange looks.

"Another fun day!" I smiled. "Might as well get to it!"

Like the prior instances where Javie, Lilly-Ann, Matt, and I worked together, today was no different. We went about our tasks seamlessly as if we'd been a team for years and not days. Good thing, too, because the morning rush never ended, and before we knew it, we were hustling through lunch.

"Listen," I said to Lilly-Ann and Javie as I rinsed off a few dishes and quickly dried them. "I thought perhaps we'd have some time to work on the charcuterie trays that we're going to need by seven tonight. Thank goodness these are small trays, and the customers will be picking them up, but I need to be home at two-thirty to let my cleaning lady in. Any chance either of you can hold down the fort? I honestly did not expect us to be this slammed, and Matt needs to leave in time for his afternoon and evening classes."

"Not a problem for me," Javie said. "Just let me know what the designs are."

"I'm in, too," Lilly-Ann smiled. "But I'd better dart across the street for a few of those edible flowers before Petals and Plants closes up."

"Whew! Thanks, guys. I should be back here by six at the latest." *Sooner if I can get Cora talking. And Edith to stay away.*

Chapter Thirty-Eight

Between the clean-up and set-up for the next day, coupled with the charcuterie board prep, I literally felt beads of sweat on the nape of my neck. At two ten, I bid everyone a good afternoon and promised to be back as soon as I could. Then, I hung my apron on one of the knobs in the kitchen and exited the place without another word.

I had one opportunity to glean information about the Billings from Cora, and I wasn't about to let it slip through my fingers. Not if it meant re-circulating dust bunnies from room to room if that's what it took.

With ten minutes to spare, I arrived home, changed Speedbump's water bowl, and gave him a handful of kibble. "We've got to be shrewd about this," I said to the dog. "Coax the information out of her without her realizing it."

"Fat chance with that. Cora's cantankerous, but she's not daft. She'll know what you're up to." I looked past the dog to see Edith in a golden chiffon gown. "Shh! Not a word. I sort of snuck off with this, and I'm hoping no one notices."

"How can they not notice? One minute you're dressed as if you're in attendance at a military funeral, and the next, you're Cinderella. Or maybe the fairy godmother."

"Not funny, Missy. Now listen up if you expect this to work."

"Huh? What?"

"Just follow my lead, and everything will be fine. Hmm, if I'm not mistaken, that's Cora's car pulling up. And don't blurt out the first thing you think of."

"No, because you'll beat me to it. Edith. We have a limited amount of time to find out what Cora knows about the Billings. And the best way is to let her think we know it, too. Or, in this case, *I* know it. Or I should know it."

"Quit rambling. That battleaxe is at the door already!"

"I'm starting in the back bathroom," Cora announced as soon as I let her inside the house. She arrived with her usual cleaning bucket, mop, and all sorts of wipes and paraphernalia. "Must say, I'm looking forward to the peace and quiet."

"Huh?"

"Let's just say I'm sick and tired of hearing about golf course drainage management. You'd think if two people were going to argue, it would be about something more interesting—like one of them cheating or maybe gambling."

"Are you talking about Deirdre and Scott Billings?" I could hardly contain my excitement.

"Those two? Heavens no. Boring as wet toast on a rainy morning. But you've got half the equation right. Not that I'm one of those gossipy cleaners who can't wait to spread the manure, but in this case, I'm referring to Stacee Thorne, that cutesy receptionist from Hidden Boulders. Next time I'm going to insist she buy me noise-canceling headsets if Scott shows up at her place to ruminate about the golf courses."

"Um, why would he show up at her place to talk about his grounds keeping job?" *And OMG—Hidden Boulders is becoming a regular* Peyton Place.

"She's his sister. Or weren't you aware of that? Guess old Scotty got tired of bringing up the matter with Deirdre. But if you really want to know what I think, Stacee is privy to lots of information, and Scott needs to get his hands on it."

"About the golf course issues?"

Cora breezed past me into the bathroom, then turned around. "Someone cut corners, and now that fancy-dancy development is paying the price."

"Do you think Stacee was in on it, Tambra found out, and then Stacee made sure it wouldn't go any further?"

Cora shrugged. "Stacee's an opportunist, but she wouldn't double-cross her own brother. No. I think she knows something, that's all."

"Did you share any of this with the sheriff's deputies?"

"They didn't ask. I didn't tell."

"But you think something, don't you?"

"Tambra was one smart cookie, and she knew how to manipulate people with the best of them. Most likely, she had information about payoffs and corner-cutting when that development was being built. I wager she leveraged it and lost. But whatever information she had, was tucked away somewhere, and Scott wants his hands on it pronto. That's where his sister comes in."

"But why Scott?"

"Because the blame game will land in his lap. Duh!"

With that, Cora closed the door to the bathroom and turned on the faucet. My cue, our conversation had ended for the day.

I ambled back to the kitchen and mouthed "thank you" to Edith for keeping her proverbial lips sealed around Cora. A lone ice cube rolled across the kitchen floor, and I chalked it up to "message received."

Then, my cell phoned dinged, and I realized it was a text from Ian. Part of me wanted desperately to ask him about any stalkers or old love interests, but the last thing I needed was to ruin a great relationship before it even had time to heat up. Instead, I decided to take a wait-and-see approach.

Ian's text was short and gave no indication he knew anything about the rock-tossing ex in his life. *If,* indeed, I was right about that. In brief, it read-CRAZY WORK SCHEDULE. SUNDAY CAN'T COME FAST ENOUGH. MISS YOU. STAY SAFE.

I read the "stay safe" sentence at least three times before I felt an ice cube hit me on the ankle.

"Next time, read it out loud. I hate hovering over your shoulder."

"Do you think he knows anything, and he's not saying it? Was he trying to give me a warning?"

"I think the 'stay safe' is right up there with 'have a good day.' Let it go. You can always pry it out of him on Sunday."

"I suppose." I put the phone on the counter, and in that second, another text came in. This time from Liam's number.

"GOT IT. CALL ME WHEN YOU ARE ALONE."

"I'm stepping outside for a minute," I shouted to Cora. She responded with a flush of the toilet as I grabbed the phone and raced to the porch.

Edith was already leaning over the railing, adjusting the chiffon ruffles on the drape of her dress. "Well, what does it say? What's he got?"

"I haven't phoned him. Give me a second."

I went straight to Contacts and tapped Liam's number. Boy, talk about "at the ready." His voice all but jolted me.

"Good. You got my text. I had to do a bit of cross-referencing, but you'll never guess who sent those texts to Scott."

"Stacee Thorne?"

"What? But how did you—"

"I didn't. My cleaning lady did. She apparently has quite the cadre of clients in Hidden Boulders. And guess what? Stacee is Scott's sister."

"*That,* I didn't know. But it all makes sense in a bizarre kind of way. Hey, once I tracked down the number, which, thankfully, was side-listed on an employee database, I was able to figure out who it was. Then, are you ready for this? I made a note of the time of the incident and was able to ascertain that Stacee had gone for the day and was replaced by Wendell Craig."

"The guy with the comb-over?"

"Uh, yeah, come to think of it. Anyway, we can pretty much agree Stacee was your stalker at Cherie's locker."

"By why would Scott be interested in what was in Cherie's locker? Unless it wasn't jewelry he was after."

"Guess we'll never know, but I wager if there is something telling, those deputies will be all over it. I'll keep you posted if anything else wafts my way. Other than the wackiness that's been going on in the kitchen ever since Javie left."

"Wackiness?"

"And then some. Apparently, one of the sous chefs has been pitching a fit since Javie left, and it's been nothing but chaos in there. But get this? Remember the server's outfit we noticed on the floor the night of Tambra's murder?"

"Uh-huh. It had to be from Hidden Boulders since it wasn't the kind

Randolph's Escapade uses."

"I found out from a source at the sheriff's office that it was one of ours. They're still testing it for DNA evidence to see if they can find out who wore it."

"Wow. Sounds like they might be close to making an arrest."

"I wouldn't go quite that far."

Just then, Cora yelled out to me, and I had to end the call. "My cleaning lady. Sounds as if whatever she found will up her prices."

Liam laughed. "Let's stay in the loop, okay? I have a funny feeling that things are about to heat up."

"Sure thing." With that, I raced back to the bathroom to see what the commotion was all about. Cora held out a small bottle of what looked like shampoo and announced, "Unless you've decided to substitute household poisons for the usual shampoo and conditioner, I'd be wondering why this was on your shower shelf. It wasn't there the last time I cleaned, and since it had no label, I thought maybe you misplaced it. But then again—"

I gasped. "What is it?"

"Hells bells if I know, but I opened it to be sure, and when I caught a whiff, I thought it could kill me. Good thing I wear these rubber gloves."

I eyeballed the bottle from a distance and gasped when I realized it was a yellowish-oily substance. "Tansy oil!"

"Is that what it is? Is it some sort of insecticide? I need to know if I'm going to be around dangerous substances."

"It's not mine. And I'm only guessing what it is. Put it down, Cora. I need to call the sheriff's office. Someone is trying to kill me."

"I'm charging overtime if this takes longer than my usual hours."

Overtime. Yes, that was my first thought too.

I had Cora put the bottle back where she found it and then dialed Deputy Vincent's number faster than I've ever dialed anyone.

"This is Katie Aubrey, and you need to come right over. Someone planted poison in my bathroom."

"Calm down, Miss Aubrey, and start from the beginning."

"Can't we just move to the part where my cleaning lady found the poison?"

"All right. I'm on my way, but if it turns out your so-called poison is an expired food item, we're going to need a long talk."

"It's tansy oil. At least, I think it is."

"Fine. Don't touch anything."

When I ended the call, my hands were trembling, and I was glad Cora was the one who put the bottle back where she found it.

"Quick!" I said. "We'd better check the kitchen cabinets in case there's more than one bottle."

"Like I said, overtime rates."

I immediately raced over to where Speedbump was napping, and he appeared perfectly fine. Then I checked his kibble and changed the water bowl before phoning The Char-Board to speak with Lilly-Ann.

"Hey, it's me. Any chance the three of you can manage until later?"

Her voice was as chipper as usual. "Sure. What's up?"

"Someone planted poison in my bathroom. With my shampoo."

"Oh my gosh. Did you call the sheriff's office?"

"Uh-huh. Listen, do me a favor. The three of you have to check every single bottle in our shop. Pantry. Under the sink. You-name-it. And wear the heavy rubber gloves. Call me if you find anything."

"I will. Are you sure it's poison?"

"Not only that, but I'm sure where it came from, too."

Lilly-Ann gasped just as I ended the call. Maybe Ian didn't want to admit it, but I was pretty certain someone didn't want me to have any part of him. Even if it meant going to the extreme. Still, what on earth did this have to do with Tambra and Cherie? And why tansy oil?

There was one big puzzle piece missing, and if I was going to come out of this unscathed, I'd have to think like Tambra and put those pesky pieces together before it was too late.

Chapter Thirty-Nine

L ess than ten minutes after my call to Deputy Vincent, his official vehicle arrived along with another one from the Maricopa County Forensic Lab. To make matters worse, when I opened the door to let the deputy inside, I spied Colleen Wexby across the street with another neighbor, and both of them stood, mouths agape, looking at my house.

Cora leaned against her broom and wasted no time introducing herself. "Cora Milbrand, in case you forgot who I was. I'll make it quick for you. I still have the kitchen, the master bedroom, and the living area to clean."

It was the first and only time I saw Deputy Travis Vincent speechless. Really speechless.

"Um, Cora is the one who found the poison. It's in the bathroom. Come on. I'll show you."

Deputy Vincent nodded at Cora, who was a few feet behind me and proceeded to follow us to the bathroom. Then, he turned and looked at Speedbump, who had positioned himself on the small rug by the kitchen sink. "How much does your dog weigh?"

"Huh? Forty-two pounds, actually. The vet's office weighed him when I brought him in last year, and his weight hasn't changed. Why?"

The deputy turned and pointed to the doggie dog. "Because the size of your doggie door is more in keeping with a Golden Retriever or even a Rottweiler."

"I don't understand."

"What I'm saying, Miss Aubrey, is that if I were to wager a guess as to how someone might have snuck into your house, that doggie door would be top of my list."

"Oh." Thoughts of intruders wafting in and out of here resulted in a sudden queasy stomach that I tried to ignore. "I'm having an alarm system installed. Honest. You can check with ADT. I'm on their schedule."

"Miss Aubrey, you are not under any obligation to install an alarm system. However, living alone with only a beagle for protection, it's a prudent idea."

"I've got a Ring device, too, but I guess it didn't record anything. And whoever tossed that rock through my open bedroom window obviously didn't bother showing up at the front door first."

"What rock? What window? Honestly, Miss Aubrey, I feel as if I've walked into the second act of a play that I had no intention of seeing in the first place."

"Sorry. I suppose I should have led with that, but I honestly thought someone was messing with me. That is, until my cleaning lady found the bottle of what I think is tansy oil."

"Are we still going to the bathroom?" Cora asked, "Or should I start cleaning in the kitchen?"

Deputy Vincent cleared his throat. "The bathroom. Show me what you discovered. I'll need the forensics crew to remove the evidence and search the house for any other substances of concern. In the meantime, Miss Aubrey, suppose you show me that rock. Unless you've removed it."

"Oh no. I saved the rock. And the message that was attached with a rubber band."

"Message?"

"It was a threat, but I thought it was a prank. I didn't want to call your office to report it."

"Let me get this straight. Someone throws a rock threw your window with a threatening note attached, and you don't feel as if our office needs to be notified?"

"I didn't want to be a pest."

The look on Deputy Vincent's face said it all. *You're well past that, Miss Aubrey.*

We walked into the bathroom, where Cora pointed out the bottle in question. Without wasting a second, the deputy took a photo of it with his phone and informed us the forensic crew would be removing it. Then he placed a call, and a few seconds later, two lab techs entered the house with evidence bags and cameras.

"Don't expect a top-notch cleaning job," Cora announced from a few yards away. "Not with all this foot traffic."

I did a mental eye roll and proceeded to tell Deputy Vincent about the rock hitting the wall.

"Do you have any idea who could have thrown it?"

I shook my head. "No."

"Our crew will be removing it as evidence, along with the bottle your cleaning lady found."

"Okay. Just so you know, I called my employees at The Char-Board and told them to scour the place for anything out of the ordinary."

"When was that?"

"A few minutes before you got here."

"Fine. When the techs finish up here, I'll send them to your sandwich shop. Better to be on the safe side. And next time, notify our office when something like this occurs. And to be clear, I'm referring to the rock."

"I know."

"I'm heading back to my office but expect a call from me later this evening."

Wonderful.

I don't know how she did it, but Cora skirted around the forensic techs and managed to do a decent job cleaning the more-trafficked areas and the kitchen. She finished up at four thirty, about the same time the forensic team wrapped things up. I thanked her, gave her a generous tip, and told her I'd see her in two weeks.

Then, once everyone had gone home, I sent Ian a text. – SOMEONE PUT POISON IN MY BATHROOM. TO SCARE ME. WE NEED TO TALK.

It was immediately followed with: ARE YOU ALL RIGHT???

I texted back: YES. FOR NOW.

A second later and Ian responded with: WORKING LATE. WILL BE AT YOUR HOUSE AFTER TEN. KEEP EVERYTHING LOCKED.

This time I responded with a thumbs up and the word THANKS.

Then, I sank down on the couch, intent on phoning Maddie. I needed a sounding board, but more than that, I desperately needed to figure things out before it was too late. However, before I could tap her number, Lilly-Ann called.

"I don't want to alarm you, Katie, but those techs are all over the place."

"Did they find anything? Did you guys find anything?"

"No. Nothing. But I'm not sure if we can get tonight's charcuterie boards done on time. It looks as if those guys will never leave, and people will be stopping in to pick up their orders."

"Okay. No problem. Give me twenty minutes, and I'll be over there."

"Are you sure?"

"Uh-huh. Not much I can do here except sit and worry."

"By the way, count our lucky stars we've got Javie. Without him, we'd still be serving lunch. And poor Matt. He really wanted to stay longer, but he has a class."

"No problem. See you in a bit."

I glanced at Speedbump, then at his doggie door. "Come on, buddy, you're going to hang out at The Char-Board tonight. I doubt the health department will be making any surprise inspections, and I really need to close up that doggie door of yours."

The dog arched his back and looked at me as if I was about to bestow a treat on him. "Maybe later. I'll toss a few biscuits in my bag, and we'll be off."

Then, I made sure all the windows were locked, the shutters drawn, and a few lights left on so it would appear as if someone was home. Ten minutes later, Speedbump and I were on Cave Creek Road headed for The Char-Board. If nothing else, the distraction of putting together those charcuterie boards would save me from conjuring up images of Ian's ex's intent on ending our relationship before it really took off.

"You should have set a trap before you left the house."

"Edith?"

"Who else? And why didn't you put the dog in the backseat? Now I have to sit there."

I turned my head, and sure enough, Edith was sprawled in the backseat, still wearing that chiffon gown.

"I didn't realize you would be joining me."

"And miss all the fun? But those charcuteries can wait. I say we go back to the house, remove the plastic slider from the doggie door, and set a few mousetraps on the floor in front."

"First of all, I don't have any mousetraps, and besides, Speedbump could get injured. Besides, I doubt whoever put that poison in my bathroom is about to make a return visit. You saw the commotion."

"The whole neighborhood saw the commotion. Especially Colleen. She was probably on speed dial with everyone in Cave Creek."

"Oh my gosh. Colleen! Edith, you're a genius! I think I may have figured a way to track down who set foot in my house. And if I'm really savvy about this, set a bona fide trap to catch the real killer, or killers, as the case may be."

"What part of 'let the deputies do their job' don't you get?"

"The part that actually solves the case."

Chapter Forty

I signaled right and pulled off Cave Creek Road.

"Time to put things in motion," I said to Edith and the dog. With cell phone in hand, I managed to find Colleen's landline and phoned her.

"Colleen? It's Katie. I'm sure you must have noticed the commotion in front of my house a little while ago. You'll never guess what happened, so I'll tell you. Someone snuck into my house and planted tansy oil in my bathroom. That's the same poison that was used to kill Tambra Wright at the Hidden Boulders Fashion Show."

"Oh my goodness. How awful. Are you all right?"

"I'm fine, but I thought you should know something. The forensic crew was able to extract a fingerprint on the spot, and they'll be able to locate the perpetrator in no time. It had to be someone in the food industry who was working the fashion show. My take is either someone on the Hidden Boulders staff or one of the servers from Randolph's Escapade."

"Heavens! Some of our part-time food service workers at Valley Wide Hospital also work for those establishments. I certainly hope it wasn't one of them. And to think, this used to be such a nice community. I'm glad you're safe. Thanks for letting me know."

"Hey, neighbors need to keep an eye out for each other. Have a good evening."

As soon as I ended the call, I laughed. "I give her all of thirty seconds, and she'll be dialing everyone on that staff directory."

"Sounds like you think her little gossip train will ferret out whoever's got designs on that hunky chef."

"That's exactly what I think. Not that it will help solve those murders, but it will let me sleep better tonight once I know who it is. I'm guessing that vixen won't stop there. Now all we have to do is sit back and wait for her next move, which, by the way, may just happen when Ian shows up later."

"Putrid aroma? Ice cascade? Or should I try something different, like high-pitched noises?"

I cringed. "None of the above. Once perpetrators are caught in the act, they usually don't have any place to go. We don't need theatrics."

"You may regret that, Missy. Theatrics are merely the staging for solid and concrete planning."

"Oh, brother." I pulled up to The Char-Board and was relieved that the road had an abundance of parking spaces. "Do you intend to hang out and watch me prepare charcuterie boards?"

"I intend to offer pertinent advice. I notice when you're in a hurry, you neglect to flute the edges on the cured meats. And don't get me started on the cheese cubes."

I motioned for Speedbump to get out of the car and then hesitated for a second before slamming the door shut. "I'll take that under advisement."

Undaunted, Edith slithered past me and leaned against the front door. The closed sign was up, but a quick look inside and I could see Lilly-Ann and Javie from the open door between the kitchen and dining area. They seemed to be working in sync, but I had no idea how far behind they were.

Without wasting another section, I unlocked the door and stepped inside. Speedbump wasted no time either. He positioned himself under one of the dining room tables and licked his front paw.

"I'm here, guys. Thanks so much for hanging in there. Give me a second to wash my hands and grab an apron."

Javie looked up from rolling the prosciutto into fancy logs. "We're making progress, but those customers will be here within the hour for their boards."

"No problem. Show me what you've done, and we'll take it from there."

As we worked, I gave Lilly-Ann and Javie more detail about the tansy oil but neglected to tell them about my conversation with Colleen.

"Do you have any idea who could have done this?" Lilly-Ann asked. "And why? Maybe it *was* the person or persons responsible for those deaths. And maybe they figured you knew too much."

I opened a fresh Genoa salami and gulped. "Thanks. That's very reassuring. So, I take it nothing was found here, huh?"

She and Javie exchanged glances before Javie spoke.

"No sign of anything, but one of the techs warned us not to get lax. Funny, but whoever planted that oil did it at your house and not here. I hate to say this, but I think Lilly-Ann may be right. Why else would they have targeted you and not your place of business?"

I tried to put their comments out of my mind, but frankly, I had to admit, it did give another spin to the situation. For the next forty minutes, I cut, chopped, designed, and polished off two boards while Lilly-Ann and Javie completed the rest.

"Whew!" Javie said when the last customer stopped in to retrieve their board. "Talk about getting down to the wire."

We gave each other high fives and took a collective breath. Lilly-Ann and Javie because they finished up in time, and me, because Edith stayed out of our way.

"Are you going to be all right?" Lilly-Ann asked as the three of us and Speedbump exited the shop.

"Uh-huh. A friend of mine is coming over."

Lilly-Ann raised an eyebrow and smiled. "A friend, huh? Good. You won't be alone."

I might not be alone, I thought, but I wasn't too sure how I'd broach the subject of an ex-girlfriend with Ian. Still, I couldn't let it go.

Needless to say, things don't always work out as planned, and the conversation I needed to have with Ian never took place. Instead, something far more chilling did.

Speedbump and I arrived home about twenty minutes later. Everything looked normal when I unlocked the door and went inside. The dog immediately gravitated to his spot on the rug by the sink, and I went into my bedroom to change into clothes that didn't smell like a delicatessen. Ian wouldn't be here for another few hours, so I figured my time could be best spent touching base with Maddie and then revisiting my murder notebook/map. That is, until I caught sight of myself in a mirror.

"Good grief, Speedbump, I look like that waif on the red, white, and blue cover for *Les Misérables.* I really need to rinse off."

The dog looked up and then put his head down on the rug. It took the water about three minutes to warm up, but when it did, the steam encompassed the entire bathroom. I could have sworn I heard something outside the room, and for the first time, I decided to make good use of Edith's on-and-off again presence.

"Edith? You in here? And don't play games. Is someone in the house?"

"Just the lazy beagle. You really think whoever left that nasty surprise for you will come back?"

"Absolutely." I reached for the rose water body wash and proceeded to slather it all over. "They left unfinished business. If they don't come back tonight, they'll think it's too late. Remember, Colleen is spreading the word like a middle schooler who just got kissed."

"A half-baked plan, for sure. How are you going to deal with it if the nutcase comes barging in here guns a-blazing?"

I rinsed off and reached for a towel. "First of all, guns aren't her weapon of choice. I think all she wants is a confrontation and agreement that I'll steer clear of her love interest. I'm actually hoping the timing works out so that Ian's here. Even it if will be awkward."

"Awkward? Try deadly. Don't you watch crime TV?"

I continued drying off, and Edith continued spouting off.

"And if he's not here and she goes berserk?"

"It's not as if I'm about to let her inside."

"Honey, if she can heave a rock through a window, she'll find a way to get in. Be prepared. Get a can of bug spray. Don't you have some Raid under the sink?"

"And what will you be doing?" *Like I need to ask.*

"I'm handy with plumbing, gas leaks, and assorted—Rosaline! What are you doing here? Get out! Get out this instant!"

And then, as if listening to one voice from beyond the grave wasn't enough,

I heard a second. "Not without my chiffon dress. You swiped it while I made a wardrobe change."

"A wardrobe change? Is that what they're calling it these days? Stay back because this gown isn't leaving my body."

And then, steam everywhere. Followed by whooshing sounds, a few expletives, and then, nothing. Edith and her wardrobe nemesis, Rosaline, had both vanished, leaving me in a humid bathroom with no recourse but to dry off, get dressed, and plan my next move. Bug spray and all.

I've never confronted love-interest rivals, let alone unhinged ones, but something about the situation plagued me more than someone's sour grapes. It was the tansy oil. That was the substance used to knock Tambra's lights out, and none of this made sense. I mean, it wasn't as if they were running a special at Walgreens for tansy oil. And odd, that it was Tambra's murder weapon as well as what I think Ian's ex put in my bathroom.

Naturally, I did what I should have done hours, if not days ago—I called Maddie and crossed my fingers she wouldn't overreact.

Chapter Forty-One

"Someone planted poison in your house, and you set up a trap for them to return? Have you lost your mind?"

"Try to calm down, Maddie," I said. "I've got this under control."

I thought I was clear and succinct as I explained the situation leading up to Cora's discovery in my bathroom, but apparently not.

"Call the sheriff's office and tell them what you've done. You've pretty much lured a killer to your house."

"I wouldn't go quite that far."

"*I* would."

"Hang on. Another call's coming in. From Javie. My new employee. Call you right back."

I ended my conversation with Maddie and answered Javie. "What's up?"

His voice sounded edgy and strange. "I got a text threatening to 'do some real damage' to The Char-Board if I didn't return to Hidden Boulders. I don't recognize the number but I'm on my way over there. I also called the sheriff's office."

"The Char-Board? Hidden Boulders? Holy moly. I've got to throw on some clothes, and I'll be right there."

Then I glanced at the dog and froze. It was *The Lady and the Tiger,* for sure. Only not a fairy tale. If I left Speedbump at home and Ian's crazed love interest showed up, who knew what she'd do to him. Then again, if I brought him with me to The Char-Board with another lunatic threatening harm, it could be worse.

At least at The Char-Board, I could keep an eye on him. Plus, Javie had already called the sheriff's office.

"Come on, dog," I said as I threw a sweatshirt over my top and headed for the front door. "Go for a ride."

The dog looked as bored as ever but ambled to the door. I nearly broke every speed limit in Cave Creek as I flew through stop signs, pedestrian walks, and heaven-knows-what else. When I reached the shop, I parked across the street and made sure Speedbump was securely leashed before letting him out of the car. Not that it did any good. He broke free and raced toward Javie, who stood adjacent to the entrance.

"Grab his leash!" I shouted. "I thought the sheriff's deputies would have arrived before me." Javie's eyes widened, and absolute terror registered on his face. A second later, I knew why. The girlish voice came from behind me, and although it sounded familiar, I couldn't quite place it. One of the bunco ladies? "I sent them racing to your house, so don't expect them anytime soon. And don't turn around unless you want to be sprayed with some lovely tansy oil."

Next thing I knew, I felt something press into my back. Then I heard Javie's voice. Sharp and focused. "What the heck are you up to?"

And then, the gruff voice morphed into a whine. "I really didn't want it to end up this way, but I had no choice with Tambra. She was going to axe you from your job at Hidden Boulders, and I'd never see you again."

Oh my gosh! A love interest! And not Ian's.

Petrified to turn around, I directed my question to the woman while looking straight ahead at the entrance to The Char-Board.

"You're the one who poisoned Tambra with that oil. But how?"

Her response was acerbic. "I rubbed the oil on a linen towel and used it to wipe down the forks at your charcuterie table. Once Tambra selected her fork, I removed the others and threw them in the back of my car for disposal later. I didn't want to poison anyone else. This was something between me and Tambra."

Terrific. A murderer with a conscience.

"Stop this now," Javie yelled. "Don't make it any worse. Drop that spray bottle."

"I can't. I have no guarantee Katie will let this go."

Then she continued talking to my back. "I thought you'd get the message when I gunned my car engine in front of your shop. But no, I had to move on to slashing your tires. Now it's too late to drop it."

I cleared my throat, but my voice was still raspy. "Oh, trust me, I'll let it go. No problem. Kick the spray bottle to the curb, and we'll call it a day." *And don't think I won't send you a bill for those pricy tires! Good Grief!*

"Very funny."

I looked to my sides, and other than the three of us and Speedbump, no one was in sight. The deputies were on their way to my place, and if they swung around to get back here, it would be too late.

Thoughts like, "Could I manage a round-house kick?" and "If I scream, would anyone hear me?" ran through my head non-stop. Then, out of nowhere, another voice. This one shrill and annoying. "Edith, I want that gown off your back and on mine, and I want it now."

Rosaline. I could actually hear her. Then, Edith retorted, "Over my dead body. Oh, wait. I am dead. Tough luck."

Then, out of nowhere, wind and dust devils like nobody's business. Edith and Rosaline were at each other with more forces of nature than I've seen on the Weather Channel. The more they argued, the more intense the change in the barometric process got. Javie's jaw dropped, and I wasn't much further behind. Then, the absolute kicker of all time—a mini burst that was in and out of the street in a nanosecond. I'd seen photos of the damage they caused, and it rivaled a small tornado. In this case, it knocked my assailant to the ground. Javie rushed toward her and kicked the spray bottle a good six or seven yards away. "What on earth?"

"Global warming," I replied. Then I turned to see who my perpetrator was and gasped. "Twila?"

She glared at me and didn't say a word. Meanwhile, I kept trying to process how jealousy could have been the motive.

"What about Cherie Simms?" I asked. "Was she trying to take Javie away from you, too?"

"What? I had nothing to do with her death. And didn't the news report she was strangled? That's not my style."

By now, Javie had latched on to one of Twila's arms and held it steady.

"Those deputies are going to be here any second," I said, "Tell me, how did you get your hands on tansy oil?"

"Hmm, I would have thought you figured that one out. You've seen my car. The red Toyota. In fact, I know you have. I saw you looking at the bumper stickers the first day you showed up at Hidden Boulders."

The faded red Toyota.

I thought back to the bumper stickers, and sure enough, herbal medicine was right there, along with Go Vegan. "You're an herbalist?"

"Oh, heck no. But I've got a cousin in Black Canyon who is. I told him I needed some real tansy oil for medicinal purposes, and he didn't question it."

He will now.

Just then, an MCSO vehicle pulled up to The Char-Board, with Deputy Vincent thundering his way toward us.

"Don't believe what she tells you," Twila announced as she used her free hand to point to me."

This time I glared at her. "Oh, save it."

Thankfully Edith and Rosaline took their melee elsewhere. Or, they were behaving themselves, but I doubted it.

Javie directed the deputy toward the spray can and explained what had ensued. Then, because the adrenaline in me had reached a nuclear level, I threw in my two cents.

"I believe I have the salient points, Miss Aubrey. You'll be needed at my office to complete some paperwork along with—" And then he looked at Javie.

"Javier Rivera."

"Mr. Rivera."

"When?" I asked.

"Anytime tomorrow. Try to pull yourself together."

Oh sure. Just what I feel like doing when someone tries to kill me.

Twila was read her rights and escorted into Deputy Vincent's car by another deputy, who pulled up a few minutes later. That's when I realized I needed to ask her something. Without wasting a second, I charged toward the deputy's car and approached her before he closed the door.

"I need to know something, Twila. Did you ditch a server's uniform on the floor by the fashion show?"

"Boy, you don't miss a trick. Yeah, I did. It was an old uniform. One we haven't used in years. I found it in the way back of the supply closet. I figured if Hidden Boulders was using its surveillance for the event, and they saw me near the charcuterie forks, they might put two and two together. But by tossing that old uniform on the floor, I created a ruse. And let me tell you, it wasn't easy. Some wacko woman in an ombre dot dress all but knocked me over on her way out of there."

And now, with Twila's confession, I learn the ombre dot dress lady isn't the killer. So much for my sleuthing skills.

"Have to admit, you are clever. Diabolical, but clever."

Twila smirked and turned away just as the deputy closed the door. Then, I walked back to Javie, and the two of us watched as they drove off.

Javie held his palms out, leash still attached to Speedbump. "I am SO sorry, Katie. I had absolutely no idea what was going on in Twila's head. None whatsoever. Are we still okay?"

"Of course."

"But that's only half the puzzle. Cherie's murderer is still out there, and I'm not very optimistic those deputies will have enough evidence to make an arrest."

"Yeah, I thought the same thing."

"Look, don't take any more chances. Tonight was frightening enough. Say, would you feel better if I followed you home?"

"Thanks, but I'll be okay. Unless, of course, you've got more lovesick women after you."

"Geez, I hope not. I still have to get my degree. I don't want to get tangled up in romance."

We both laughed and agreed to share the details of tonight's incident with Lilly-Ann and Matt in the morning. I drove home with Speedbump curled up in the passenger seat and Edith nowhere in sight.

The second Speedbump and I got in the door, I locked it. Then I phoned Maddie.

"You were supposed to call me right back. I figured some order got messed up for your charcuterie catering when you said one of your employees called. What happened?"

"You won't believe this in a zillion years, but my new employee had a stalker, and she was the one who killed Tambra."

"What? What happened?"

"I guess I didn't need a plan to lure the killer after all. She was intent on doing whatever she had to in order to keep me as far away from him. Long story."

"I'm in no rush. Tell me."

When I finished, it became evident I'd missed so many clues. Twila pitching a fit in the Hidden Boulders kitchen when Javie left. Twila, gunning her car engine up and down the road in front of The Char-Board. Not to mention those black Sharpie warning notes. And the rock. If I could miss all that, surely, I missed a whole lot more regarding Cherie's killer. And that's when I began to really worry. What if they thought I knew more than I did and this was only the beginning?

Good thing Ian was coming over, but that was still a half hour away. Then again, what could possibly happen in thirty minutes?

Chapter Forty-Two

I opened a can of Coke and sank down on the couch. At least my heart stopped racing, and I was able to think clearly. Knowing that Twila was the one responsible for Tambra's death, it now became a process of elimination to find out who was responsible for sending Cherie off to the great unknown. But first, I had to revisit my Tambra speculations.

Easy enough to eliminate Eric since he obviously didn't kill his wife over information she might have had. Even though it was a good theory. So much for the divorce settlement idea. As for Cherie, whatever game she played as she raced out of the fashion show in that ombre dot dress, it didn't matter. I moved on to Scott.

And while he wasn't Tambra's killer, he most definitely was on my case and colluding with his sister. Go figure. I reasoned it all had to boil down to whatever they thought was in Cherie's locker. I took a sip of the Coke and thought back. Sure, the pawned jewelry was there along with a canister and a sweater, but so what? Then I remembered something else. Something that slipped by me altogether. It was that business card. The one for waste management/construction. And, if I remembered correctly, there was a scribbled note on the back. Something about "staying on schedule with payments."

At the time I thought it was a note Cherie had written on some business card she found, but now I realized how far off I was. Given Scott's involvement with the locker's contents, and the fact he used his sister to scope things out, I wagered that card had to do with him, and somehow Cherie got her hands on it. Then, the fact I snooped around gave Scott all the more reason to get me out of the way, even if it was only by intimidation. And payments? For what? Not a business service or it would have gone through Hidden Boulders.

I downed another sip of my Coke, and that's when it dawned on me. Scott wasn't trying to find out who cut corners on that golf course installation. He was intent on keeping that secret to himself, even if it meant paying off someone and lying to Liam and me the day he thought he had a heart attack. *Thank you, Edith.*

At this point, I was pretty certain I knew who Cherie's killer was. It had to be Scott. Somehow Cherie got wind of what he did, and he had to shut her up. But how to prove it?

I tossed my Coke can in the recycling basket and nabbed another one from the fridge. This time is sticking it in my pocket. That's when I heard the knock on my door. "Ian?" I'll be right there.

Without thinking, I opened the door, but instead of Ian, it was Meredith who stood there.

"Merry? What's going on?"

She stepped inside, and then, like a thunderbolt, my mind kicked back in gear. I *did* see the name on that business card in Cherie's locker but must have thought it was so insignificant as to blot it out. It was Mason. Mason! Mason Waste Management and Construction. Oh my gosh. This was her company. But that wasn't the worst. Nothing like having my mind recall with absolute clarity the things it should have. When I last spoke with Meredith about Cherie, Meredith said, "At least I didn't wind up face down in a dumpster."

Why oh why didn't I catch it then? No one knew except me and the forensic techs that Cherie's body was face-down. It was never on the news and never disclosed. Only the killer would know.

Fantastic. I'm face-to-face with Cherie's killer, and I have no idea how to get out of this.

It would be at least twenty minutes until Ian made an appearance and who-knows-where Edith was. Not as if I could conjure her up.

Then Meredith spoke. "I should have kept my mouth shut when you phoned me. I knew it would be only a matter of time for you to figure it out, and I wasn't about to wait."

Of course not. Only I wait until it's too late.

Merry inched closer to me, and that's when I saw her reach for something in her pocket.

"I wouldn't do that if I were you." *What am earth am I saying? Of course, she'll do it, whatever it is she's going to do.*

I looked around to see if there was anything within my reach I could toss or throw her way but other than a few decorative pillows and the TV remote, I was stuck. I couldn't even pull the cell phone from my pocket and tap 911. Too time-consuming.

"Tell me," I said, "Since you aren't going to let me walk out the door, how did you kill Cherie and get her into that dumpster? It couldn't have been a one-person job."

Meredith laughed. "One person? Try three."

Boy, when I'm wrong, I'm wrong.

In the back of my mind, I figured if I could keep Meredith talking, I might be able to think of something to get me out of this predicament.

"Three? I figured it had to be you and Scott. Scott knew Cherie had information regarding his involvement with the original cost-cutting plans for the golf course. That would bite him, for sure. But Cherie found out about your involvement since it was your company that was getting a payoff to keep things quiet. Isn't that collusion? And isn't that why you had to get her out of the way? As for the third person, I'm lost."

"Really now? It was right in front of your eyes. It was Tambra. Tambra had suspicions Cherie wanted her dead but never got the chance to act. She, did, however, share those suspicions with me, so that's why I'm counting her as the third person in our little "murder club.""

"Oh my gosh! So that's why you were never on her blackmail list."

"Bingo! She trusted me. Can you believe it?" Anyway, Cherie needed to keep Tambra quiet. And one night, when we had too much to drink, I found out Cherie planned on poisoning her. In public. At the fashion show. Too bad she never got the chance. Had it all worked out, too. She planned on using Digitalis from an old prescription her mother had. Even went so far as to disguise herself with an ugly wig and ombre dot dress. Who wears those anymore?"

I shrugged as Meredith kept talking.

"Cherie planned on putting the Digitalis in Tambra's drink but never got the chance. Someone beat her to it. That meant she had to get the heck out of there and fast."

It was all making sense, but that wasn't going to do me any good with an unhinged psychopath ready to add me to her murder list. With no available weapons for me to grab, my only recourse was to keep her talking.

"Wow. Very interesting. But where does Eric fit in? I did a little snooping around myself and found out Cherie and Eric were into something."

"You didn't snoop enough. Eric was getting a take on Cherie's little entrepreneurship. Or should I say "lending library?" That's how she referred to it. But he took advantage. I wager she would have axed him first if Scott and I didn't get her out of way. Real easy, too."

By now, I could feel small beads of sweat trickle down my neck, and I wondered how long I could keep this up. I swallowed and looked Meredith in the eye. "So, how did you strangle her and get her into that dumpster?"

"You really do want all of my little secrets, don't you? Well, I suppose it doesn't matter now. I knew Cherie had an appointment with her colorist, so Scott broke into her car and waited in the back seat. She was parked behind the building with no one around. He used one of Deirdre's scarves and came at her from behind. You don't want all the gory details now, do you?"

I shook my head. "I suppose not."

"Good. I was in my car a few yards away. When the deed was done, Scott texted me with a thumb's up emoji. I went to Cherie's car, and together we shoved her out of the driver's seat and into the passenger's seat. Then, a quick spin to the dumpster out back, and you know the rest."

What I did know was that my time had run out. What more could I ask? And why, of all nights, did Edith choose to be elsewhere? I thought about lunging toward Meredith, but if she had a gun in her pocket, it would be too late. Heck, a sharp knife would be too late. All I had were pillows and—oh my gosh! My Coke can.

I slipped my hand into my pocket and slowly pried the tab from the can of Coke. Then, I moved as if I'd seen a roach crawling my way. I flung the can from the pocket and spewed the liquid in Meredith's face.

Please don't let her whip out a gun.

The distraction was enough for me to race to the kitchen to reach for the landline. Unfortunately, Meredith was on my heels and furious as hell. I figured she didn't have a gun, but who knew what on earth she *did* have.

Then, without warning, a cascade of ice cubes flew from the fridge and coated the kitchen floor like Kansas after a hailstorm. I inched my way to the table, but Meredith was caught off guard and slid to the ground. That's when I made a move I'd only seen in slapstick comedies. I grabbed a kitchen chair and held it over her. "Make one move, and this comes down over your head. And believe me, it's a heavy sucker."

Meredith squirmed and tried to stand, but the ice cubes kept coming, and no matter how hard she tried, she couldn't get any traction. Meanwhile, I inched my way to the counter, reached for the landline, and dialed 911.

"It's over," I said.

"Not necessarily. Scott knows I'm here."

If Meredith said that to unnerve me, it worked. But only for a minute. The rational part of my brain told me the sheriff's deputies and/or Ian would beat him to it. Still, those weren't the most pleasant words to hear.

"Good. The county can make two arrests."

My arms got tired as I held the chair over her head, but finally, I heard a knock on the door.

Don't let this be Scott.

"Miss Aubrey?"

"In the kitchen. With Cherie Simms's murderer. Oh, and the floor is slippery."

A loud groan, and Deputy Vincent thundered his way toward us. "You can let go of the chair. I don't think whoever is on the floor is about to make a move."

"Meredith Mason," I replied. "And she and Scott Billings were the ones who killed Cherie."

"You're insane," Meredith said. "I came over here to discuss some charcuterie ideas, and that woman went nuts."

"Not *that* nuts. I couldn't use my cell phone to reach 911, but I was able to activate the record app. Guess what? Your entire confession is on my phone." With that, I placed the chair upright against the table and handed Deputy Vincent my phone.

Within the hour, Meredith was read her rights and escorted out of my house. Just in time for Ian to arrive and witness everything.

He walked through the open door and raced toward me. "Please don't tell me someone tried to attack you in your own house." He pulled me close, and I latched on to his shoulders for what seemed like hours.

"My house, my place of business…it's been a horrible night."

"I'll need you to report to my office tomorrow and give us a statement," Deputy Vincent shouted as he exited the house.

"Haven't I given enough statements?" I whined. "And you're not taking my cell phone, are you?"

"Evidence. You can pick it up in the morning."

Amazingly, Speedbump didn't budge from his rug during the entire fiasco. It was only when Ian said "Hey, buddy" to him that the dog got up and nuzzled him non-stop.

Then, a burst of persimmons haze followed by a familiar raspy voice, "See, even the dog thinks he's a keeper."

Epilogue

L iam was astonished at the turn of events and couldn't believe what had been going on at Hidden Boulders. Seemed everyone had a piece of the deceit, and now the sheriff's office had to sort out the details.

I never did have that conversation with Ian. No need. It was pretty obvious the only woman in his life was now me, and I intended to keep it that way.

Edith and Rosaline still fought over that chiffon gown, and lamentably, the only way I could console her was to agree to pay Imogen a visit with her. I should have had my head examined. Still, I owed Edith more than I cared to admit.

Lilly-Ann, Matt, and Javie continued to make an amazing team, resulting in five new charcuterie designs that brought the old-world flavors from Spain into Cave Creek. Business continued to grow, and I toyed with a new endeavor – teaching charcuterie skills to emerging chefs.

Who knows? It sounded like fun, and after my experience with the Hidden Boulders, I needed some fun. After all, how hard could teaching a class be?

Charcuterie Tray Recipe

(Plan 3 ounces of meat and 3 ounces of cheese per person)

Ingredients for Baltic Charcuterie Tray

- Wedge of Jarlsberg or Swiss cheese
- Diced Havarti cheese
- Slices of Gouda cheese
- Small dish of black caviar
- Rolled lox (cured salmon)
- Small dish of cream cheese or tiny cream cheese balls
- Small dish of red caviar (optional)
- Small dish of pickled herring – (VERY optional)
- Small dish of almonds
- Small dish of red onions
- Small dish of tiny dilled pickles

- Sliced hard salami
- Sliced smoked sausage or Polish sausage
- Slices of dark rye bread or marbled rye bread
- Plain crackers – Use at least two different types and shapes
- Small tomatoes or dilled tomatoes
- Small radishes or sliced larger ones (You can cut these to look like roses)
- Sprigs of dill and parsley for accent – Optional

Design

Begin with the larger items first. Place the chunked and wedged cheeses in the center of the tray and surround them with the meats – hard salami and sausage. Surround with mixed crackers on one side and small dishes of almonds, dilled pickles, radishes, tomatoes, etc. on the other. Then surround with folded lox and small dishes of caviar. Place cream cheese near the lox and caviar. Put the bread on the outside edge of the tray.

Use little round dishes for the smaller items or they may fall off!

Don't forget to have serving utensils!

Use the parsley and dill sprigs for accents around and in the tray.

Have fun! Play around with the placement so it looks aesthetically pleasing. If it is too overwhelming, cut out some items or lessen the quantity.

Serves 5 – 8 people, but can be adjusted to fit your number of guests

Acknowledgements

Somehow the word "Thank-you" doesn't come close enough when we think of all the support, encouragement, time, and work that these amazing folks have given us. In short, our agent, Dawn Dowdle from Blue Ridge Literary Agency, has made it all possible for us!

Susan Schwartz from Australia continues to edit and critique long before we'd ever dare to submit the manuscript to our publisher. Her skills are phenomenal! And Gale Leach has rescued us numerous times when it comes to technology and computer snafus. She's amazing!

Special thanks go out to our editor at Level Best Books, Shawn Simmons, and the entire team at Level Best Books for giving us this opportunity to shine with our quirky ghost in this paranormal cozy series.

About the Author

Ann I. Goldfarb

New York native Ann I. Goldfarb spent most of her life in education, first as a classroom teacher and later as a middle school principal and professional staff developer. Writing as J. C. Eaton, along with her husband, James Clapp, she has authored the Sophie Kimball Mysteries (Kensington, Beyond the Page Publishing), the Wine Trail Mysteries, (Kensington Lyrical, Beyond the Page Publishing), The Charcuterie Shop Mysteries (Level Best Books) and the Marcie Rayner Mysteries, (Camel/Epicenter Press). In addition, Ann has nine published YA time travel mysteries under her own name. Visit the websites at: www.jceatonmysteries.com and www.timetravelmysteries.com

James E. Clapp

When James E. Clapp retired as the tasting room manager for a large upstate New York winery, he never imagined he'd be co-authoring cozy mysteries with his wife, Ann I. Goldfarb. His first novel, *Booked 4 Murder* (Kensington) was released in June 2017 and followed by ten other books in the series. Non-fiction in the form of informational brochures and workshop materials treating the winery industry were his forte along with an extensive background and experience in construction that started with his service in the U.S. Navy and included vocational school classroom teaching. Visit the website at www.jceatonmysteries.com

SOCIAL MEDIA HANDLES:
https://www.facebook.com/JCEatonauthor/
https://www.instagram.com/j.c.eaton/
https://www.twitter.com/JCEatonauthor
https://bookbub.com/authors/j-c-eaton

AUTHOR WEBSITE:
www.jceatonmysteries.com

Also by J.C. Eaton

The Sophie Kimball Mysteries
Booked 4 Murder
Ditched 4 Murder
Staged 4 Murder
Botched 4 Murder
Molded 4 Murder
Dressed Up 4 Murder
Broadcast 4 Murder
Railroaded 4 Murder
Saddled Up 4 Murder
Grilled 4 Murder
Strike Out 4 Murder

The Wine Trail Mysteries
A Riesling to Die
Chardonnayed to Rest
Pinot Red or Dead?
Sauvigone For Good
Divide and Concord
Death, Dismay and Rose'
From Port to Rigor Morte
Mischief, Murder and Merlot
Caught in the Traminette (to be released 2023)

The Marcie Rayner Mysteries
Murder in the Crooked Eye Brewery
Murder at the Mystery Castle
Murder at Classy Kitchens

The Charcuterie Shop Mysteries

Laid Out to Rest
Sliced, Diced and Dead

Printed in the USA
CPSIA information can be obtained
at www.ICGtesting.com
LVHW041641210324
775159LV00002B/28